DAY of the
KOMODO

To, Robin

With my best wishes

Hugh Ainsworth

J. H. Ainsworth

Published by

MELROSE
BOOKS

An Imprint of Melrose Press Limited
St Thomas Place, Ely
Cambridgeshire
CB7 4GG, UK
www.melrosebooks.com

FIRST EDITION

Cover designed by Jeremy Kay

ISBN 978 1 907040 11 5

FSC
Mixed Sources
Product group from well-managed
forests and other controlled sources
Cert no. SGS-COC-2953
www.fsc.org
© 1996 Forest Stewardship Council

Printed and bound in Great Britain by:
CPI Antony Rowe, Chippenham, Wiltshire

DEDICATIONS

In memory of my late mother who fell asleep peacefully.

I WOULD LIKE TO OFFER MY THANKS AND gratitude to Louise Stewart of the BBC and Anne Carmichael for keeping a sharp eye on the manuscript, to John Leonard, Andy Morrison, Lincoln Wee, Giuseppe Perrone for their contribution and to Shona Gammack, Linda Thirde, Lesley Robertson and my daughter Sarah Ainsworth for their infectious enthusiasm. The events of the Tsunami and 'troubles' in the Aceh province of Sumatra have been recorded in the annals of history, but this story and the characters within it are all entirely a figment of my imagination.

CHAPTERS

PROLOGUE

THE LINCOLN SEDAN CRUISED SLOWLY BY ALONG Ludlow Street, a run-down thoroughfare in one of Manhattan's less affluent areas. Situated between Lower East Side and Chinatown in New York, it certainly lacked the glitz of Times Square. Stopping by a nondescript apartment block, a silver-haired man got out and walked towards the building. He spoke briefly into the intercom before the black door buzzed opened. Peeling wallpaper clung forlornly in the lobby for want of a makeover. As he climbed the stairs, he could feel the excitement build up like it always did. The decaying obsolescence somehow added to the seedy vibrancy of the establishment. He hardly noticed the dirt, focusing instead on his host. The greeting was friendly as per usual.

'Hello, how are you today, my friend?' the Latino asked in his sharp Puerto Rican accent.

'I'm very good, Carlos. Do you have something special for me?'

'Of course! Would I ever let you down?' he replied with a pained smile.

'No, because I pay you too well. Where is this one from?'

'Mexico. Just came in the other day.'

'Fresh meat, huh?' the man chuckled.

They walked the short distance along the red-carpeted corridor. It was a good-sized apartment block, sitting above a clothing workshop. The row of rooms at the front looked down into Ludlow Street. At the back, the yard was surrounded by more ugly buildings. Protruding metal fire escape stairs jutted out like extra-terrestrial carbuncles. Maybe the spiders from Mars had invaded after all. In the mind of one drug addict, they had. The powerful hallucinogen had made him shoot from the rooftop but the customers had become nervous when bullet holes started to appear in the windows. It was bad for business and Carlos had known what he had to do. The punk had to pay the ultimate price for his stupidity. The clingfilm around his face showed no fingerprints or foreign DNA, just the saliva from a dying man. The crystal meth had finally got him nailed because Carlos couldn't allow the crazed drug addict to shoot up his place any more. The body ended up in the trash can with the other garbage as life had become cheap.

The Puerto Rican opened one of the bedroom doors and ushered his guest into a semi-darkened room. There was a distinctive red glow from the solitary bedside lamp. The young naked body hardly moved at all, lying face down on the bed as the narcotics flowed through his veins. The client felt relaxed already in the familiar surroundings. He removed his jacket and tie in anticipation. Carlos had never failed to produce the goods. The man liked what he saw already. Very much so.

Chapter 1

Edinburgh

The Scottish capital has its share of famous bars, from The Dome in George Street to the Oxford Bar. The Canny Man's in Morningside was no different. Established in 1871, entry was through the side door. The performing artists from a bygone age had even called it the 'Stage Door', adding a certain panache. Now serving as a watering hole for the well-heeled Morningside set, it did not welcome football supporters or backpackers. It said so outside. Refusal of entry was also non-negotiable. The Four Ale Bar and Smoke Room were tinged with old tobacco smoke, giving a patina to the numerous memorabilia hanging from the ceiling. Scribbled words from the ghosts of yesteryear added poignancy to the little pub, especially above the urinals in the men's toilets. Go-go dancers had even pranced around on the counter at one time but that had been a mistake. Genteel sensibility had now returned to the fine establishment.

Nick Forbes had finished his training in London as an orthopaedic surgeon with a cloud over his head. His torrid final year in the big city was at an end, or so he thought. He now sought work as a hospital consultant, knowing the past had to be buried if he was ever to move on. Returning to Edinburgh had seemed like the best option, even if it was for a short period. With fate being such a bitch, it had struck one of the orthopaedic surgeons at the Royal Infirmary. The man had suffered from a heart attack and his survival now depended on the powers of human recovery. Nick's own brush with death at the hands of a psychopath had been a severe test of his mental reserves but somehow, he had managed to remain sane. The creamy pint of 80 Shillings beckoned as never before. It was served chilled, unlike the more rustic English ales down south. It certainly felt good to be back in Caledonia as he prodded his old friend in the back.

'Is that your second or third?' Nick asked quietly.

'Hey, it's the big man himself! You know the first never touches the sides! How are you?' Stuart replied in his distinctly non-Morningside accent.

'Better for being back,' Nick replied, giving his mate a good hug.

'You'll want a pint then?'

'No, make that several. How are things here?'

'Nothing new to tell. I gather you've been through the wars,' Stuart said, sticking two fingers up to the barman to indicate his order.

'It could have been worse.'

'Could it? The paparazzi seemed fond of you.'

'Actually, the boys were just doing their job.'

'Care to explain that one to me?'

'It's too complicated.'

'You can take your time because we have all evening.'

'Do we have to talk about this?'

'Yes. Just tell me how they got involved.'

'Come on, you must have read about it in the newspapers,' Nick said hopefully.

'I did but how many people did you say this chief executive person murdered?'

2

'Let's drop it. I didn't say anything about that.'

'So what was your involvement?'

'I was stitched up. Somebody died but it had nothing to do with me.'

'Sounds like we have to talk about this over a good bottle of malt,' Stuart suggested.

'I've got a bottle of Johnnie Walker Blue Label which needs some attention. It's not quite a malt but it'll do,' Nick said, deliberately playing down the cost of the liquor.

'Life can't be that bad after all! We must have a proper chat sometime,' Stuart replied, contemplating the exquisite blend.

'How many properties do you own now?' Nick joked, changing the subject.

'Just the four. The new parliament has now made property prices too expensive to buy,' Stuart replied, handing a ten pound note to the barman in the bowtie.

'Shame. How much did the Parliament cost at the end?' Nick asked with a sardonic smile.

'About four hundred million. It's the eighth ugliest building in the world.'

'Says who?'

'The whole world. Even the windows aren't straight,' Stuart replied with an authoritative air.

'I thought that was the whole point.'

'Not for a Scottish Parliament it's not. It's a bloody mess. Anyway, cheers. It's good to have you back.'

'Thanks. How are Mary and the kids?'

'They're fine, apart from eating me out of house and home.'

'That shouldn't be a problem for a property tycoon,' Nick mocked.

'Hey, that's great coming from a rich surgeon!'

'Don't believe the hype. People earn more money from changing a tap washer these days.'

'Your job is like fixing things which go wrong, isn't it?' Stuart asked, carrying on with the banter.

'At least I don't work where people play,' Nick replied.

'What, like a gynaecologist?'

'Yes,' Nick laughed.

'How long are you back for?'

'It could be for a few months. I'm covering for somebody with a heart attack.'

'And how's the love life?'

'There could be somebody around.'

'Oh, for God's sake, Nick, cut the nonsense and tell me her name.'

'Meg.'

'And what does she do?'

'She's a nurse.'

'And?'

'She's blonde.'

'What a surprise. You've not changed much, have you?'

'It was purely coincidental,' Nick replied with a smirk.

'So what what does Meg look like?'

'A bit like a young Helen Mirren. You know, with all the right bits in the right places,' Nick teased.

'Oh God, I'll definitely have to meet her,' Stuart groaned in anticipation.

They had been friends for a long time, having lived on the same estate and gone to the same primary school. Things kicked off between them only after Nick had given the school bully a good pasting behind the dining hall. Like most bullies, the boy had been nothing more than a bigmouth. He begged Nick to keep the fight a secret in order not to lose face but Stuart had seen it. When word had finally got out, respect from the younger boys came quickly. The odd stone was still thrown at him by the older boys as if to challenge his new standing but there had been no real malice in it. By the time Nick went to secondary school, he had enroled in karate classes. There was never a chance to use his new found skills because the bullying had stopped by then. He chose to go to medical school but Stuart had decided to leave further education altogether, eventually becoming a self-employed joiner. Owning four properties didn't need a university degree. Nick clung on to his vocation and got through the lean years of medical school without any parental support. It had been a tough lesson in his life but the final hurdle of becoming a hospital consultant still beckoned. Having almost achieved his ultimate ambition, he was only too aware that he wasn't quite there yet.

The pub had filled up quietly with the regulars without the mad rush. Amidst the background babble they had become inconspicuous. Nick was still facing the bar when he felt a tap on the shoulder. In some Edinburgh pubs it could be followed by an approaching fist, but in The Canny Man's the thought hadn't cross his mind. He turned round to see a woman grinning at him.

'Hi, Nick.'

'Emma! What are you doing here?' he replied in total surprise.

'I suppose a daft question deserves a daft answer. I'm having a drink!'

'Why in Edinburgh?'

'We've not spoken for a while, have we?'

'No, I suppose not.'

'I got the job at St John's.'

'What, as a consultant?'

'Yes, of course. What else?'

'Congratulations. Meet Stuart, an old friend from school,' Nick said graciously.

'Hi. Just in case Nick doesn't tell you, I'm Emma and we went out together in London,' she informed him with a cute smile.

'No, Nick hasn't mentioned it. We've just met up,' Stuart answered.

'Well, I suppose I'm just one of his ex-girlfriends.'

'Surely not,' Stuart replied, not knowing what to say.

'And what are you doing here Nick?' she asked her old flame.

'I'm from Edinburgh, in case you've forgotten.'

'No, I haven't. Job hunting?'

'Maybe.'

'Aren't you pleased for me?'

'Yes, of course. Well done. What else should I be saying?'

'Knowing you, that's probably enough. I'm sitting in that corner over there with Ed so why don't you come over?' she asked.

'Who's Ed?' Nick asked, wondering if she was mocking him.

'He's my new boyfriend.'

'Yes, sure. I'm still trying to catch up with all the local gossip but we'll come over in a short while.'

'I'm just trying to be friendly, Nick,' she said with a deliberate smile.

'I know that,' he replied, looking straight back at her.

'Well enjoy your gossip boys. I'm sure you'll have things to talk about. Perhaps I'll get a chance to speak with you again Stuart,' she said, before walking off.

'Yes, indeed,' he replied.

Nick felt totally bemused by the encounter. This wasn't exactly Casablanca but life certainly had a funny way of springing surprises. After their breakup in London there had been a mutual decision to avoid each other whilst working in the same hospital. Now back in

Edinburgh, he wasn't sure if that agreement still applied. He suddenly wondered if her apparent friendliness had a deceptive air about it. Perhaps she wanted to flaunt herself with her new man as some kind of payback for being scorned.

'Wow, what was all that about?' Stuart asked.

'I think she's mocking me. What do you think?'

'Perhaps, but she's actually quite stunning,' Stuart replied observantly.

'She could eat you alive and not lose any sleep over it,' Nick answered.

'What? Like some horrible female spider after mating? I wouldn't care!'

'Don't be an idiot.'

'Were you involved with her and Meg?'

'Sort of.'

'What, at the same time?'

'There may have been a slight overlap.'

'You little devil! No wonder she seems a little brassed off.'

'It's another long story which I won't go into.'

'I don't rate her boyfriend much though,' Stuart said, taking a sip of his beer.

Nick had to turn around surreptitiously to see. He saw some balding chap in his mid-thirties, not ugly but not a painting either. Nick was surprised by her choice. It certainly wasn't her usual clean-cut rugby type as this one looked more like a geeky academic.

'I see what you mean,' Nick replied.

'Well, maybe he's good in other ways.'

'Now I know you're definitely an idiot,' Nick replied with a smirk. He enjoyed Stuart's sense of humour, most of the time.

In London, he had been an emotional wreck fighting with the NHS management. Emma's indifference to his mental state at that time had pushed him close to the edge of a mental breakdown, something Meg had wryly observed. She had kept in the background, not wanting to interfere until the situation had made itself apparent. When Nick's relationship was officially over with Emma, she felt the time had come to make her move. The two women had probably drawn daggers at each other in the casualty department but Nick had been too preoccupied to acknowledge the situation. Any sense of perverse satisfaction he may have gained from knowing that two of the most attractive women at the hospital were vying for his attention had gone unnoticed. Meg had always been supportive to him as a casualty sister and had maintained her own high standards of personal integrity at all times. She had kept her thoughts about Emma to herself but the converse may not be true. With Emma now back in Edinburgh, the rules of engagement could be different.

'Shall we go across and annoy them?' Stuart suggested mischievously, suddenly interrupting his thoughts.

'I think it's she who's winding me up,' Nick replied pensively, still mulling over the surprise encounter.

'So what if she is? Play the game and be cool.'

'OK, let's go over,' Nick suddenly decided.

'What does she do?'

'Obs and gynae.'

'So she really does work where other people play!' Stuart said with a high inflexion.

'You're not just an idiot but a pervert as well,' Nick replied in a deadpan manner.

Stuart laughed as they picked up their pints and walked over to the other side of the bar. Emma smiled as they approached but the boyfriend was less sure, looking uncomfortable like some balding tomcat sitting on a hot tin roof.

'This is Ed,' Emma said, introducing them to him.

'Hello,' Nick replied with as much élan as he could muster.

Ed put on a shaky smile as he stood up. He was a little taller than Nick. His manners were impeccable as he shook hands with both the interlopers. Emma had clearly primed him about Nick.

'I believe you're doing orthopaedics,' Ed said, to break the ice.

'Yes, I am. What about yourself?'

'I'm in general practice.'

'And how are things in GP land these days?'

'Good and bad, I suppose. The new contract means the day job has just got a lot harder. We're trying to offload some of the pressure from you hospital boys,' Ed replied with a slight lisp from his badly shaped teeth.

'And that's the bad bit, I suppose?' Nick replied in a conciliatory manner.

'The good bit is we don't work seven days a week anymore. Apparently you hospital consultants do quite a lot of private work these days.'

'I wouldn't know as I'm not a consultant. I'm just doing a locum job at the moment,' Nick said, unsure if Ed was being deliberately antagonistic.

'Sorry, I just presumed you were. Emma did say there was some trouble in London.'

'Oh, did she?' Nick retorted, feigning surprise. He wondered what was coming next.

'Yes. She mentioned something about somebody dying from a morphine overdose.'

'Is this leading up to anything in particular?' Nick asked, his hackles now truly raised.

'I just need some advice, that's all,' Ed replied blankly.

'Fire away,' Nick replied, ready to punch the man if he said anything insulting but professional courtesy wouldn't allow him to do that.

'Actually, it's not our problem at all. It concerns a neighbouring practice.'

'Go on,' Nick encouraged him, intrigued by what the man had to say.

'Naturally it must remain confidential,' Ed said, looking across at Stuart.

'Listen, you guys carry on with your talk whilst I get the drinks in. What are you all having?' Stuart asked, taking the hint.

'You don't have to on our account,' Ed replied, feeling suddenly embarrassed.

'I need the loo anyway,' Stuart replied, with a strained smile for effect.

'Thanks mate. I think Ed's having the same as us and Emma's a G and T if I remember correctly,' Nick replied, handing his friend a twenty pound note.

Emma put on a pained expression but didn't refuse the gin and tonic. Nick knew his friend wouldn't be offended by playing the waiter.

'I hope Stuart didn't think I was being rude,' Ed said, conscious of the faux pas.

'No, he's fine. Carry on.'

'You don't mind if I talk shop?' Ed asked.

'Why should I?'

'Some people like to switch off when they're not at work,' Ed replied.

'Just relax, Ed. Tell me about this medical practice.'

'For your information, I'm in partnership with a group of other GPs outside Edinburgh but we share the same building with another single-handed GP. We had discussed the possibility of joining our two medical practices but it came to nothing.'

'So, what about it?' Nick asked, still trying to fathom where the conversation was going.

'Recently, my senior partner was given an ultimatum by the medical director to compile a report about the present incumbent at our neighbouring practice.'

'For what reason?'

'I believe many people have lodged complaints to the Primary Care Trust about the poor standard of care at that practice. They needed some corroborative evidence and came to us about it.'

'Why your medical practice?'

'Because we had provided cross cover at weekends in the past.'

'And was there any justification for the complaints?'

'There were the usual stories.'

'Such as?'

'This is where it gets difficult. Apparently, several people had been given large doses of morphine.'

'Are we talking about another Shipman?' Nick asked, referring to the mass killer.

'No, not exactly.'

'So what's the problem then?'

'We think this doctor is using certain drugs inappropriately but we don't believe he is trying to kill people.'

'In that case, how can I help you?' Nick asked coolly.

'I'm keen to know how we could cover ourselves against any possible litigation for complicity. We suspect he does use high amounts of morphine on his elderly patients.'

'For what purpose?'

'To relieve chronic pain.'

'How is he using it?'

'Usually by intramuscular injection. His patients are often left alone after he has visited.'

'This is beginning to sound more like Shipman. Are you saying he has got away without killing anybody so far?'

'Yes, but we know the patients' relatives have started to ask questions. It could be more a case of medical incompetence rather than any true malicious intent. As you know, the pharmacodynamics of any drug in the elderly is affected by various conditions. I would normally give a lower dose, not higher.'

'I know that too.'

'But this doctor didn't. We had some concerns one weekend when he visited one of our elderly patients who was already on a huge number of medicines. In this situation, morphine should have been used with great care but it was given quite liberally. Perhaps he didn't have all the necessary information to hand but as you know yourself, it can be quite difficult to assess somebody who is not your regular patient.'

'Regardless, any competent doctor would have taken a good medical history first.'

'I accept that but sometimes even the patients don't know what's wrong or what medicines they are taking.'

'True, but are you saying this doctor is negligent?' Nick asked.

'Perhaps incompetent is a better word.'

'It amounts to the same thing. So why has he not been reported before?'

'That's just the point. He has been. The medical director has been told about his clinical incompetence by several hospital consultants over a number of years.'

'And nothing was done about it?' Nick asked, to confirm the story.

'Exactly. This is where our dilemma begins. We know that the Primary Care Trust management has all the necessary information they need to take action.'

'But they won't?'

'That's right. Conversely, it can clearly be seen from the prescribing data over many years that this doctor has been under prescribing the medicines needed for treating chronic conditions such as heart and lung diseases. His prescribing data showed a worrying trend, especially when it came to treating diabetes.'

'And how would you get that kind of information?'

'That's the easy part. Every medical practice gets its own set of data from the Primary Care Trust on a monthly basis. It also compares prescribing data with other medical practices. The results are clear to see and there is even a breakdown of the numbers and types of medicines prescribed by each doctor. The data in this case showed this person has not been doing the job properly.'

'So, the Primary Care Trust knew about this and did nothing?' Nick asked again.

'Yes. We think the management themselves are incompetent.'

'Is that the whole reason?'

'No.'

'You said earlier on that the medical director had asked your senior partner to submit a written report.'

'That's right.'

'How did that request materialise?'

'It came through as a personal phone call to the house one evening.'

'From the medical director?' Nick asked, to clarify the story.

'Yes.'

'Is this single-handed GP foreign, by any chance?'

'Yes.'

'So there a possibility of litigation for racial discrimination?'

'I suppose so.'

'It sounds to me that somebody is being rather clever.'

'We thought as much but I wanted your opinion. You have dealt with NHS management before.'

'What will your senior partner do now?'

'We have no options but to submit a report on what we know. The NHS management will then just say they were acting on information they had been given.'

'And consequently save themselves from the possibility of getting sued?'

'Yes.'

'How long have they known about this problem?' Nick asked.

'About ten years.'

'You've told me about the morphine business but do you think anybody has died because of the lack of medical care?'

'It's quite possible some lives may have been lost prematurely if people hadn't been treated properly. That's common sense.'

'What other evidence do you have to back your report?'

'We know of one patient who had his dose of warfarin increased when his blood was already over-anticoagulated. He could have bled out. Several other patients with very obvious cancers had been misdiagnosed which any competent doctor would have picked up. We're not talking about a small skin freckle which develops into a melanoma.'

'This sounds like a fitness to practise issue. The General Medical Council directive is quite clear about this. Your medical practice has no options but to report it,' Nick said.

'We know that.'

'So why did you feel it was necessary to ask my opinion?'

'I just wanted somebody else to confirm that we've been shafted by the medical director.'

'You have. Welcome to the dirty world of medical politics,' Nick replied.

It had crossed his mind earlier whether the conversation would get difficult but thankfully it didn't. So far, Emma had said nothing as Ed had done all the talking. He seemed like a straight talking chap with no obvious hang-ups. Try as he did, Nick could not discern any animosity from the man despite the shaky start. He presumed it was just Ed's manner of speaking, direct and to the point. Ed may have known about Nick's past involvement with Emma but he hid it well once the chat had started. The surreal situation had given way to a strange bonhomie, greatly helped when Stuart returned with the drinks. It was Emma's turn to speak.

'So where are you in terms of your own career?' she asked.

'I'm doing a short stint for one of the orthopods at the Royal Infirmary.'

'Yes, I heard about the heart attack. If it were me, I'd quit. Would you think of going back to work if that happened to you?'

'Perhaps.'

'Well I wouldn't. There may be a job available soon.'

'Why, have you heard something on the grapevine?'

'That's the general talk. Being a locum should put you in a good position, if the job did come up,' Emma added.

'Maybe,' Nick replied, still unsure how genuinely encouraging she was being.

'Life is full of uncertainties. Look, I'm normally here on a Friday. Why don't we meet up again? I'll keep my ears to the ground for you.'

'We could do that.'

'Will you be here next Friday?'

'No, Meg is coming up.'

'How is she?' Emma asked, without showing a flicker of emotion.

'She's well.'

'Good, I'm glad to hear that.'

Nick felt he needed to clear the air between them, as no doubt she did, except now was not a good time. She had a look of smug satisfaction about her, perhaps as a result of being a hospital consultant. Nick struggled to see what she had found so attractive about Ed but it was not his place to ask. He could be wrong but he thought he could feel an emotional undercurrent coming from her as she had gazed in his direction for much of the evening. Perhaps she had become human again, no longer bitter about chasing a career in a male-dominated speciality. For Nick, meeting up with her again at The Canny Man's was a coincidence he had not envisaged. His emotions had started to become confused again as Emma applied her feminine charms. She looked radiant with her chiseled features accentuating her natural beauty. He was determined not to fall into her trap again as no doubt many men already had. Somehow, it was difficult not to.

Chapter 2

The Interview

THE SURGEON WITH END-STAGE HEART FAILURE KNEW he could never operate again. He was breathless doing nothing, let alone attempt to hold a scalpel again. The job did come up quicker than Nick had anticipated and he had been short-listed. However, there were others in the queue. As the rank outsider he knew his chances were slim but he tried to cling onto Emma's words. Perhaps he was in the right place at the right time. The interview panel was composed of the usual mix, including the medical director of the Acute Hospital Trust, the chief executive, a manager from human resources, a representative from the Royal College plus two orthopaedic consultants. When the time came, he faced them with as much aplomb as he could, answering all the questions without any preamble. There had been the usual range of questions, including the one about his strong and weak points. Banking on the predictable, he had to bite his tongue to stop saying anything too effusive. His particular expertise lay in anterior cruciate ligament reconstructions and knee replacements but they already knew that. It was a growth area as more people outlived their joints. His weak points were more difficult to answer, such as a penchant for disliking pompous bureaucrats. His relative lack of experience as a newly qualified orthopaedic surgeon would go against him but overall, the interview had gone well. They would let him know of their decision later on that day. The woman from HR had looked like the bitch from hell with her false smile.

His nervous tension had quickly melted away after the interview. Standing up, he gave an unconvincing grin before the medical director fired off a parting shot. The man mentioned knowing Bob McLean, his now deceased counterpart working at Nick's last hospital in London. It was an ominous sign. Both men had apparently been to Edinburgh Medical School, something Nick hadn't considered before. He simply presumed Bob McLean was English, but then again, McLean was a Scottish name. Bob had spoken English with a cultured accent as one did in Morningside or Stockbridge. Perhaps Nick had read too much into the small talk. It was really up to the panel to decide, not just the medical director but the shadow of doubt remained. Perhaps past events in London had caught up with him.

With a slightly troubled mind, he drove away from the hospital in Little France, going through Gilmerton with ease. Edinburgh was relatively easy to get around without the congestion charges. He had traded in his blood-spattered Audi for a second-hand Porsche Boxster from a dealer in Essex. The compact little roadster with its massive 265 mm rear tyres had enough rubber to chew tarmac and certainly handled much better than the Audi. There was a reassuring level of feedback through the steering wheel as he hammered up Frogston Road, easily taking the bend at sixty-five before easing off at the Marie Curie Centre in Fairmilehead. He turned right at the next junction before heading down into Buckstone Terrace. The rented flat was in a modern block, looking out towards the north end of the city. It went some way to justify the outrageous rental fee. The phone call came through after 7 p.m.

'Hello. Is that Nick Forbes?' the woman asked.

'Yes, speaking.'

'It's Julie Dow from HR.'

'Hi.'

'This is let you know about our decision. I'm sorry but you didn't get the job.'

'Thanks for letting me know,' Nick replied, taking the hit calmly.

'Well, better luck next time.'

'Just before you go, may I ask who did get the job?'

'Yes, it was Joseph Sharma.'

'Was there anything I could have done to improve my chances?'

'No, you interviewed well but there were some strong candidates.'

'And did the medical director say anything about me in particular?' Nick was curious to know.

'I really can't go into that. It was a general decision.'

'Thank you, anyway.'

'Goodbye,' the woman said, sounding like some dreadful woman from a games show.

The news came as a bitter blow despite knowing that at best he was a wild card entry. Walking into a job at one of the world's most respected hospital and medical schools would have been a dream start to his career but reality had now kicked in. Technically, he was just as competent as any other surgeon at the interview but he had lacked research experience. That was something clever people did to get their names into medical journals. The two orthopaedic consultants on the panel had been very positive about his work but it had not been enough to get him the job. Now convinced that past events had definitely caught up with him, it felt like the ranks had started to close in. It could all be in his imagination but the the medical director must have put a negative spin on his reputation. It was true he had sought some payback for being the fallguy for somebody else's mistake in

London but he wasn't a whistleblower. Now feeling like a modern exile from the NHS, he understood Ed's dilemma. At least Ed wasn't acting alone because he was in a medical partnership. Nick felt very vulnerable at that moment. There would be other jobs, he thought to himself.

CHAPTER 3
OLD TIMES

THE NUMBER 11 BUS STOPPED THIRTY YARDS across the road from The Canny Man's outside the parade of shops. It was hardly a walk before the welcoming cosiness of the pub pulled him in. Nick peered in both bars but couldn't see her. Emma had been there on most Fridays unless she was on call for the hospital. He bought his pint of beer and nibbled on the free snacks, except they weren't free because the drinks were pricey. Several men stood on their own by the bar but the 'long coat' brigade were already there in numbers, boisterous and in obvious rude health. The old boys from George Watsons mingled with their own ilk, part of the thriving ex-public school contingent of Edinburgh. Emma suddenly appeared with a female friend and pointed to the inner bar when she saw him. She preferred it there. They found a small free table and ordered drinks from the waitress. It had to be the Bombay Sapphire.

'This is Lucy,' she introduced her.

'Hi,' he replied with a smile.

'How did the job interview go?' Emma asked.

'I didn't get it.'

'Why, what went wrong?'

'I don't know. I thought it was all sewn up. Maybe the others were better.'

'Did you know any of them?'

'No, but the chap who got it was somebody called Sharma.'

'What, Joe Sharma? He was a complete idiot. We worked together in Glasgow as junior doctors. How the hell did he get the job?' Emma asked.

'No point asking me.'

'He is about the same age as us so you couldn't exactly say he had that much more experience.'

'Maybe he had more research experience to offer.'

'Well, I got my job with next to no research experience.'

'But you're not at the Royal.'

'Spare me the sour grapes. Who interviewed you?'

'The usual suspects; the medical director, the chief executive, a couple of orthopods, somebody from the Royal College and the HR manager.'

'Was it Julie Dow from HR by any chance?' Emma asked.

'Yes, how did you know?'

'She was there at my interview, sucking up to the medical director. Normally she hasn't got a clue what she's doing.'

'That sounds like situation normal. The medical director said he knew Bob McLean. They had gone to medical school together in Edinburgh.'

'So who else was not on your side?' Emma asked with a mock laugh.

'How should I know?'

'Come on Nick, you can be a bit of an arse sometimes.'

'Thanks for telling me. Do I look like I'm an arse to you, Lucy?'

'I wouldn't know what one looked like,' she replied sincerely.

'Good answer. And what do you do?'

'I work in the operating theatre as a charge nurse. Emma does her gynae list there on a Thursday.'

'I've not seen you here before.'

'No, it's my first time.'

'And where do you live?'

'In Bathgate. Emma's putting me up tonight.'

'At The Grange?'

'Yes. I'm slumming it,' she replied, deliberately teasing her friend.

'Did you ever manage to sell the flat in Hampstead?' Nick asked his ex.

'Yes and before you ask, it did make a nice fat profit. Isn't it time you bought a place?'

'I'm working on it. Is Ed coming tonight?'

'No, he's doing a shift for the out-of-hours service.'

'How long have you known him?'

'We met recently at Champany's when I was giving a talk there.'

'How is Champany's these days?'

'Much the same.'

'How much do they charge for a steak now?'

'About forty pounds a pop.'

'What!' Lucy said, astonished.

'And the vegetables are extra,' Nick added, smiling at her naivety.

The waitress arrived with their drinks.

'Is this your local?' Lucy asked, casually.

'I come here sometimes,' Nick replied.

'Nick's a regular. When is Meg coming up again?' Emma interrupted.

'Tomorrow, actually. She's on a late shift tonight. Why do you ask?'

'Just curious.'

'I've not seen Ed for a while. Did he get the problem sorted?'

'You'll have to ask him yourself.'

'I didn't think he was your type,' Nick said without thinking.

'What exactly do you mean by that?' Emma asked, coldly.

'Well, you know, at university you seemed to hang around with the rugby guys,' Nick replied, struggling to find the right words.

'And Ed doesn't fit in to the stereotype I suppose?'

'Well, not really.'

'That is none of your business.'

'Sorry. I shouldn't have said anything.'

'Then why say anything at all?' Emma replied.

'It's just that he looks very academic.'

'And that's a bad thing?'

'No, not at all.'

'Look, I've never made a comment about Meg so I would really appreciate it if you didn't talk about Ed.'

'OK, point taken. Let's drop it.'

The conversation had gone the wrong way within a short space of time. Raking up the past was definitely not a good idea, especially when emotional wounds were still raw. Lucy had picked up on the signals and decided to intervene before things really went pear-shaped.

'Hey, I thought we were on a night out. If you two want to have a bunfight, just tell me and I'll go.'

'No, don't be silly. Nick was just being his usual inconsiderate self,' Emma replied.

'And I suppose you're the fairy godmother?' Nick asked.

'Really, you can be such an idiot at times..'

'Hey guys, let's call a truce here,' Lucy said.

'Maybe I'm an idiot but at least I know it,' Nick said, riled by her comments.

'Look, I have a much better idea. What's there to eat around here apart from Indian or Chinese?' Lucy asked to break the impasse.

'Fish and chips,' Nick replied.

'OK, let's have some fish and chips later. Just stop arguing.'

'Fine! Whatever!' Nick replied, knowing he had to have a proper talk with Emma.

Morningside was much poorer compared to other parts of Edinburgh when it came to restaurants. With little else to choose from other than Indian or Chinese, they agreed on having a fish supper. After several more drinks, they wandered next door to the local take-away. The traditional establishment was ideally placed to serve great food, so long as it was fried in beef dripping. They ordered their meals. The aroma of freshly cooked fish and chips wafted into the air, perfumed by the liberal application of vinegar. They ambled up Canaan Lane as steam gently percolated from the wrapper against the chill of the night. The food was piping hot.

Within the dark shadows, the entrance to the Astley Ainslie Hospital could be seen at the point where the road swung sharply to the left. The Grange was situated in a genteel part of Edinburgh which looked out onto the Braid Hills. It was not beyond imagination to believe one was in the countryside rather than in the city. Many of the grand buildings had been converted into flats as people couldn't afford to buy them apart from bankers. Emma's own converted flat in Hope Street had been part of an imposing building until it was divided up into two. Nick noticed the new Porsche 911 sitting on the gravel drive. It looked fabulous, even in yellow.

'That thing yours?' he asked, wiping his greasy fingers on the wrapping paper.

'Yep,' Emma replied, scarcely giving it a second look.

'Nice.'

They went into the apartment. It was immediately apparent how tastefully everything had been decorated. Even the furniture exuded quality and the antiques had been deliberately placed to lend an air of natural grace. Emma pulled the curtain closed and lit the gas fire to take the chill away. Despite the central heating, the Scottish winter had made its presence felt.

'I've got a Dalmore if you want, Nick,' Emma offered.

'Thanks, that's a good choice of malt,' he replied, surveying the room.

'Still got the TT?' Emma asked as she walked through to the kitchen to fetch the drinks.

'No, I traded it in for a second-hand Boxster. Can't affort a 911,' he replied.

'That's not a real Porsche. I hope it's the S model at least,' she said in a perfunctory manner.

'Yeah, I'm happy with it,' he replied.

There was no reason not to, especially with a cracking 3.2 litre straight six-cylinder engine pulling some incredible torque from low revs. He just wondered if Emma was reverting to type by her snide comment. It certainly sounded snobbish.

'Do you still smoke cigars?' she asked as she handed him the whisky.

'Now and again,' he replied, thinking she was going to offer him one.

'They're bad for you but somebody told me that whisky is made for cigars.'

'That's what it says on the bottle. Are you still banging on about my cigars?'

'No.'

'Then why make a comment about it?'

'Oh, for heaven's sake, Nick, just relax! I'm only trying to make conversation.'

'Look, maybe this is not such a good idea for me to come here,' he replied.

'And why not?' Emma asked.

'Because you're beginning to annoy me.'

'Why? Just because I mentioned your silly cigars?'

'Work it out.'

'You're angry about not getting the job but don't take it out on me.'

'Well, I don't need your patronising attitude,' he replied.

'Not everybody lands the first job they apply for, Nick.'

'You did.'

'I work very hard at what I do. Maybe I deserved the break.'

'Are you saying I don't work hard?'

'Oh, drink your whisky and lighten up.'

'I'm leaving.'

'Suit yourself.'

'Just tell me one thing. How do you always land on your feet?'

'Maybe I bring my own good luck.'

'You've never had a disappointment in your life, have you?'

'How about when you left me?'

'I left you because you never understood what I was going through. You didn't try to understand nor did you care. Everything just centred on your career.'

'That's rubbish. Nick, get yourself sorted out because I'm not listening to this nonsense any more.'

'You never do. I'm going,' he replied, putting the whisky glass down on the fine antique table.

'Well go then,' she replied unceremoniously.

Nick walked out and heard her close the door with a slight bang. He had felt irritated by her condescending remarks. Deep down, he knew it was the job, or lack of one, which was getting to him. Rather than taking the bus home, he decided to walk back to the flat. It was still busy on Comiston Road as he walked past the chip shop, noting the hungry queue staring patiently at the greasy offerings. Crossing Jordan Lane, he remembered the happier times. One of his female friends from Dundee had got a job as a lawyer in Edinburgh and bought a flat there. The dinner parties had been legendary. An American guest had even got so drunk one night she struggled to remove the bucket from her head after throwing up. The surreal sight could have led to a tragedy but they had been unable to help her, paralysed by hysterical laughter. He loved his friends and this part of Edinburgh. Despite coming from a modest background, he moved in privileged circles. It was a difficult cross to bear at times, watching how other people with money lived their lives. At the opposite end of the social spectrum, he had also seen poverty. Growing up on a council estate, he had known many people who survived on benefits. At least he had a career and good prospects, unlike many other people who had consigned themselves to a life of drink, drugs and domestic violence. He just needed a slice of good luck to change his life for good and it wasn't too much to ask.

Chapter 4

The Blonde

N ICK DROVE DOWN BIGGAR ROAD, HEADING TOWARDS the bypass. The airport was only ten minutes away, unlike in most other major cities keen to distance themselves from noise pollution. Edinburgh was a great place to live but the secret was out as thousands of Poles and Eastern Europeans had already discovered. Now Auld Reekie was seeing a flood of Nigerians and Ghanaians doing the same thing. Asylum seekers from Iraq and other far distant shores had already depleted the capital's council housing stock, leaving many local natives irate and homeless. Scottish nationalism was on the rise as even the English pushed north of the border to escape the crowded south. It remained in the annals of folklore that the Scots had invaded England many times before to steal the women but came back with sheep instead when hunger proved more important. Meg was the quintessential English blonde who enjoyed coming to Scotland.

The two-lane bypass had got busier over the years, frequently becoming gridlocked in the rush hour. Nick managed to arrive in good time, it being a Saturday. The solitary Spitfire at the entrance reminded people that the war had reached the Scottish capital but for some reason the Luftwaffe had chosen not to bomb it. The city was blessed, unlike Glasgow, which had been bombed. Now the airport was set to overtake its rival as Scotland's busiest, linking up to more destinations around the world. The BMI baby flight from Heathrow had been on time as Nick pulled up in the dropping off area. It saved paying a parking fee in the short stay car park. He popped open the rear boot lid door of the Boxster as Meg quickly dumped her small travelling bag into the snug space.

'Hi,' she said as she climbed in, reaching across to give him a kiss.

'Good flight?'

'Yes, brilliant. How are you?'

'Good. Top down?' Nick suggested. It was a crisp November day with diluted sunshine from a cloudless sky.

'Show-off! Just turn the heating up,' Meg giggled.

He took that as a yes and opened the roof. It was a neat piece of German engineering. Nick suggested they went to South Queensferry for lunch, only a short drive away. The small village by the Firth of Forth lay between the world famous Victorian iron railway bridge and the more modern road bridge. The newer structure was already at risk of collapse as the suspension wires were corroding, something the Japanese engineers were trying to fix. It was one up to the Victorians. They stopped at one of the quaint sea food restaurants overlooking the water with an amazing view of the old bridge. The restaurant was semi-busy but they managed to get a decent table.

'I waited for you to call last night. How did the interview go?' she asked.

'I thought I'd tell you today. I didn't get it.'

'What happened?'

'It was their decision. I'm staying on until January which gives me another six weeks here.'

'And then what?'

'I don't know,' Nick replied.

'Would you consider working down south again? There are more jobs there.'

'I know that but I like it here. You also know how I feel about London.'

'Nick, my job and my home is in London so you have to tell me where we stand. I'm prepared to consider my position but remember I've got a job whereas you don't at the moment,' she said logically.

'Would you move up if I got a job?'

'You also have to remember that all my friends are in London.'

'Does that mean you won't move up?' Nick asked.

'No, I didn't say that.'

'So what are you saying?'

'Why don't you get a job first and then we'll see.'

'Is that a maybe?'

'Yes. Let's not spoil the weekend by talking about it. I've missed you.'

'Well, I'm glad you're here too,' he replied, touching her hand.

'I suppose one casualty department will be pretty much the same as another,' Meg reasoned, trying to put a positive spin on things.

'Except there are probably more drunken idiots here.'

'What in Scotland? Surely not?' Meg replied amusingly.

'Apparently, it's our national culture.'

'Well, you can get me a nice big glass of that Australian sauvignon blanc.'

The lunch was good with scallops served in truffle oil for starters. The bream had been perfectly grilled too, matching the crisp white wine. They strolled along the small rocky beach after lunch before driving off to the arts galleries in Bedford Road. The Dadaist and Cubist paintings left something to the imagination but the room full of balls was just that. Nick was glad for Meg's company, especially for the way she laughed at the absurdity of what they had seen. It was as bad as a pile of bricks at the Tate gallery but no doubt somebody would call it art. They went back to the apartment in Buckstone having filled their culture lust. Even her ruffled blonde hair looked good. It has been quite a few weeks since she last came up as Nick kissed her passionately. He desperately wanted to forget about yesterday. Despite his seemingly charmed life of being a young surgeon with the sports car and pretty women by his side, there was still a feeling of emptiness, of perceived failure. It was a strange mix of emotions which had stemmed from a childhood devoid of love or encouragement. It would take a very special woman to fill the void as Meg pushed him against the wall with a hungry look. It was all he needed just then. He kissed her even harder. The wine had removed all her inhibitions as Meg took a commanding position. She was in charge and he would let her do anything she wanted. Life felt good again at that moment.

CHAPTER 5

DILEMMA

S HE CAUGHT THE LAST FLIGHT BACK TO Heathrow on Monday evening. It was all too brief a weekend but since coming back to Edinburgh Nick had been working flat out. He had gone back to London twice but found little time to relax. It always felt better when Meg came up because there was so much of Scotland he wanted her to see. It also felt good not to work that day, mindful that winter was not a good time for getting temporary work. He would need the income soon when his current contract finished. It was enjoyable working at the infirmary and many patients had wished him well, except his luck had run out on the day of the interview.

Despite their frosty parting, Emma sent him a text in an attempt to be friendly. Even in the tough back-stabbing world of medicine, she knew how devastated he must have felt about not getting the job. There was a kindred spirit of being at the same medical school but he was also an ex-lover. She needed to know that Nick still considered her to be attractive in a way all vain women thought men did, despite flaunting a new boyfriend. He replied to her text.

They agreed to meet at the Scotch Malt Whisky Society on the Friday night rather than at The Canny Man's. The Society was in Queen Street, part of the New Town area of Edinburgh. The regency-style building rested between Hanover and Frederick Street overlooking Queen Street Gardens. The main restaurant was on the ground floor with the members' lounge upstairs. It displayed a huge array of cask strength malt whiskies selected by a panel of experts. For the connoisseur, savouring the delights in the comfort of one of the leather chairs was a blissful moment of escape.

From Princes Street Nick walked along Hanover Street, past Milnes bar, once a haunt for the poets of Edinburgh. A fine drawing of Hugh MacDiarmid hung by the entrance, drawn by his long-term friend Rosalie Loveday, an English artist. Crossing over George Street, it was downhill to Queen Street and the Whisky Society. He planned to wait for Emma in order to sign her in but was surprised to see them already there. Lucy had obviously decided to come. After signing them both in, they headed up to the members' lounge.

'What would you both like?' Nick asked, surprised to see Lucy again so soon.

'We'll have what you're having,' Emma answered surprisingly.

'I didn't know you liked whisky,' Nick replied.

'We've acquired a taste for it.'

'Excellent, in that case the Cragganmore is absolutely superb.'

Lucy just smiled as Nick ordered the drinks. Both women looked around, noticing things a man normally wouldn't. The place certainly had a relaxed clubby atmosphere but the ceiling light was simply ghastly.

'It's lovely here but I'm not sure about that thing,' Emma said quietly, referring to the ugly lighting unit.

'Not the most pretty is it?' Nick agreed.

'How long have you been a member here?'

'I joined several years ago. There's even a branch in London. Let's get a seat,' Nick indicated, handing them their whiskies.

They sat by the window looking down onto Queen Street. Nick poured a little water to 'open up' the whisky, releasing the delicate aromas. He indicated the women should do the same as the fiery liquid was 60 per cent alcohol by volume.

'Lucy managed to find out something which may be of interest to you,' Emma said, swirling her glass gently.

'What's that?' Nick was curious to know.

'My mother works for the Council for Healthcare Regulatory Excellence in London. I told her we met recently,' Lucy answered.

'Who are they?' Nick asked.

'It's a government-based agency which helps to oversee the GMC, amongst other things.'

'I've never heard of them. How did your mother get involved with that lot?' Nick asked.

'She was a nurse before heading towards the management side of things. She trained in Glasgow and worked there before moving down to London when she and Dad split up. That was only a few years ago but she climbed the ladder quickly.'

'Why go over to the management side?'

'She wanted to make some changes.'

'That's original.'

'Let's face it, most nurses hit the ceiling pretty quickly as far as a career goes. She didn't want to get bogged down with nowhere to go.'

'OK, I can see that. What do they do exactly?'

'The organisation helps to validate complaints against doctors and nurses.'

'Did you say they oversee the GMC?'

'Yes, something like that.'

'Who came up with the bright idea to set this up?' Nick wanted to know.

'It's another government initiative to have an independent review body to oversee what the GMC or the NMC does, especially when it comes to disciplinary matters involving the medical or nursing profession. I can't give you all the answers because I don't know much more than this.'

'It may be cynical but it sounds like the government wants to legislate the abolition of the GMC, and perhaps your nursing body the NMC for that matter. They probably want bad doctors and nurses to be punished by lay people of the government's own choosing.'

'I don't think it is as radical as that. The GMC and NMC will always have a major role to play.'

'So where does your mother come in to all this?' Nick asked.

'She reviews the reaction from members of the public regarding any major medical and nursing issues and sees how these problems had been dealt with by the GMC or NMC. In particular, the GMC is under great scrutiny.'

'Let's face it. The government will do anything to pander to the press. From their point of view, they will always add some spin to try and keep doctors under control because they know people still trust us. Can anybody trust a politician? When was the last time people looked at their expense claims? The GMC has been doing a good job for over 140 years so why change a fundamentally good system when it's not broken?'

'What about the Shipman murders?' Lucy replied.

'There was no way in the world the GMC could have foreseen that. No, this is another sign that the government just wants to undermine the authority of the medical profession. I'm sure your mother is doing a good job but as far as I'm concerned, the GMC is already doing that.'

'OK, think about this from another angle,' Lucy suggested.

'What's that?'

'Regarding the trouble you had in London. Apparently everybody knew about it.'

'So what?' Nick asked.

'The problem remains that you will struggle to get a consultant's post anywhere in the country.'

'Why, because I stood up to corrupt management?'

'Yes, exactly. You fought the system by trying to be a maverick. People don't like that sort of thing.'

'I stood up for what I believed in.'

'I know that, Nick. For exactly the reasons you believe, the Council for Healthcare Regulatory Excellence also monitors for discrimination within the medical or nursing profession. Their aim is to make sure that discrimination in any form does not exist but unfortunately it does, as you well know,' Lucy explained.

'So, are you saying that I will never get a job because some chief executive of a hospital trust has lost her job?'

'Work it out for yourself. These people stick together, it's a closed shop. If one chief executive goes, so can the others. Somebody did get fired in London when the hospital consultants had a vote of no confidence but that was done as a mass action. Things are different when you rock the boat by yourself. It can be looked upon as troublemaking. Medical directors also don't like junior doctors upstaging them.'

'And you think me not getting the job had something to do with all this?' Nick asked.

'Look, if this is of any consolation to you, the system is changing. There is now more openness and people are starting to ask questions about decisions made by the hierarchy,' Lucy said.

'Is that just to make me feel better?'

'No, but if people can see how the GMC or the hospital trusts work, they will be more reassured. The government will then have less ground to take their powers away.'

'It makes sense. It's time you nurses fought for your own recognition too.'

'Why do you think my mother is there?' Lucy replied.

'God, I'll get another whisky whilst you two carry on,' Emma suggested, feigning despair.

'Why don't you ask for one of the darker malts?' Nick suggested.

'Which one?'

'The Bowmore fifty-year-old is rather nice but check your bank balance first,' Nick advised, smiling to himself.

As Emma walked over to the bar, he thought about Lucy and what she had tried to say to him. She had seemed very confident, perhaps coming from the Glaswegian school of hard knocks. She was petite, about five foot two, with short cropped brown hair. It was her infectious grin and perky hair style which had slowly endeared her to him, plus the accent. He appreciated her take on medical politics, no doubt enlightened by her mother. Her friendship with Emma was a little more difficult to fathom out. He had expected Emma to fraternise with the Morningside crowd, join the Porsche club or play touch rugby with the medical fraternity but she had seemed very friendly with the articulate Glaswegian. As they worked together, perhaps it was enough to keep their friendship up but something didn't stack up. Was he looking too deeply for an answer?

The barman had recommended the eighteen-year-old Linkwood. It was a dark amber-coloured whisky with lots of sherry character but Nick was right, the Bowmore fifty-year-old was just too pricey. The second whisky was very different in character to the Cragganmore. The women compared notes as Nick savoured his dram. Afterwards, he suggested they went to one of the Italian restaurants in Hanover Street for a meal, a family-run affair serving some of the best south Italian cuisine. The friendly head waiter could easily pass for a flamboyant Italian despite being Turkish but all that was irrelevant as he welcomed Nick like a long-lost friend. The lady of the house also treated him like a celebrity, Nick having eaten there for many years as a student and then as a doctor. The talk of medical conspiracies had melted away in favour of talking about good food and Italian wine. Things seemed to be going well.

After the meal, they managed to find one of the Edinburgh taxis, elusive at that time of night, just outside the restaurant. They headed back to Emma's flat rather than to one of the noisy discos where girls wore skimpy dresses, oblivious to the cold outside. Once back at the flat, Lucy suggested putting on Pink Floyd as Emma fetched the coffee. She then sat next to Nick on the big settee, suddenly looking quite meaningfully at him without smiling. The mellow intro to 'Shine On You Crazy Diamond' continued as Nick shut his eyes, aware he was being watched. The effect of the whiskies and red wine had dulled his mind but it was a welcomed intrusion as Lucy paid him close attention. He could feel his personal space being invaded, especially with her scent. The gentle fingers suddenly ran through his hair, which felt reassuringly calming, but she had now definitely invaded his space. Before he realised what was happening he felt her mouth pressing onto his. Instantly he froze on the settee; he had been unprepared for this. He wondered if this was the action of an intoxicated woman, concerned that Emma would hit the roof when she came back to find them so intimately connected. Somehow, rather than pushing Lucy away, he simply allowed her to carry on, feeling her tongue explore his mouth. She became more passionate, as if hungry for a man. He did not match her ardour, still waiting for the shock-horror which would undoubtedly be coming from Emma. The music carried on, masking Emma's silent footsteps. She laid down the coffees silently and slipped in beside them. Nick felt her presence as another cool hand slipped around his face. He felt her pulling him towards her, before a familiar mouth engaged his. It was a pleas- ant surprise, a new experience. Strangely, he felt no shock as it all seemed so natural.

He opened his eyes to see both women grinning at him. He wondered if this was a game as they took it in turns to kiss him. Shutting his eyes again, he heard the music riding the gravy train until the riffs slowly died, leading into 'Wish You Were Here'. The women were by now more passionate, running their hands over his body. He showed some self-restraint as he thought of Meg but the alcohol had weakened his resolve. The pressure was suddenly off his lips despite the girls being intimately close to him. He opened his eyes again and saw them kissing each other. The penny had finally dropped. All the while in London, he had felt Emma's lack of passion. Their physical relationship had felt mechanical but he always thought it had been due to her personality. Now he knew better. It was her sexuality which had been the invisible barrier to their relationship. Nothing had made sense until now. He was seeing Emma in a different light, now here with her friend. They stood up suddenly, pulling him off the settee. He could only presume where they were heading. Like some meek lamb, he followed them to the bedroom.

Chapter 6

White Lies

NICK DECIDED TO GO TO LONDON THE following week, out of a sense of guilt. The Easyjet flight had left an hour later than scheduled due to delays building up over the course of the day. Despite being unable to make up for lost time, there would be no compensation. It was easy to access the M11 motorway from Stansted airport but at peak times it became chaotic. Pressure for landing slots had also made Stansted very busy, adding to the passenger load. Nick didn't say much until they were on the M11, allowing Meg to concentrate on the road.

'Have you heard about the Council for Healthcare Regulatory Excellence?'

'No, who are they?' she replied.

'Well, I met somebody in Edinburgh who was telling me about it. Apparently this organisation looks at how various healthcare organisations are regulated, including the GMC and your nursing and midwifery council, the NMC.'

'What about them?'

'These people apparently have a very good idea about how medical politics work.'

'Nick, can you please tell me what this is all about?'

'Well, I'm just wondering if there was some other reason

why I didn't get the job.'

'And what makes you say that?' Meg asked.

'Maybe I'm just reading between the lines but I've been told that challenging the hierarchy wasn't a good career move.'

'That's rather obvious. And who told you that?'

'I was just speaking to somebody at the Whisky Society.'

'Somebody who knows a great deal about medical politics I suppose?'

'Yes, in a way. Do you believe the medics would close ranks, just like some secret society?'

'Do you mean like the Freemasons?'

'Yes.'

'Perhaps you've been watching *Murder by Decree*.'

'I'm not talking about Jack the Ripper.'

'It sounds like you are. Wasn't he a surgeon?' Meg asked with a straight face.

'Oh come on. Since you mentioned the Masons, what do you know about them?'

'Absolutely nothing except it involves a bunch of men who do some very silly things just to be one of the boys.'

'Well, just who are the Masons?'

'I really don't know, Nick. Are you still annoyed about not getting the job?'

'You know I am. My point is that there could be many people in the medical profession who are in the Freemasons. If Jack the Ripper was a surgeon, he would have been protected by them. The loss in public confidence would be unimaginable.'

'You must have a vivid imagination. I still don't see what all this has to do with your job interview.'

'What if both the medical directors had been Masons, don't you think one would have made sure I didn't get a job?'

'That is theoretically possible but still unlikely,' Meg replied.

'Well, it would make a lot of sense. Let's take police for an example. Many of them are in the Masons. Only a few years ago the government wanted everybody in the police to declare if they were a Mason or not but it was met with some very strong objections, not surprisingly. How do we know that senior doctors and NHS managers are not in secret societies? How come the NHS has been so badly run and yet the people running it have not lost their jobs?'

'Something to do with lunatics running the asylum, I guess.'

'This wouldn't happen in a big corporate organisation. Heads would roll if a company kept making a financial loss. Even bankers lose their jobs during a recession but how many NHS managers lose theirs when wards are closing?'

'The NHS would argue they can't attract good managers because the pay is so poor compared to the finance industry. What has this to do with you seeking a job?' Meg asked.

'My point is quite simple. If the NHS doesn't want me, I'll never get a job unless I go abroad or try the public sector.'

'And you're convinced there is a vendetta against you?'

'I just don't know but it seems like that.'

'Who were you speaking to about this?'

'Oh, I met up with Emma and a friend. It was her friend who knew about the Council for Healthcare Regulatory Excellence.'

'Is there more to tell?' Meg asked in subdued tone of voice.

'Not really. Emma's got the consultant's job at St Johns, a hospital outside Edinburgh.'

'When did you meet her?'

'I bumped into her at The Canny Man's.'

'And then at the Whisky Society?'

'Yes.'

'How often have you seen her, Nick?'

'Oh, just a few times. She has a new boyfriend. I'm sure she still hates me.'

'Does she? I wouldn't know.'

'I'm sure she does,' he replied, deliberately avoiding the mention of her bisexuality.

'Well, that's unfortunate for you. Why did you decide to come down this weekend?'

'To see you, Meg.'

'I thought you're always too busy to come down. There is something going on, isn't there?'

'Maybe I'm just confused about my career.'

'Well, you have to make your mind up soon about what you are going to do, Nick, because I don't think I'll be moving up to Scotland. You know there is more of a chance of getting a job down here. Let me know what you decide to do, sometime soon.'

They finally reached her flat in Southgate after a seemingly long drive in an uneasy silence. Nick knew Meg's feminine intuition had kicked in, sensing something was wrong. He felt pangs of guilt after spending that night at Emma's. At least she had been an ex-girlfriend. Lucy had been an added distraction but these things happen. Being in London again had brought back a sense of reality as he knew he was being torn in two, between the excitement of a new life in Edinburgh or the comfort of having Meg at his side in London. Things were becoming complicated.

CHAPTER 7

CHRISTMAS DAY

AVING HAD VERY LITTLE TIME TO PREPARE for the Christmas period, the actual day rushed up at Nick without him noticing it. The night frost had left a thin layer of ice on the roads, including the Wisp, a notorious road on the south side of Edinburgh. Stretching from Niddrie to join the Old Dalkeith Road, accidents frequently happened at the bend, especially when it was icy. The transit van had been travelling east towards Niddrie when it hit the black ice and lost control. Slamming into the road barrier, a rectangle cross section broke off and impaled itself into the left side of the van. The driver was unhurt but his passenger was not so lucky. He was skewered. The metal road barrier had gone through his pelvis, taking out his bladder, genitals, rectum and sacrum. He was still very much alive when the trauma team got to him. With multiple drips in his arms, the fluids ran in as the blood poured out. The firemen had to cut him free quickly, sawing through the section of metal barrier. The vibration transmitting up his spine was mercifully dulled by the ketamine anaesthetic. It was the same medicine they used for horses.

Nick was working on Christmas Day and took the call from the trauma team. He had nearly finished the morning ward round when the call came in. Luckily there were only a few patients around as all routine operations had been called off for the festive period. The emergency operating theatre had been prepared to receive the casualty but the trauma team wanted Nick out there on site to give instructions. He was rushed by a paramedic in a fast response car just as the other specialists gathered in the hospital. The general surgeons, urologists and neurosurgeons would be needed. Nick had to assess the situation on the orthopaedic front. The man's pelvis had shattered with a metal structure going through it. After cutting the barrier free, the man was rushed to the hospital, now fully anaesthetised. He was assessed by the panel of specialists who decided the metal barrier should be removed first before stabilising the pelvis. The bleeding remained a problem despite clamping off the major blood vessels. Nick's first task was to drill pins into both sides of the pelvis to brace the structure with metal bars. He knew what he was doing was totally pointless but it had to be tried. Mercifully, the man died on the operating table as the injury was beyond repair. Christmas was over for his family. The men in the van had only been out for a beer before dinner.

Having long since learnt the art of emotional detachment in order to do the job, Nick still felt the sense of loss when somebody died. He was free to get away from the hospital after the emergency but it had taken over six hours of hard battle to try and save the man's life. Buckstone was only ten minutes away from the hospital if he had to get back for another emergency.

Meg had agreed to come up for Christmas knowing she would be working the shift on New Year's Eve. The turkey dinner was spoilt but there had been no further interruptions during the night. Too many Christmases had already been wiped out working for the NHS for him to worry any more. This time, he wouldn't be working on Boxing Day. His friends in Edinburgh had a tradition of having a post-Christmas party. Offering to cook for Stuart and Mary would be a welcome distraction.

CHAPTER 8

BOXING DAY

I T HAD ALL GONE QUIET AFTER THE big drama yesterday. Boxing Day felt good, especially with Meg there. They walked down to Greenbank where the old City Hospital used to be. It was now a desirable residential area for the upwardly mobile. Stuart had wisely invested in another property, this time as the family residence. Nick quickly ensconced himself in his friend's kitchen and busied himself with making the food. The Cullen Skink smoked haddock soup took no time to make but it would taste better with some maturing. The next chore was to pipe the choux mix for the profiteroles. With the sea food linguine the last thing to do, everything was under control. He slurped down some wine in a Floydian manner just as Stuart shouted from the living room.

'Hey Nick, come and see this!'

'What? I'm busy,' he shouted back, having reached the crucial stage. Choux mix could not be left alone for too long.

'We just saw you on the news!' Stuart shouted again.

Nick came through in time to see the brief footage on TV. It showed a badly smashed-up van surrounded by fire fighters and paramedics. He saw himself advising the emergency team as the local BBC crew reported on the crash. His real work only started after they had got the man to the operating room but they didn't show

47

that. He returned to his profiteroles without saying much despite the inevitable questions. Mary followed him through.

'It looked awful. Did he live?' she asked.

'No,' he replied pensively.

'Here, do you want me to do that?' she offered, referring to the profiteroles.

'Yes, why not? I'll get started on the linguine. The oven is ready to go.'

'You must see a lot of that sort of thing.'

'Sometimes. Most of the work is routine.'

'What will you do after this current job?'

'Look for another one?' Nick replied with a whimsical laugh.

'Don't be an idiot. I'm sorry you didn't get the job.'

'I'm working on it but there aren't many permanent posts out there.'

'Stuart said you didn't get the job because of what happened in London. Is that true?'

'I don't really know but it's a possibility.'

'Can't you complain about it to somebody?'

'No.' Nick laughed slightly louder this time at her innocence.

'It's not funny, Nick. I mean it. Why don't you complain to the Scottish Health Minister for instance?'

'What for? He would just argue the Hospital Trust has every right to make its own decision. The only way I can lodge a complaint is if I was the only candidate and didn't get it because I was gay, black or ugly. Anyway, they gave the job to a Scottish Indian guy born in Glasgow.'

'So why him and not you?'

'I'm not a mind reader, Mary.'

'It's all sounds like a pantomime. You've worked so hard all these years that I've known you. Why didn't you become a vet or something? I'm sure it would have been so much easier.'

'Maybe you're right. Animals don't talk back and it's always the humans who create all the trouble.'

'Would you think of working abroad?'

'I may have to. There's less of this sort of nonsense in Australia. The old boy network is not so rife out there.'

'What if there was a major world disaster? Would you consider working for *Médecins Sans Frontières* or a similar organisation?'

'I've never thought about it. Working in a war zone has never appealed to me.'

'It doesn't have to be a war zone. It could be helping out some poor people in Africa or Bhutan.'

'Hey, I need to live as well! They don't pay foreign medics in Bhutan. Some people work there for free on a six month sabbatical.'

'But I can just see you operating in some disaster area or other. You'll be good at it. If I was a nurse, I would wipe your brow.'

'If you were a nurse Mary, nobody would get the right dressing put on! Now shut up and pass me more of that wine,' he said, amusingly.

'Just think, Nick, it could be another one of your wonderful adventures!' she teased in reply, knowing his lust for foreign travel.

'I think I'm going to break one of your legs.'

'Then you'll have to fix it!'

'OK! Come here,' he said, chasing her with his pastry filled hands.

'Get away from me!' she screamed with laughter.

'You'd better take over if you don't want this pastry all over you. Just don't get any on the ceiling.'

'Nick, you bastard! I'm not that hopeless.'

'Pipe it out neatly. We're making profiteroles, not eclairs,OK?'

'Right, I'm definitely going to kill you with this piping bag!'

'No you won't. You wouldn't know how. Where's that wine I asked for?'

'I'm going to get you back! Is the primitivo OK or do you want some white wine?'

'It'll do for the linguine.'

'So, are you and Meg quite serious?' she asked, pouring wine into his glass.

'Maybe. What do you think of her?' Nick asked.

'She's pretty nice.'

'Is that all?'

'I hardly know her Nick.'

'You'd better get those profiteroles in the oven because we'll be eating soon.'

'Are you in love?'

'Oh for heaven's sake, don't ask daft questions.'

'I think you are!' she said, flicking a piece of choux pastry at him.

'Right, I'm really going to break your leg this time!' Nick shouted, chasing her with his garlicky hands.

She ran away screaming again.

The food had gone down well, especially the pudding, a mountain of choux balls covered in chocolate sauce. The children had done their best to eat up, even after their big Christmas Day lunch the day before. The adults busied themselves with consuming a small wine lake, enough to keep the producers happy. There were other friends there and their children, making Nick and Meg the only couple without any. Meg had looked a little broody. Nick saw the cheeky grin on Mary's face as they left. As the best man at Stuart and Mary's wedding, he had had a brief dalliance with the brides-maid later on that evening. Undoubtedly, she had spilled the beans to Mary, regreting the liason had not materialised into a meaningful relationship. Mary knew better than most that Nick had to settle down for his own good. He was now over thirty and couldn't keep having different relationships. She and Stuart had met at eighteen and were married soon after. She was like a sister to him.

Meg flew back the following day. With only two weeks left of his locum work, Nick knew he had to find other work soon. Perhaps something else would turn up in the New Year but it had been a good Boxing Day after all. Nobody had bothered to turn on the television to watch the late news as turmoil reigned on the other side of the world.

CHAPTER 9

NEW YORK

A FEW MONTHS EARLIER, A MEETING HAD TAKEN place in secret at the Waldorf Astoria Hotel in New York. It sat on Park Avenue, between 49th and 50th, just uptown from Grand Central Station near the Rockefeller Center. Besides the famous salad, the hotel was also known for its Art Deco and marble floors. Ornate chandeliers hung from the ceilings, giving an air of ostentatious exuberance. The place oozed class, unlike the man who had hired the private dining room.

The meeting had been arranged by Bill Frazer, the CEO of the New England construction company. The big man knew his way around the business, from laying concrete to erecting steel. Now being in his late fifties, the designer suit could barely cover his girth and getting his hands dirty these days meant eating seafood. He had arrived well before his guest, ordering a large Scotch before settling down in the deep leather chair. A quaint notion had occurred to him. Somehow, he had actually been invited to give the lunch. His guest was without doubt one shrewd player.

The Assistant Secretary-General for Programme Planning, Budget and Finance of the United Nations had deliberately engineered the lunch to discuss the multi-billion dollar deal to renovate the UN headquarters. It was not going to be done cheaply. The building on New York's East River looked tired, having been completed in 1952. It was hailed at the time for its modernist design but, it being technologically out of date, the demands of the twenty-first century had dictated a redesign. Muslim fundamentalists were now on a jihad to kill the infidels. A fanatic with a machine gun could easily shoot everybody dead without pause behind the scallop-shaped information desk in the lobby. Nostalgia for retro kitsch had no place in a modern world. Even the wavy white pine ceiling in the Woodrow Wilson Reading Room of the library had to go. The whole building would be stripped down and rebuilt and nothing was ever going to be that uber-chic again, especially not at the UN. There was serious work to be done.

Walking in with an air of confidence, the financial director met his host and shook hands warmly. The men sized each other up mentally and smiled, acutely aware of what was at stake. Bill Frazer had been surprised to get the call at all, coming unexpectedly as it did, leaving him almost duty bound to suggest they had lunch. He ordered another Scotch on the rocks for his guest just to break the ice. The pre-chosen menu was Norwegian Gravilax, Beluga Caviar and Confit de Canard served with a Foie Gras salad. It was washed down with Cristal Champagne and Puligny Montrachet. Small talk had certainly helped the lunch go down as both men considered their strategies. They adjourned to the lounge, settling comfortably in the deep leather chairs with the 1942 cognacs warmed to the correct temperature. They were accompanied by Cohiba cigars. The seven-inch Esplendido was indeed very splendid, burning slowly and evenly, just as the maker had intended.

'That was a great lunch, Bill. Good choice,' the man from the UN said cordially.

'Glad you enjoyed it,' the CEO answered, looking straight at his guest.

'So, shall we get down to business?'

'That's what we're here for, I guess.'

'I'll come straight to the point. The UN building renovation programme is going to be one of the biggest deals right now, bar Ground Zero. We want a technologically competent structure that will take us forward for the next fifty years and I like your company's design.'

'I'm glad you see it our way!' the big American said, beaming confidently.

'The other companies also have good designs.'

'Is that a problem for us?'

'I don't know. That would rather depend on how much this deal means to you.'

The CEO eyed the other man carefully, considering the opening gambit as he slowly sucked on his cigar. He knew only too well the contract would be fought for tooth and nail. All the competing bids would be scrutinised by a panel of experts from the UN. There was no doubt the contract would be awarded on the basis of technical merit and cost. So, what was all this about? he wondered.

'Obviously I want my company to win. So, what are you proposing?' he asked.

'I like your submission very much. I am keen to personally back it but as you can guess, it's not just my decision.'

'Just how much say do you have in all this?'

'What I say goes a long way but it may take some work to persuade the panel. I think I can get them to come round to my way of thinking.'

'And why would you want to do that?'

'I just want to see a good job done,' the financial director replied with a confident smile.

'Where's the catch?'

'Let's think of it as collaboration,' the financial director answered, contemplating his cigar.

'How much do you need to persuade the panel?' the CEO asked without flinching, correctly guessing there was a personal angle to all this.

'I don't want to be crude, so you tell me how much you think it is worth to your company.'

'I figured about one half of one per cent of the contract deal.'

'That would amount to about eight hundred thousand.'

'I guess that's about right.'

'I prefer a round figure, say a million,' the financial director replied coolly.

'That's a lot of money.'

'Suppose we gave the contract to the Marello group?'

'On the same basis? Do you really think you would get a million from those guys?' the CEO answered.

'Oh, I think we might.'

'I'm going to call your bluff. The UN will never deal with a company which has links to the mob,' the CEO gesticulated. He felt irritated at the gamesmanship being played right then.

'They're clean. All the bidding companies have been vetted. You know they have,' the UN man replied coolly.

'So you really think the mob has no influence in New York? You think the Marello group has really moved on?' the CEO asked, thinking the man opposite him was being rather naive.

'Of course we know some companies are linked to the mob, but not them. Right now they're doing some work near Ground Zero. Tell me, what's your company doing?'

'Hey, let's not get personal here. We've done some big developments in this city and you know it. Take my word for it, stay clear of Marello.'

'Why? Because they may do a deal with me?'

'Are you trying to put the pressure on me or something?' the CEO replied.

'Like I said, I like your company's design but the Marello people have also put a good package together. I can either help your bid or theirs. It's as simple as that.'

'You're asking for too much.'

'I can do a deal with nine hundred thousand,' the financial director replied.

'Maybe I can live with that.'

'So do we have a deal for real or not?' the financial director asked, pinning the man down.

'Sure, but my company will need some guarantee on getting this thing,' the CEO replied.

'I cannot give you anything in writing but since I pull the strings when it comes to money, just consider it as a done deal.'

'What about your office of internal affairs? Don't these guys sniff around?'

'What's there to sniff around if there's nothing smelly?'

'You seem pretty sure about this whole business, huh?'

'Just relax.'

'OK, this deal had better be good because mob or no mob, there are other people who'll play this game rough and I'm not kidding you when I say they play for keeps. How do want the money?' the CEO asked.

'It's to be paid into my Swiss bank account.'

'I figured that. Do you have the number?'

'As matter of fact, it's right here,' the financial director indicated, patting his suit pocket on the left breast.

He reached into his jacket pocket and pulled out the wallet, carefully removing the small piece of paper. The CEO saw the neatly printed numbers from a laserjet printer. There was no handwriting on it and probably no identifiable fingerprint on it either.

'The money will be wired over to you once the contract is in the bag,' the CEO said.

'I'm prepared to take your word about the money. There is just one other small matter,' the financial director added.

'What's that?'

'If I can't persuade the committee to give the deal to you, I'll return half of the money.'

'Can I think about this for a minute?'

'Take your time.'

'So what you're saying is that for nine hundred thousand, you're going to speak to a bunch of people to give my company the contract. If they don't agree with you and give it to somebody else, we'll still be paying you whether we get this deal or not,' the CEO said to clarify the position, dabbing his forehead with a handkerchief. He had suddenly taken an instant dislike to the arrogant man in front of him.

'Yes, that's just about it,' the financial director replied, nosing the complex aroma of the cognac.

'If we don't get the contract, what's to stop me from discussing our little meeting with the whole world?'

'Nothing except your company will probably find it hard to get any work in New York or anywhere else. As they say, we all go down together,' the financial director replied with a smile.

'Something tells me you've got this whole thing worked out.'

'I suppose I have. Do we concur?'

'I'll need to speak to some of my people in the company. It won't be easy to come up with that sort of cash in a hurry. They'll need to know something,' the CEO replied.

'Oh, I'm sure you'll think of something. Why don't you tell them there are over a dozen companies who want this contract? Damn fine cognac,' the other man said, draining it to the last drop.

The CEO knew that the multi-billion dollar contract needed some fragrant grease, as the Chinese would put it, to make things happen. It was not impossible to clinch the deal on their own merits but this was a real opportunity. He had rightly perceived the financial director to be a shark, a wheeler-dealer in one of the biggest organisations of the world. It was no less than the United Nations. Over the short space of a lunch, several construction companies had lost the chance of getting the contract. None would be the wiser for it but industrial espionage had a sneaky way of revealing even the closest kept secrets. The prestige for winning the UN contract was huge within the building industry, something the financial director knew only too well. He chuckled to himself as he left the hotel, knowing it would soon be time to play the game again. The CEO, for all his experience in the building industry, had been a total walkover. He was a lightweight and business had been done for the day. The lunch had clearly been well over the top.

Chapter 10

Insurance Policy

THE DEAL CONCLUDED AT THE HOTEL HAD no legal validity and Bill Frazer knew it. The contract to renovate the UN building was the biggest thing his company had ever gone for and the cost of the lunch matched what was at stake. Clinching the deal suddenly seemed very important and took up all of his waking hours just thinking about it. Having been in the construction industry all his life, he was damn sure this deal was going to happen. He preferred to talk tough like a man but the financial director had been too smooth for his liking. He was annoyed with himself for being outmanoeuvred so easily and he knew it.

The size of the contract could easily cover the kickback and it was just a cash flow issue. Technically, the job was more difficult because it would involve stripping out the entire building. With the General Assembly Hall standing over the old New York slaughter-houses, it contained lots of asbestos. The foundations were impregnated with the cancer-causing material, creating a potential biohazard such as Mesothelioma. The unusual type of lung cancer was caused by inhaling tiny asbestos fibres. It could take many years before the grey-white tumour developed around the lungs, obliterating the space between the chest wall and the lungs themselves. It was a bad way to die and Frazer already knew several people who had. The health insurance bills would be astronomical and it all had to be factored into the contract price.

The informal agreement between two men and the Swiss numbered account was all he had to show for the deal. No bank worth its salt would ever divulge its secrets. For that reason, he needed an 'insurance policy' for a rainy day. Besides, he hated the man. The old address book contained a special telephone number. No name had been written down next to it. Even his mobile had not been pre-programmed. It only took a few seconds before somebody answered.

'Yeah, who's this?' came the voice at the other end of the phone.

'You know who it is,' the CEO said without introducing himself.

'Hey, how are you?' the tough-sounding, laconic voice answered.

'Let's skip the chat. Did you get the package?'

'Sure. What do you want me to do?'

'Just get some dirt on the sucker.'

'When?'

'Like now.'

'You didn't say who it is,' the investigator replied.

'The Assistant Secretary-General for Programme Planning, Budget and Finance at the UN. I know it's a mouthful but you've got the photo of him.'

'Wow, that's big cheese! So what's the deal?'

'Just find out what does it for him. I don't care if he is married but I need to know if he is screwing around with mistresses, hookers or whatever. You need to give me something good.'

'What if he ain't got no vices?' the investigator asked, thinking that his target may turn out to be pretty humdrum.

"Ain't" and 'no' is a double negative. Come on, everybody has their own thing. Even if he doesn't, make something up,' the CEO suggested.

'And what's yours?'

'Don't get smart with me! Do you want me to put the word out that you're a jerk?' the CEO demanded angrily.

'Hey, OK already! Where's your sense of humour? It will cost you ten grand this time,' the investigator said calmly. He wasn't scared of the CEO.

'How come? The deal was for five grand the last time.'

'It's the inflation, plus your man is in the UN. This job will be a lot harder.'

'Son of a bitch! You're trying to screw me. Just get on with it or this is the last time I deal with you!'

'Yeah, whatever. I want half the money now, half later,' the investigator replied, as if bored with the conversation

'My man will see to it,' the CEO replied, feeling very annoyed.

'Just one more thing. Why this guy?' the investigator asked.

'That's my business. I pay you to do a job, not to ask dumb questions.'

'I need to know the score before I get my ass in a lot of trouble.'

'You get paid to do this job. I just want that material asap!'

'Hey, that's bullshit and you know it. I need to have something.'

'There's a deal going down and this is for backup. That's all you need to know.'

'Yeah, sure. It must be something big, huh? Maybe I should charge you more.'

'Go to hell!'

'Hey, you need me!' The investigator laughed out loudly to annoy the CEO.

'Fucking ass! Just do it,' the CEO said before pressing the 'end' button. The man was becoming intolerable.

The chain-smoking private investigator was an ex-US Marine. After years of cultivating the habit he definitely needed to quit before it killed him. There was no way he could run five miles now without stopping. The ten grand was nice, like taking candy from a baby. Tailing people around was certainly easier than going to war. He lit up another cigarette and took a big lungful of smoke before starting to plan the mission. Just like any military exercise, you need a plan. Otherwise it will go to jack shit. The coffee percolator bubbled away gently in the corner, keeping him supplied with a stream of caffeine. His time with the boys in the Marines always brought back good memories but this job was as good as it could get for a middle-aged man.

He smiled again and looked at the face of the man in the photograph. This one seemed to be more personal than usual for the big CEO. As the man said, everybody had his own thing. All he had to do now was to find out if he was screwing around. Most people did.

CHAPTER 11

THE INVESTIGATOR

THE FINANCIAL DIRECTOR COMMUTED BETWEEN HIS PLUSH apartment on Fifth Avenue and the UN headquarters on Franklin D Roosevelt Drive on most days. This time, he stayed on a little later than usual. The routine was different but it was easy enough to follow the Lincoln sedan as it proceeded down FDR, past the heliport. It carried on down to East River Drive and did a right at East Houston Street, cruising past ten streets before turning left into Ludlow Street. Parking outside another ordinary-looking building, he got out. The investigator immediately recognised where he was. He knew rent boys hung out there, some definitely underage. Many were from the gutters of Venezuela or Mexico, smuggled in to supply the sordid trade. Nobody would miss the diaspora where a shoot-to-kill policy already existed to exterminate the glue-sniffing kids. Somebody somewhere had obviously forgotten these children had a mother. The investigator could only wonder why the place was never busted, but he wasn't there on a crusade.

The whole street looked dilapidated, tired and run down but it was cheap enough for backpackers to crash there. For fifteen dollars a night they could buy some floor space. No blankets, just a mattress. Doped-up junkies frequently emerged from the shadows to ask for money. They usually moved on when instinct told them that even pond life had reached rock bottom when nobody threw them a dime. The crack cocaine addicts just sat on the doorways rocking back and forth, but it was the premature ageing effect of crystal meth which said these people had a limited time left on this earth. In some South American countries, rehabilitation was unnecessary. Police death squads just eradicated the problem with a bullet through the head. The dregs of humanity would never survive and Ludlow Street was full of them.

The ex-marine stopped his own car and parked up. Scanning the scene, he could see it was fairly quiet, the street being nearly deserted. He was still fit enough when it mattered, having no hesitation in shooting some son of a bitch if they dared pull a knife on him. The sanctity of life did not extend to scum as far as he was concerned. He had seen too many decapitated bodies committed by death squads in Iraq to feel emotional any more.

The financial director stayed for a little over half an hour but it had been enough to feed his weekly fix. Molesting children had become a drug. While psychologists debated long and hard whether it was mad or bad, the investigator had already made up his own mind. For now, he simply noted the place, time and day. The veneer of respectability ensured by high office and a marriage would not keep the financial director's reputation safe for long. The ex-marine wasn't surprised to see him there. As Bill Frazer said, everybody had their own thing. This certainly wasn't turning out to be humdrum after all. As the Lincoln sedan pulled away, he considered his options. He had correctly assumed that men like that were creatures of habit. They would be back, usually at the same time and same place, drawn by the allure of erotic, risky sex.

He lit a cigarette before getting out of the car. The street was eerily quiet except for the odd car going past, illuminating the garbage bins briefly, brimming with detritus. He ignored the vacant stares from the doorways and walked up to the black door. There was just a solitary door buzzer, a letter box, but not much else. Walking a few metres away, he spotted a nearby alleyway. More garbage littered the place, with pools of offensive liquid lying stagnant beside them. Even junkies and dogs needed to urinate. He gripped the automatic in his coat pocket and headed up the dark walkway. A slurred voice suddenly asked for money but it didn't sound menacing. Even the word 'asshole' didn't sound offensive. He ignored the woman and carried on further. A smaller road ran behind the apartment, running parallel to Ludlow Street. The ubiquitous fire escapes dangled from the buildings, which he quickly spotted. It could offer one way of entering the building. Having surveyed the lie of the land, his job was done for the night. He walked past the drunken woman again but refrained from telling her how ugly she was. There was little point in starting a scene, especially when he would be back.

Chapter 12

Evidence

J UST AS THE INVESTIGATOR PREDICTED, THE FINANCIAL director had his night out with the 'boys'. It was always at the same time, the same day. His wife kissed him goodbye in the morning, little knowing he would be busy later on. Gullibility was no excuse, unless she played away too. The investigator knew this was good information. Already the assignment had run into the second week and the CEO was not a patient man. It was difficult for the ex-marine to explain he needed just a little more time.

Having cased the joint already, he suspected the place was run by Puerto Ricans. It was the wrong part of town for the Italians. The old Mafia hated the newcomers for muscling in on their business, especially the sex trade. They particularly despised the Latinos for their lack of style. Whilst a Sicilian necktie had certain style, boiling people alive was crude. The investigator knew how the game was played. The man from the UN was certainly living dangerously.

This time, he parked fifty metres away from the other car. He saw the man entering the building just as eagerly as he did last week. There would be no diplomacy tonight, he thought. He checked the automatic and digital camera. The street looked deceptively empty but he could feel the eyes following him. Pulling down the black woollen hat as far as it would go, he covered his head and ears. Probably no drug addict would remember his face. After waiting ten minutes, the ex-marine got to the door in under a minute. A tinny distorted voice spoke on the entry system.

'Yo! Who's this?'

'I've been told to come here for something special,' the investigator replied.

'Yeah? And who told you this?' the thickly accented voice replied.

'Some guy called Ari.'

'Ari?'

'Yes, he's with you right now.'

'The Dutchman?'

'He told me to come and join him.'

'You better not be shitting me!'

'We'll pay you a special price.'

'Get in!'

The investigator was buzzed through. He found himself at the bottom of the stairs. Even in the poor light, he could see the Latino watching him. Once in the apartment, the Latino assessed the tall American with a careful eye.

'What kind of thing are you looking for, my man?' he asked.

'You have boys here?'

'How do I know you ain't the cops?' the man replied suspiciously.

'If I was, you would be busted by now.'

'And Ari told you about this place, huh?'

'Yes, let's go find him.'

'Maybe, I don't like the way you look.'

'I'm beginning to feel the same way,' the investigator replied with a cold stare.

'Hey, I just want you to get out of here, mister,' the Latino replied menacingly, suddenly suspicious of the intruder.

'No, I don't think so,' the investigator replied, pulling the automatic from his coat.

The Puerto Rican didn't expect to see a Browning High Power 9 mm staring him in the face. Rather than being scared, he felt angry. This man was out of control. Nobody busted in and pointed a gun in his face.

'Believe me, you're a dead man already.'

'Just tell me which room Ari is in.'

'Listen, you piece of shit, my people will cut you up for this unless you go right now,' the Latino said venomously.

'We'll do it the hard way. Put these on your legs,' the investigator ordered, handing the sweaty man a plasticuff restraint.

'What you gonna do if I don't? Shoot me?'

'Yes, you're going to lose both your kneecaps if you don't shut the fuck up. Put it on.'

The man reluctantly took the plastic restraint and sat on the floor, before strapping it around his ankles. His hands then received the same treatment from the ex-marine.

'Is there anybody else here?' the investigator asked.

'No, there ain't no other person here, you punk,' the Latino replied in bad English.

'Which room?'

'The second one down there,' he replied with a filthy stare.

'You be a good boy now!'

'Screw you, man!'

The tall ex-marine stood up and put the automatic away. He presumed the Latino was not that stupid to start shouting the place down, knowing he would get a slug in his head if he did. Fishing out the digital camera, the investigator walked down the corridor and stopped outside the second door. Listening hard, he heard the unmistakable sound of somebody in pain coming from the other side. He felt sick already. The heavy weight of the automatic in his pocket reminded him that he could end all this right now. He presumed the Puerto Ricans would never call the police in. However, he wasn't being paid to execute the Dutchman, just to get some evidence. He tried the door handle, turning it without making much noise. The door gave way slightly, telling him it wasn't locked. Steadying his nerves, he prepared himself to go in. With one swift motion, the door opened and he was in. The bemused- looking man looked up in surprise as he straddled the unfortunate creature beneath him. He tried to cover his face with one arm but the investigator had already taken several pictures. It was no use; the game was up. His pale white flesh contrasted against the dark-skinned boy. It was the evidence the investigator needed. The Dutchman started to curse and the stranger headed back into the hall.

The Latino watched it all. He swore out loud, which made the investigator stop in his tracks. It was followed by a swift kick in his side. The man groaned and shouted out more obscenities. On the small reception desk by the door, the investigator found a variety of condoms and a tin of air freshener. There was also a Mace spray, presumably reserved for unwanted guests. He took the Mace and knelt down on the Latino's back. Jerking the man's head back by the hair, he squirted the Mace into his face. The Latino screamed as he felt the pepper spray enter his eyes, feeling the burning liquid hitting the supersensitive cornea. He coughed and choked, writhing in pain with both hands and feet bound together. Feeling satisfied, the investigator threw down the small canister and walked out. He had got what he came for, and made sure nobody followed as he drove off. The drunken woman was still there, swigging from a bottle in a brown paper bag. She did not remember him.

CHAPTER 13

MARELLO CORPORATION

THE MARELLO CORPORATION WAS BASED IN NEW Jersey, across the water from Manhattan. It was originally started by a group of hard working Italian immigrants during the boom time. Through major construction, the company helped to create modern New York from its rocky foundation with much sweat and tears. Many men died in the process. Boom time was also good for the Mafia. Organised crime crept in like unwanted weeds around a flagstone. Initially innocuous, the interweaving roots had spread until it became part of the social fabric. The waterfront had been taken over, dominating the extortion racket. Class A drugs then became the number one merchandise but the construction industry had not escaped. The old guard clung to their empire, leaving internet fraud to the modern generation. They had well established links with the local politicians and police, enough to legitimise the industry. An iconic city such as New York would not have been what it is today without the Mafia connection. The Marello Corporation now ranked as one of the big players in the top league, except its tenuous links with the mob in the past had all but evaporated in a sea of respectability.

The company had to fight for large capital projects like anybody else. It was still a close-knit family business with roots in the hills of Sicily. Back then, the peasants had carried double-barrelled shotguns to guard the properties of the rural Bourbon landowners. In a modern twist, the younger Americanised generation waged war over pricing contracts. The tender for the UN contract had to be above board. Of the original dozen tenders received, half had been eliminated, leaving the other six to sweat it out. Tony Marello, the CEO of this company, had received a personal phone call from the UN financial director. He was curious to hear what the man had to say, in private. It was odd when the man suggested having lunch in Chinatown. Luckily, he liked Chinese food.

Marello had no difficulty in finding the right place. Little Italy was over the other side of Canal Street, heading up towards Midtown in a part of Manhattan he knew well. Having worked on numerous building sites throughout the city, he found the restaurant with no problem. As most Chinatowns went, it was like any other and could have been found anywhere in the world. The restaurant served cheap, tasty food with barbecued pork and wind-dried ducks hanging by the shop front window. It looked authentic. The man from the UN knew his food.

It was packed with Oriental faces but several Caucasians were also using chopsticks to push rice into their mouths from the little bowls. Marello quickly saw his host, a well-dressed man sitting at a small table. He looked like somebody with authority, despite Marello having never met him.

'Hi, I'm Tony Marello. You are Ari, I presume,' he said, approaching the man.

'Hello, Mr Marello! It's good of you to come,' the financial director said, standing up to shake his hand.

'Please, call me Tony.'

'And you call me Ari. Sit down. I hope you like Chinese. This is a good place.'

'I love it nearly as much as Italian.'

'Good! I'll order if you want. Anything you don't eat?'

'No, so long as it's legal,' Marello replied.

'Hey, I like that! The roast duck and crispy pork is first class. Why don't we have some deep-fried oysters too?' the man suggested.

'Sure, why not?'

'My normal and some fried oysters. We'll have Chinese tea to go with it,' the financial director ordered in a perfunctory way to the waitress standing nearby.

The waitress nodded and scurried away. She knew the customer well. The man always ordered the same thing and it had become a standing joke with the chef. Whilst other eaters were happy to tuck into stewed chicken's feet and pig's intestines, the chef always knew when the financial director was in. The piping hot tea arrived as if by magic.

'Well, Tony, how is business?' the UN man asked, pouring the tea into two little tea cups with no handles.

'We're doing good trade right now,' Marello replied in his clipped New York Italian accent.

'You must be wondering why I asked to speak with you.'

'Is it about the contract by any chance?'

'You've read my mind already,' the man smiled.

'So what about it?' Marello was to the point.

'Well, I thought we should talk. It's important,' the UN man replied.

'Go ahead, I'm listening,' Marello replied, watching the other man with interest.

'You see, Tony, with an organisation as big as the UN, this building work is going to cause an awful lot of disruption and reorganising.'

'So?'

'Well, the day-to-day stuff is going to be a major logistical problem and I just need to know if your company can finish the work on time.'

'We've given you a fixed timescale on the tender. We always try to finish when we say we will.'

'That's good to know but what happens if you don't?'

'I thought the penalty clauses are quite clear regarding this.'

'Yes sure, that is standard practice. I need some sort of guarantee that the work will be on budget.'

'You know as well as I do that unexpected things can happen in this business. There is a lot of asbestos to take care of first and this stuff needs careful handling. The whole building needs to be gutted before we can start the reconstruction phase.'

'I hear you but…'

'But what? Is there something else I need to know first?' Marello asked suspiciously, interrupting the man quickly.

'I was going to say that despite the considerable obstacles, there are over a dozen companies bidding for this work. Since you asked, how much is this contract worth to you personally?'

'You don't mean what my company's profit share is going to be, right?' Marello clarified.

'That's right.'

'You're asking how much it would personally cost me to win the contract?'

'Yes, something like that. There are ways of recouping your outlay from the company,' the UN man replied unashamedly.

'Are you talking about creative accounting practices here? I didn't think you guys played these games,' Marello said in a disappointed tone.

'Well, big money is involved. It could mean a lot to another company. Don't tell me your company has never done this sort of business before.'

'Don't insinuate that my company does bribes. How much are you asking for?' Marello asked out of curiosity.

'The figure we're talking about so far is nine hundred thousand.'

'You're kidding me! That's big money.'

'You've made me put it very crudely. Think of the bigger picture.'

'And what happens if I don't play your game?' Marello asked.

'Then I push the contract in some other direction,' the man said bluntly.

'I know you don't run the UN by yourself and this thing needs to be decided by a group of people. What makes you so sure you can just give the deal to one particular company?'

'As the financial director, I can swing things in any way I want.'

'What's to stop me from going to the Secretary-General and telling him about what you just proposed?' Marello suggested.

'Let's just say he has enough problems on his plate just now. You've heard of the Oil-for-Food programme?' the UN man asked.

'Yeah, sure. Were you involved with that too?'

'No, but I'm sure the Secretary-General doesn't want to deal with another problem right now, especially anything to do with the rebuilding work. The UN is a big organisation but there is only so much he will accept.'

'So why are you risking talking to me like this?'

'Because we can both win out of this situation. Your company stands to make a massive profit from the work if I guarantee you the contract. This job could go to any of your competitors and they are willing to pay. It is just a question of how much you want it.'

'If we played things your way, there would be no proof of anything we said, right?'

'Yes, absolutely. I'm glad common sense has come to you.'

'What if we went along with your idea, how and when do you want your money?' Marello asked.

'Swiss bank account. I should add the price is now one million.'

'Why one million when you said the other company was paying nine hundred thousand?'

'That's your price for getting the contract. The bid has just gone up.'

'What if we don't get it?'

'I'll return one half of the money.'

'On the same terms as the other company?'

'Yes, but for your higher bid, I will guarantee it.'

'So if I said yes, this other company has already lost out. That sounds like a bad deal for them,' Marello decided.

'Perhaps, but there is something else you should consider.'

'Like what?' Marello wanted to know.

'We have checked all the companies tendering for the contract. Your company is the only one with any previous connection to the mob. That could go against you.'

'But there is no Mafia involvement. We would not have won several major government projects if we did. In case you didn't realise, we're living in the modern world. Just because I'm Italian doesn't mean we're Mafia,' Marello said indignantly.

'Our background checks have raised some concerns about your company. I know you are doing some of the work around Ground Zero but you're not getting any of the big deals.'

'That's rubbish. How do you know we're not getting some of the 9/11 work?'

'Just accept I know these things. You won't stand a chance of getting the UN contract without me.'

'How are these other people going to take it when you tell them they just lost out on the deal?'

'Very annoyed, I would imagine. So how do you want to play this?'

'How about I went to the press?' Marello said, throwing down a challenge.

'Oh, come on. With all the publicity, do you think your company will ever work again in this city? I don't think so,' the financial director replied.

'We could win without your help.'

'You have no chance when somebody else is already willing to pay up. If you spill the beans, your company will still be out of the loop for the re-tender.'

'You say one million?'

'Yes, Swiss bank account. Nobody will ever know. It will be as safe as houses.'

'I don't care for your pun but we'll get the contract for sure?'

'That's a 99 per cent certainty. I'll do everything I can to push it your way but, like you said, there's the committee to go through. Assure me you can do this thing on time and budget and we should be good to go.'

'Just one more thing. I want all the money back if we don't get the deal.'

'No, I can't do that.'

'Losing half the money for nothing is not smart.'

'That's your choice but you're either in or out. This conversation never happened.'

'Some choice. I don't like it,' Marello explained himself.

'Come on Tony, you know it makes sense. It's your call,' the man replied, picking up a fried oyster with his chopsticks.

'So if we get the deal, you'll get our million and half the money from the other company?'

'I really wouldn't worry about the small details but I do need your answer now,' the Dutchman replied, biting into the crispy delicacy.

'I have to talk about it to the other directors first.'

'Can they keep their mouths shut?'

'We're Italian.'

'I know that and I trust you on this one. The way I see it, you have no choice. I'm offering you a great deal.'

'Only if it's a waterproof guarantee.'

'Look, here's my account number in Switzerland. Just let me know when the deal's confirmed. The payment has to be in by two weeks from today. We decide on the contract shortly after that. Relax, I'll make sure it'll go your way.'

'Out of interest, isn't the other half of the UN in Geneva?' Marello asked.

'Yes, it is as a matter of fact.'

'How often do you go there?'

'Quite often,' the man answered, feeling irritated at being asked personal questions.

'Your accent sounds German.'

'No, Dutch actually. Perhaps I have been in New York for too long.'

'Somebody has obviously made a big mistake by employing you.'

'I won't take that personally. Finish the food. It's very good,' the Dutchman replied.

'We will renegotiate if we don't win the contract.'

'I'm sure that won't be necessary. The contract is already as good as yours,' the financial director said confidently, still eating his char sui pork.

'It had better be.'

Marello had quickly lost his appetite and left the table without saying another word. Perhaps it was the excitement of doing an illegal deal, knowing the company now stood a real chance of winning a multi-billion dollar deal. He also knew he had his work cut out to explain the deal to the others. They might not buy it. It was a big risk to the company. They could either win the biggest deal in the company's history or they could go down in flames. Sixth sense told him that things could go wrong very quickly. For that, he needed another plan. Walking away, he looked around the busy Chinatown Street. Just how much of the activity was controlled by the Chinese Triads? he wondered. What would they do to protect their interests? Everybody from the food delivery men to the restaurant owners was controlled by somebody. They were just the pawns, the suckers who had to pay up or lose out. Marello knew he was taking a big gamble with the Dutchman.

Driving off towards New Jersey, he thought about what he was going to say to the other guys in the company. Something about the smart-suited Dutchman made him dislike him. Perhaps it was the smoothness or the overconfidence of the man. Marello felt he needed to talk to an old acquaintance first, for the sake of his own peace of mind. Some of the old-fashioned way of doing business was tried and trusted and it never failed. It was also far less messy and complicated.

Chapter 14

Winner Takes All

A MONTH PASSED BEFORE ANYTHING HAPPENED, LATER THAN the Dutchman had anticipated. The committee for the rebuilding work was scheduled to meet again for the final analysis of the remaining bids at 10 a.m. that morning. The winning company had to be chosen as decisions had been deferred for too many years. The financial director had been set to recommend the Marello proposal until the timely delivery of the package to his office. His secretary had been told it was for his eyes only, after it had been cleared for explosives by security. The sophisticated bomb detector could analyse traces of explosives, including the odourless Semtex. It could detect one molecule of any commercially known explosive amidst several billion air particles. Having placed the package on top of his pile of mail, she advised him to open it straight away as the courier said it was urgent. Without much thought, he ripped open the manila envelope. There were several photographs to remind him of the unusual night in Ludlow Street. He broke out in a cold sweat.

With the meeting due to start in half an hour, he had to think quickly. Thoughts of the Oil-for-Food scandal came to mind but he had had very little involvement with that. It was ruled out. There could only be one conclusion and it had to be linked with the rebuilding contract. With such timed delivery, it could only be one of two people who could have sent it, knowing the final decision was about to happen. The incident in Ludlow Street had happened in between his meetings with Frazer and Marello. That left Marello clear. Logic dictated it must have been Frazer, sending him a decidedly unfriendly reminder. He knew there was no option now but to push the contract in his direction. The man wasn't such a pussycat after all. Damn him.

Throughout the meeting, nerves had eaten away at the Dutchman. Against his own intuition, he had to argue in Frazer's favour. The committee agreed. Mentioning the Mafia link to Marello's company was all it took to make it game over. The other bidding companies had come in too high with their costs and had been ruled out. For that very reason the financial director had deliberately targeted Frazer's and Marello's company in his scheme. It hadn't all been a total disaster. The phone call to Marello would be awkward but worth every penny.

'Hello, Tony, it's Ari. Can you talk?'

'Yes, sure, go ahead,' Marello answered, expecting to hear good news.

'I am sorry, Tony.'

'What do you mean?'

'The deal went to another company. I really tried to push it your way but it just didn't happen.'

'What went wrong?'

'As I feared, the Mafia thing wouldn't go away.'

'Did you say our company was clean?'

'Of course I did. They had already made up their minds.'

'In that case I want all the money back.'

'We did agree you would get only half back.'

'No, Ari, you agreed to that. Not me.'

'I thought I had made it quite clear.'

'The final words were we would renegotiate if this thing fell through.'

'Well, I'm sorry but that is not going to happen. I already told you that your company had no chance without me. At least this way, your bid got to the second round. It was a close run thing but they wouldn't believe me you had no Mafia dealings. It was out of my hands, Tony.'

'Like I told you, I want all the money back. This thing could go to the press. How would that look?' Marello barked, suddenly losing his composure.

'Tony, listen. Do that and your company will be out of business in no time. Nobody will ever trust you again. They will see you as somebody who did a deal with the UN financial director. It won't be good for me either but your company's reputation will be gone for good. Think about it. I know people here in New York. I can get you other work here if you keep this quiet. Trust me on this one.'

'We can get that without your help. Now you listen to me. I want you to you wire transfer all the money into my Cayman account.'

'I was going to do that in any case but the deal is for half.'

'No, that is so not going to happen.'

'Oh, it will and you are going to be sensible, aren't you, Tony?'

'No, I'm going to see you in hell,' Marello replied, slamming down the phone.

The Dutchman stared at his phone in silence, considering the veiled threat. He quickly dismissed the thought, knowing Marello had no other options. Half of the money would go to the Cayman account. It was a done deal.

CHAPTER 15

TROUBLE

TROUBLE UNDER ANY GUISE SPELT DISASTER AND the UN was no different. Regional conflicts had led to big wars, sucking in the superpowers to bolster fledgling new governments like those in Afghanistan and Iraq. Tensions continued to simmer in the troubled areas of the world such as Darfur, Tibet and East Timor. Africa was slowly killing itself through civil war. If not, it was AIDS or starvation. Global warming had led to droughts, shrinking even the once mighty Lake Malawi. The emerging nations of Brazil, Russia, India and China had started to gobble up unsustainable resources at a furious pace, stripping oil and minerals from the ground whilst encouraging widespread deforestation. Several simultaneous global conflicts remained a real possibility. Nonaligned countries such as Iran and North Korea raced to produce ballistic missiles capable of delivering an atomic bomb. North Korea had closed its doors to weapons inspection. Iran had remained a signatory of the Nuclear Non-Proliferation Treaty but they were proud to boast of their nuclear processing facilities. Reports from the International Atomic Energy Agency were a cause for concern. Israel had been denounced as a stain on the Islamic world, to be wiped off the face of the earth by the Iranian president. The Iranian uranium enrichment programme now continued under the direct supervision of the Revolutionary Guards, answering directly to the president. Battalions of suicide bombers had been trained to strike Israel and the West if their nuclear sites were ever bombed in a pre-emptive strike. The UN Baghdad office had already been blown up with ease by an al-Qaeda suicide bomber.

The UN headquarters in New York had already witnessed the destruction of the twin towers at close quarters. To destroy something so big in the American heartland had shown the massive threat posed by international terrorism. The UN headquarters remained a prime target for any fundamentalist movement hell-bent on demonstrating the wrath of Allah. They could use light aircraft to crash into the building. With hundreds of small aircraft flying through Manhattan airspace every day, each one could represent a potential flying bomb. The Air National Guard may have been given permission to shoot down hijacked airliners but there was no easy way of identifying small rogue planes.

The need for extensive security measures had been passed on to all the competing construction companies. No building could withstand a hit from an airliner but there had to be a survivability factor included in the design against smaller aircraft. Frazer was suitably pleased to be told his company's design had been the most robust and cost-effective. It stood to make millions from the deal and he was a a major share holder after all. The photographs of the financial director had been worth more than the ten thousand dollars he paid. He opened a very expensive bottle of whisky to celebrate.

CHAPTER 16
THE UNITED NATIONS

FOLLOWING THE MASS MURDER OF SIX MILLION Jews by the Nazis and another fifty million estimated dead during the Second World War, the world had to be united. The Treaty of Versailles in 1919 was intended to stop future wars in Europe but it proved to be useless. Nazi Germany was allowed to rise in power during the great recession when hungry people believed in Adolf Hitler's Thousand Year Reich. Europe had destroyed itself again, but this time it also dragged in the rest of the world. President Roosevelt realised that peace between nations could only be achieved in the event of a new style of world politics. From a memorandum of understanding between twenty-six allied nations, the Axis Powers of Nazi Germany, Italy and Japan had first to be defeated. After the war, representatives from fifty countries came forward to sign up to the United Nations Charter on 26th June 1945, including the former Axis Powers. By 24th of October 1945 in San Francisco, the United Nations had been born. It was to mark a new chapter in the history of mankind.

The UN was by now a huge organisation based in New York. It had been sub-divided into three main parts; the General Assembly (all member states), the Security Council (five permanent and ten non-permanent member states) and the Economic and Social Council (fifty-four member states). The aim of maintaining peace and security throughout the world was simplistic in concept but complex in execution. With currently more than 190 sovereign member states, the inflexible behemoth had stretched communications between member states to dizzying levels, holding them together through an army of interpreters. When the Security Council dithered, people died. Examples had already been seen in many countries such as Bosnia, Kosovo, Rwanda, Congo, Sierra Leone, East Timor and the Aceh province of Sumatra. The killings began when pleas of help were ignored. With an ever growing mandate, the UN had found it harder to police areas of the world where corruption and kickbacks were a normal way of life. The UN itself was not an organisation beyond reproach.

Mike Turner was a forty-eight-year-old English lawyer chosen to head the department of internal affairs within the UN. His brief was to shake up the organisation, to get rid of unwanted controversy. The UN badly needed to regain its reputation as a trustworthy organisation after years of corruption and incompetence. Having worked in The Hague on major show trials, his credentials were not only good but squeaky-clean. They had to be. All eyes had been focused on the UN following the disastrous Oil-for-Food scandal in Iraq. The year-long investigation concluded that the UN had been guilty of 'illicit, unethical and corrupt behaviour' in running the US$64 billion Oil-for-Food programme, which had been set up to help Iraq's poor during a decade of sanctions. The head of the programme had siphoned off US$160,000, whilst politicians and journalists had also received bribes from the Iraqi regime.

Turner already knew that the humanitarian aid relief to 27 million Iraqis after the first Gulf War had benefited the isolated Baghdad regime and many others. With an estimated 80 per cent of the population sick and malnourished, the country had badly needed help to deal with the outbreak of cholera, tuberculosis and meningitis. Oil money would be used for the US$42.7 billion needed for the humanitarian aid but that still left some change from the US$64.2 billion generated over an eight-year period. The country's huge oil reserves had hardly been dented. The Iraqi government under Saddam Hussein's control had conveniently siphoned off approximately US$10.9 billion from the illicit revenue whilst his psychopathic son Uday drove around Baghdad in Ferraris killing people for fun. It had all gone on under the eyes of the Security Council as the oil flowed out of Iraq. Now with irrefutable evidence available, the Security Council had no option but to co-operate with an Independent Investigation Committee led by the US Federal Reserve Chairman.

The report when it arrived had sent shock waves throughout the UN. The Secretary-General knew the UN had to clean up its act. No further unfavourable disclosures must come out of the woodwork, especially when gossip had started to emerge about his own family being involved in the Oil-for-Food scandal. The Secretary-General had summoned Turner to the 38th floor for a personal chat.

As an experienced player in the European circuit, Turner knew what he was there for. To stay alive politically, he needed skill and tenacity, something he had already acquired in the international law courts. He had to keep ahead of the game in the new harsh environment in which he found himself. The rules were different. He tried to work it all out beforehand, much like a game of chess, but despite that surprises had a funny way of turning up. He loved it.

The private meeting with the Secretary-General had given him plenty of food for thought. The Secretary-General had mentioned the Potomac Two-Step, dropping the phrase casually into the conversation. Turner learnt it was a game politicians played in Washington before their careers went tits up. He had to wonder if this was some kind of discreet warning. His job within internal affairs was to wipe the UN clean of corruption but he still wasn't sure if there was some glass ceiling beyond which he could not investigate. He had been specifically headhunted for this job, but what if somebody from the 38th floor was also willing to close him down? The Potomac Two-Step was not a game unique to Washington. Everybody played it: dish the dirt on me and I'll do the same. What did anybody have on him? He had led a clean life until now, unless there had been something he had forgotten. Even with absolutely clean credentials, he knew how easy it would be for somebody to throw the spanner in the works. It didn't take much to destroy a reputation. He had to be very careful.

CHAPTER 17

RUMBLINGS

FOR OVER TWO HUNDRED MILLION YEARS, PANGEA existed as the supercontinent on earth. It broke up to give the world its continents, but America had at one time been part of Africa. The rich and poor were now divided by the Atlantic. Plate tectonics had become a new science but the fundamentals were as old as the planet. The earth's surface remained in a state of dynamic flux as the continental plates continued to push and pull against one another. Some plates rifted and expanded in a divergent manner, causing hot plumes of magma to rise from deep within the mantle to create an upward crust. The Atlantic ridge reached 2000 metres above the sea floor and continued to grow. Rifting continents also broke up through plate separation, just like in the Rift valley of Africa, now programmed to split the continent in two. Tectonic plates also destroyed each other by a process of subduction when one converging plate submerged beneath the other. The Nazca plate riding beneath the South American plate had pushed up the Andes mountain chain onto the latter. Similarly, Mount Everest had got taller each year by the action of the Indian and Australian plates pushing against the Eurasian plate to create the High Tibetan Plateau of the Himalayan Mountains. Now, worryingly, the Australian plate rotating against the Indian plate had caused considerable stress to build up. The combined Indo-Australian plate advancing on the Eurasian plate at a rate of sixty-one millimetres a year was creating huge seismic activities at the point of contact. Cataclysmic events were imminent.

Near to the island of Sumatra, the area of subduction between the Indo-Australian plate and the Eurasian plate was demarcated by the great Sunda trench. It stretched some 5,500 kilometres from Burma down to the western coast of Sumatra and Java before turning east to head in the direction of New Guinea. An additional fault line ran down the length of Sumatra to give the island an extra level of instability with a strike-slip fault. When the two sections of rock passed by each other in opposite directions, they generated a large frictional force. The Sunda trench and Sumatran fault line were a frequent cause of large earthquakes. Deep down in the Sunda trench, the plates continued to push against each other. Pressure within the megafault line was building up. Small but regular rumblings had already started to occur, invoking memories of Krakatoa, which disappeared in a fireball in 1883. The idyllic charm of the equatorial sun had lulled people into a false sense of security, but the Sumatran tectonic system released major earthquakes every 130 to 200 years. Some 36,000 people had drowned in the tsunami that followed the eruption of Krakatoa. Once again beneath the waves the fish were getting restless. As for the fishermen, they would do better by staying out at sea. The signs were ominous.

CHAPTER 18

TSUNAMI

THE RUMBLINGS HAD BECOME MORE FREQUENT AS the tectonic plates tried to hang on. As if in some slippery handshake, they had to let go eventually. Plates were pushed up in a massive displacement as the frictional coupling failed. Energy many times more powerful than the atomic bomb was released in a short space of time. The existing fracture system on the sea floor suddenly rose twenty metres high, displacing the water above it. Concentric waveforms had started to radiate outwards from the epicentre, travelling at several hundred kilometres per hour. It grew faster as it headed towards land. Now compressed against the sloping seabed it started to slow to seventy kilometres per hour just as the height of the wave grew enormously. In a bizarre phenomenon, it had even pulled water away from the beach, leaving the fish to flap around on the waterless seabed. The mesmerising sight had rooted many onlookers to the spot when they should have been seeking higher ground. When the moment came, something had clearly been lost to translation as fascination turned to horror.

Huge waves crashed into the shore like demented demons, pushing several billion gallons of water over beach front properties. Houses were smashed up like matchboxes just as huge trees were uprooted like daisies. Foaming water pressed on relentlessly inland, destroying all before it. People died in their thousands, powerless to escape their watery graves. Like some unrepentant serpent, the tsunami suddenly vanished, leaving a devastating legacy.

The Indian Ocean region had quickly become a disaster zone. No surrounding landmass had escaped with Sri Lanka, Thailand, the Andaman Islands and Sumatra bearing the brunt of the disaster. In Banda Aceh at the northern tip of Sumatra the dead and missing numbered 225,000. It had been a major humanitarian catastrophe; a Boxing Day to remember. Christmas was definitely over as the huge juggernaut of the UN started to roll. Many people now had to be fed, treated and accommodated as a matter of urgency. The UN would use up its resources quickly until foreign governments and public donations refilled the UN coffers. Somebody would have to take charge of all the money flooding in.

CHAPTER 19

MERCY AID INTERNATIONAL

THE UNITED NATIONS HIGH COMMISSION FOR REFUGEES (UNHCR), based in Geneva, Switzerland had received news about the tsunami. Personnel on Christmas vacation had to be called back quickly. As part of the UN, they responded to major humanitarian disasters when displaced refugees needed urgent assistance. Often, with destroyed local infrastructure and non-functioning medical services, these disaster areas quickly became toxic dumps without immediate assistance. Communicable diseases spread quickly, leading to epidemics. The UNHCR served as an organisation to marshal aid from the international community. Any delay in getting aid to the disaster zones increased the number of deaths dramatically, mitigating the effectiveness of subsequent rescue efforts. Seriously injured people often died within the first hour unless they were treated. This was known as the golden hour but help often arrived several days later due to logistical reasons. Nobody could survive beyond the boundaries of human endurance when trapped or injured without food or water. Many earthquake victims survived in pockets of collapsed buildings but most people drowned in a tsunami. The UNHCR had to act fast as huge numbers of bodies had already started to rot.

With a large area to cover, the organisation targeted countries least able to mount a disaster relief programme. The region of Banda

Aceh had been totally destroyed with the greatest number of deaths. Advance teams from the UNHCR base in East Timor had already begun to arrive in Aceh within a day of the disaster. They were the vanguard of the much larger team heading from Europe. The first load of aid, consisting of 400 tonnes of emergency relief material, had already left the UN depot in Dubai with more coming from Copenhagen. Shelter material for 100,000 people had been requested, including portable warehouses to store the incoming supplies. Tonnes of plastic sheeting, jerry cans, and 20,000 sets for cooking were being mobilised. Money to pay for the short-term non-food items to supply a population of 175,000 people had to be released, amounting to US$60 million. The UN, with an annual budget of US$1 billion, was going to be hit hard by the scale of the disaster. With another 17 million non-tsunami refugees in 120 countries to look after, the maths dictated that more money was urgently needed.

Over 200 aid agencies independent from the UNHCR had also decided to head for Aceh Province. A worldwide tsunami appeal had gone out as many governments had pledged several billion dollars for the relief effort. Many major cities throughout the world had started their own tsunami appeal, including Edinburgh. The Lord Provost of the Scottish capital had appealed for financial donations and medical supplies. Newsletters had been circulated to hospitals and medical centres. Feeling horrified at the disaster, Nick remembered the conversation with Mary on Boxing Day. It had just seemed too much of a coincidence. The newsletter appealed for aid workers to volunteer their services. He decided to give one of the locally based charities a call.

'Hello, Mercy Aid International. Linda speaking, how may I help you?' a pleasant female voice answered.

'I'd like to speak to somebody about the tsunami appeal,' Nick replied.

'Yes, of course, may I take your name?'

'Yes, it's Nick Forbes.'

'I'm just putting you through to our manager. Please hold,' the receptionist answered. It took a few seconds to be transferred.

'Hello, I'm Hilary Carmichael. What can I do for you, Mr Forbes?' the woman asked quickly, as if busy on another matter.

'I am responding to your appeal for volunteers.'

'Oh, I see. Have you worked for us before?'

'No, but I am an orthopaedic surgeon.'

'Perhaps you should know what we do first of all.'

'Thank you. That would be useful.'

'Our charity mainly deals with post-traumatic stress, helping people cope as victims either from a general disaster or from civil wars and genocides. Is that something you can help us with?'

'I've dealt with traumatised patients.'

'Well, we offer counselling and psychological therapy as a practical way of helping them readjust back to normal life. Perhaps as a surgeon, this isn't your line of work.'

'No, you are correct. I'm not a psychologist but I could help with any physical injuries. '

'Yes, I'm sure you can but this is not what we do. The aim of our charity is to help women and children who have been traumatised. Often they have been victims of rape or torture and we also take care of orphan children. I'm just not sure how we could use your skills,' the woman replied.

'Could you at least get me out to one of the tsunami areas?'

'We may be able to help you but what we need are qualified psychologists with field experience. Would you know of anybody?'

'No, sorry. I would still like to offer my services,' Nick urged.

'Do you have any previous experience of working in disaster areas?'

'No, but I work with trauma all the time. The casualty department can resemble a disaster zone,' Nick replied light-heartedly.

'Yes, I'm quite sure, Mr Forbes, but this is totally different. Despite your medical experience, you'll need to have knowledge of public health matters relating to working in disaster zones. Much of the disease prevention work will be done by the World Health Organisation and the Red Cross. Perhaps you could tag along with our people until you find a more useful organisation to join out there. Have you tried *Médecins Sans Frontières*?'

'No.'

'Are you up to date with your vaccinations?'

'I don't know.'

'We'll give you a list of things you should be vaccinated against. There will be a lot of mosquitoes there.'

'I'll go to a travel clinic,' Nick replied, having no idea what his immunisation status was.

'OK, send me your CV and contact details by tomorrow.'

'I could bring it down to your office personally.'

'Are you able to take time off work at such short notice?'

'That won't be a problem as my short contract is due to expire next week.'

'We close at 6 p.m. tomorrow. I shall look forward to seeing you before then. Do you know where we are?'

'Yes, the address is on the leaflet.'

'I suggest you read up about Sumatra. That is where we'll be sending a team.'

'Thank you very much,' Nick replied.

He felt neither elated or worried, just glad there was something else to do after finishing his work at the Royal Infirmary. Sumatra was a place he had never considered going to. Many people flocked to Bali as a holiday destination but very few people ever sent postcards from the large Indonesian island. He would soon find out why.

CHAPTER 20

SUMATRA

S UMATRA IS THE SIXTH LARGEST ISLAND IN the world covering over 470,000 sq km of land space. The Bukit Barisan Mountains stretch across most of the western side of the island, dropping steeply into the sea on the west but sloping gently to the east. Nearly 100 volcanoes spread out along the mountain range, of which fifteen remain active. The low-lying eastern aspects consist of swampland and estuarine mangrove forest bordering the Straits of Malacca. The island of Sumatra is just one of 17,000 which make up the fragmented equatorial archipelago of Indonesia.

The mainly Malay population is closely related to the people of Malaysia and the Philippines, sharing genetic similarities. The gene pool had diversified when trade links with India were established from the fourth century. It had brought Hinduism and Buddhism as religions to the area. By the seventh century important trading posts had grown to become powerful kingdoms within Java and Sumatra. The Buddhist Sriwijaya Empire had ruled southern Sumatra and much of the Malay peninsula for several centuries. The Hindu Mataram kingdom had encompassed most of central Java. The spread of Islam into the area by the fifteenth century had usurped the dominance of these established powers and as a result Java was split into separate sultanates. A strong Muslim empire had developed in the region by then with Malacca as its epicentre on the Malay peninsula.

The island of Sumatra contains forty million people. The diverse mix of indigenous Malays, Indian and Chinese settlers make this a true jewel of the orient. With continued transmigration between Sumatra and Java, the cultural diversity has amplified. The economy thrived on oil, natural gas, timber, rubber, and now palm oil. Swathes of prime jungle have been chopped down but other crops such as tea, coffee, and tobacco have been added to the valuable exports. The Portuguese first recognised the importance of these islands and had monopolised the spice trade. By the sixteenth century they had established other enclaves in Malacca and East Timor. The Portuguese were subsequently displaced by the Dutch through colonisation of Indonesia by the 1600s. Malacca ceded control to the Dutch by 1641 as a result of their sea supremacy and control of the trade routes. The British ascendancy over Indonesia only occurred for a short period between 1811 and 1816 during the Franco-Dutch war. An agreement between Great Britain and Holland gave the British control of India and Malaya, leaving Indonesia to the Dutch. This had led to a war of independence with the Javanese, initiated by Prince Diponegoro, which lasted many years. The whole archipelago only fell into Indonesian hands after the Second World War. Following Japan's defeat, the strong nationalist movement led by Sukarno called for independence on 17 August 1945. The Dutch fought back until realisation dawned that foreign rule had gone for ever. It was the start of a new era.

CHAPTER 21

THE SUHARTO REGIME

WHEN COLONIAL POWER SUDDENLY GAVE WAY TO the Republic of the United States of Indonesia (RUSI) in December 1949, Sukarno, the military leader, was proclaimed president. In keeping with Javanese tradition, Sukarno only had one name. He had engaged with the PKI communist movement and the armed forces (ABRI) to assist with his plan of introducing a guided democracy. The newly vested powers granted to the PKI-controlled unions and officers of the ABRI saw to the nationalised takeover of many former Dutch-owned companies. These had included the Royal Packet Ship Company which had controlled the shipping industry for centuries and also Royal Dutch Shell, the petroleum company. Some 46,000 Dutch nationals were forcibly expelled from the country and headed back to Holland.

Sukarno was eventually forced from power in 1966 by Mohamed Suharto, the independence activist who had fought against the Dutch with distinction during the attack on Yogyakarta in March 1949. As the regional military commander of the Diponegoro Division in Central Java, Suharto had funded his command by conducting various business ventures, in common with other high-ranking officers within the Indonesian military. Subsequently found guilty of smuggling sugar amongst other corruptive practices, he was temporarily relieved of his command until reinstated. Now promoted to Brigadier-General following a spell at the Army Staff and Command School in Bundung in West Java, he saw his chance for seizing power during a period of political instability. Various political parties including the Islamists and the communist PKI party had vied for power. When President Sukarno proclaimed martial law in 1957 to prevent the breakup of the republic, Suharto acted decisively and brutally.

He had already risen through the ranks after commanding 'Operation Mandala', a military operation designed to drive out the Dutch in West New Guinea in 1960. A full-scale war nearly erupted, prevented by the intervention of the UN through a United States-brokered settlement, which saw the territory handed over to Indonesia. He became a major-general in 1962 during a low-level conflict with Malaysia, drawing in Britain, the United States and the Soviet Union. Suspicions of a communist takeover of the country had been feared when the PKI, with backing from China, had attempted to raise another force of armed peasants and workers. The military had by now divided into two factions with one group supporting President Sukarno and the PKI, the other supporting General Suharto. On the 30 September 1965, pro-communist military officers had kidnapped six pro-Suharto Generals and a Lieutenant before killing them in an apparent coup d'etat. Suharto had known about the plot but did not prevent it, despite knowing he would lose several of his generals. It had been a convenient excuse to wipe out the opposition, namely the PKI communists, in a bloody reprisal. An estimated two million mainly Chinese PKI were brutally killed, or imprisoned. Many were innocent victims.

President Sukarno had been isolated both politically and militarily, giving General Suharto the opportunity to seize control of the country by 1966. The PKI had now been ousted from parliament and their organisation smashed. Suharto was now the supreme commander, placing the whole military under his direct command. Most of the PKI leaders were sentenced to death by military court or served long prison sentences, with executions continuing until 1990. Diplomatic relations with China had ended and all the Chinese-language newspapers were banned. The time had come to focus his attention on the troublesome population of Aceh province in northern Sumatra, who had sought their own independence from Indonesia. Suharto would continue his bloody suppression of these people, using an army which loved to kill.

Chapter 22

Medan

Mercy Aid International had been right as Nick quickly realised that working in a disaster zone was going to be very different to operating in a well-equipped hospital. Humanitarian aid involved providing food, shelter, medicines and disease prevention. This charity was different. It didn't provide any of these things but concentrated on rehabilitating victims of mental trauma. Natural disasters and wars both left devastated communities. Nick was simply glad to be a surgeon, fixing the parts he could see and not tinker with people's heads. With many local doctors dead from the tsunami, he knew surgeons would be needed. The cholera jab had left a reddened area on his arm. At least it should prevent him from catching the disease, which could cause death from dehydration through profuse diarrhoea. He also took a good supply of antibiotics with him just in case. Mercy Aid had given him a return ticket to Medan. He would be met out there.

Medan remained the third largest city in Indonesia, the capital of Northern Sumatra. The international airport was south of the city, a gateway for the two million people living there. Nick flew in from Kuala Lumpur on a Garuda flight, having changed flights in the Malaysian capital from London Heathrow. He was met at the airport by one of the Mercy Aid representatives, brandishing a placard bearing his name. The local man was charming as he extended a warm welcome, unlike the unfriendly immigrations officer.

'Hello, Mr Forbes. Welcome to Sumatra. I am Ryamizard,' said the balding man.

'Hello, nice to meet you. Sorry, I didn't catch your name,' Nick replied.

'Ryamizard,' he said again with a broad grin.

'Please call me Nick. Do you mind if I called you Rami?' Nick asked politely, having no idea how to spell the man's name.

'Yes please, no problem. You can call me Rami. Easier for you that way. Please, give me your big bag, lah,' Rami insisted, lapsing into local speak.

'Thanks,' Nick replied, handing over the large rucksack but holding on to the smaller one.

He had been hit with the stifling heat already, made worse by the high humidity. The area had seen torrential rain just hours before, creating humidity as the sun burnt off the moisture. Perspiration formed even before they had left the airport. It was just as well that nobody was burning off the jungle for crop cultivation right then as the smog would have made life completely unbearable. People in Malaysia were also affected by the smoke across the Straits. Vast tracks of the jungle had been cut down to grow palm trees, just as in Borneo. It was an ecological disaster.

'We go this way to the car. You have nice trip, Nick?' Rami asked in his pidgin English.

'Yes thanks. I changed over at Kuala Lumpur. It's very hot here,' he added.

'This not hot! Wait till very hot weather come,' Rami laughed.

'I shall look forward to it,' Nick replied with a hint of sang-froid.

'You funny, lah. Why you want look forward to hot weather?'

Rami asked, totally missing the point.

'Well, I don't actually but never mind,' Nick replied, sensing the confusion creeping in.

They wandered over to the car park as Nick contemplated Rami's pidgin English. The local man slid the side door open of the Honda mini people carrier and put the rucksack in. He beckoned to Nick to sit in the front. Nick was surprised to see it was right-hand drive, thinking everybody drove on the wrong side apart from Britain, India, Japan and the antipodes. Rami jumped in and started the engine.

'I take you to hotel, OK? You stay there and rest,' he said invitingly.

'That sounds good. How long have you been working for Mercy Aid?' Nick asked.

'Long, long time. They do a lot of work here,' Rami replied, without elaborating.

'I believe Mercy Aid is a charitable aid foundation working in various parts of the world, but what do they actually do in Sumatra?' Nick probed.

'Your English is too good, lah!' Rami laughed as he negotiated the little people carrier through the airport, finding it difficult to explain exactly what they did there.

'Sorry, it's my fault. I should really be speaking your language.'

'No, no, it's OK. I have to learn a little bit more.'

The genial man spoke reasonably good English but Nick couldn't speak a word of Malay. It was impossible for everybody to speak all the known languages. There were even more Mandarin speakers in the world than English. Nick would try to keep the conversation simple. He thought of telling the joke about the intellectually challenged footballer from Manchester who spoke English very slowly when playing for Madrid, thinking it was Spanish. That would have taken too long to explain.

'What does Mercy Aid do here?' Nick asked simply.

'We help sick people. Many people in Banda Aceh very sick in the head,' Rami replied, without laughing this time.

'From the tsunami?'

'Yes, from tsunami now but before, from the war.'

'Which war do you mean?' Nick was curious to know.

'Civil war. Many bad things go on in Aceh. People there get killed also.'

'By whom?' Nick persisted.

'Government soldiers,' Rami replied.

'I thought Aceh was part of Indonesia, so why are they fighting?' Nick asked, feeling a little ignorant.

'Aceh people want freedom from government. They don't want Jakarta to tell them what to do. Maybe plenty oil up there, I don't know.'

'I've heard something about the troubles there but I didn't realise there was a civil war going on.'

'For now the fighting stop because of tsunami but the government want to kill all the guerrillas there,' he said in all seriousness.

'Do they have a proper cause?'

'It is like the people in Tibet who don't want the China government there.'

'And the people in Aceh want to be separated from Indonesia?'

'Ya, people there want this.'

'I'm sorry I don't know much about your country. The tsunami is awful.'

'Newspaper reporters not allowed there until now so maybe that's why.'

'I just presumed Sumatra was a peaceful country.'

'Peaceful until government soldiers start shooting people but don't tell anybody I told you this.'

'Why, are you scared?'

'Everybody scared. Many, many people get tortured.'

'And you know this for sure?'

'That is what we do here.'

'You mean the organisation?'

'Yes.'

'Thank you for telling me this, Rami. How have you managed to keep out of trouble if you know these things?'

'I keep quiet, pretend I know nothing. Also this is a foreign charity. They protect me.'

'With diplomatic immunity?'

'Huh? I don't understand.'

'These people can't touch you if you work for a foreign organisation.'

'I tell you these people can do anything. People disappear.'

'That's awful.'

'OK, we are going to Bukit Lawang now. That is where you stay,' Rami said, suddenly sounding cheerful again as he continued to drive towards the hotel.

Despite feeling tired, Nick tried to absorb the views of the bustling city as they drove along. The traffic was heavy with swarms of little vans, cars and motorbikes all trying to head somewhere. The puny air conditioning unit in the van struggled to keep the temperature down as they fought with the traffic, losing out badly. Maybe it needed a good service or perhaps a total replacement.

The Bukit Lawang district, where many tourists and backpackers headed, was just north-west of the city. The accommodation ranged from cheap to moderately expensive, but the main place to stay was at the Bukit Lawang Cottages, comprising a large bungalow complex. Rami stopped by the main lobby.

'OK, we are here. I will check you in,' he said, jumping out of the vehicle.

Nick did the same and was instantly hit by the stifling heat again. Rami refused to let him carry the big rucksack, struggling to the desk with it. It wasn't the weight but the size of the rucksack which made it look comical. It was as if the man could disappear inside it himself to be carried around. There were still many questions Nick wanted to ask Rami, particularly about the tsunami, but there hadn't been time. He was sure all the information would be forthcoming over the next few days. Rami fired off in his native tongue to the woman behind the desk. She looked at Nick and smiled.

'Hello, Mr Forbes. Welcome to Sumatra. I hope you will have a pleasant stay with us.' She spoke English well.

'Thank you,' he replied.

'I believe you are with Mercy Aid International. Your room and meals will be supplied for you. I just need your credit card for any other drinks or services that you may require.'

'Of course,' Nick replied, giving her one of his most charming smiles. He thought he saw her blush.

Nick knew the score. All his accommodation, food and travel costs would be met by the charity but anything else would be down to him. As a volunteer, he would be giving his services for free but that did not include getting his drinks bill paid. Hopefully there wouldn't be any petty-minded bureaucrats out here but he knew every organisation had them. Being in Sumatra suddenly felt like being a million miles from home. There was definitely a buzz about the place as the woman spoke again.

'I'm sure you already know many other agencies are also using this hotel, Mr Forbes. For now, there is a problem getting to Aceh as the main roads have either been blocked or destroyed by the heavy rain. Do let us know if there is anything we can do to make your stay more comfortable.'

'Thank you. Is there anybody else from Mercy Aid here?' Nick asked.

'I will check for you,' she said, looking through a sheaf of printed paper rather than on the computer screen.

'Yes, there is one other person, called Halcyon Cooper. She is in room 201.'

'Thank you. I will call her.'

'Your own room is 406. The porter will take you there,' she said, beckoning to the local man standing by the porter's desk.

Nick nodded his thanks as the man took his luggage away. He had to ask Rami something, noting he was still there.

'Rami, is the road to Aceh still blocked at the moment?' Nick asked.

'Yes, in many places, there is no road at all!' Rami laughed, despite the seriousness of the situation.

'Well, that's good to know.'

'Why?' Rami asked, missing the point again.

'It's just a figure of speech,' Nick smiled.

Most of the coastal roads in Aceh had simply been washed away by the tsunami, made worse by the following heavy rains. Getting to the disaster areas was a major problem, with only helicopters having the freedom of access able to bring in the much-needed emergency aid, especially food and fresh water. Several air forces had provided helicopters in a joint rescue effort but it was the US Navy which provided serious lifting power by ordering one of its carrier task forces into Indonesian waters. Despite more airlifting capability, it wasn't enough. Many of the aid agencies had to sit tight in Medan until the roads became accessible. The airport continued to handle large volumes of material coming from the UNHCR but shifting this to the affected areas would take time. Many trucks hung around the airport and other marshalling areas, waiting for the order to head north. There was little else to do until a passable route to Aceh had been constructed.

Nick thanked Rami once more for getting him to the hotel, before heading to his room. The little man said he would be back when there was more news about the road situation. It was now 5.30 p.m., 11.30 a.m. GMT. Nick felt very awake despite sleeping badly on the plane. The air conditioning in the room felt very inviting as he unpacked. It was clean, but nothing spectacular, as with most decent three star hotels. It would just be wrong to be extravagant at this time. His thoughts were interupted by the phone.

'Hello?' Nick answered.

'Is that Nick Forbes?' a female voice asked officiously.

'Yes it is.'

'I'm Halcyon Cooper from Mercy Aid. I heard you've arrived.'

'Oh yes, the receptionist gave me your name. I was going to give you a call,' Nick replied, wondering if this woman walked around with a clipboard.

'I'm glad you're here safely. We should meet up later after you've had a short rest, say about 7 p.m. at the main bar? It's best if you don't go to sleep now with the jet lag,' she suggested.

'OK. What do you look like?' Nick asked.

'See for yourself,' she replied, taken aback by his direct question.

'No, I meant in order to recognise you,' he clarified quickly.

'Short brown hair, a few freckles.'

'OK, I'm sure I'll recognise you.'

'I'm wearing a cream coloured tee shirt and green combat trousers.'

'I'll look forward to seeing you later,' he said, ending the short conversation.

Nick showered and changed into a light blue short sleeved shirt and an off-white coloured pair of chinos. He slipped into a pair of canoe saddle boat shoes without socks. Gelling his hair had been a mistake in the sticky heat. Whilst the room was air conditioned, the rest of the hotel was not. It had been designed with an open layout, allowing the warm air from outside to permeate through. It was made pleasantly bearable by the rotating fans overhead. The perfume of tropical flora wafted through.

The bar was easy to find. It being only 6.45 p.m., there was time to kill a Tiger beer before meeting up with Halcyon. He noticed several groups of people chatting amongst themselves, consisting of various nationalities. No doubt they were also waiting to get to Aceh. It wasn't long before a white female made a beeline for him. She did have short brown hair, with a robust looking figure bordering on the chubby side. Nick guessed she was in her late twenties.

'Hi, are you Nick?' she asked.

'Yes,' he said, standing up from the bar stool to offer his hand.

'How was the trip?' Halcyon asked, shaking his hand.

'Good. Edinburgh to Heathrow, then out to Kuala Lumpur before getting to Medan.'

'Some hike. Do you want to grab a bite here or do you want to eat in town?'

'I'm not fussed. You decide.'

'The food here is paid for and it's not bad. Is that OK with you?' Halcyon asked.

'Yes, sure.'

They walked over to the restaurant and found themselves a table, nodding to the waitress for attention. The menu contained mostly Indonesian dishes but steak and chips was also an option. Nick recognised satay but the other dishes were new to him.

'What do you fancy?'

'What are you going to have?' he replied, searching for ideas.

'I'm going to have the rojak for starter, and then the nasi lemak with sambal ikan bilis.'

'Fine, I'll have the same. What is it?' Nick asked.

'Rojak is a pineapple salad with tossed sesame seed and nasi lemak is rice cooked with coconut milk. The sambal ikan bilis is fish cooked in a spicy sambal sauce.'

'Good, I love spicy food.'

'This is staple fare out here. So tell me about yourself.'

'I'm an out-of-work surgeon looking for a taste of adventure.'

'Is it really as simple as that?'

'More or less. What about you?'

'I've been with Mercy Aid for over four years.'

'In Sumatra?'

'No, I've only been here a week. Before that, here and there.'

'Working as a psychologist?'

'No, not really. More of a field manager, setting up facilities, clearing the red tape, that sort of thing.'

'What do you make of the situation up north?' Nick asked.

'What, the tsunami?'

'No, the political situation.'

'Oh, that. All I know is there's a small civil war going on. We have lost touch with our team in Aceh.'

'You have people there already?' Nick asked.

'Yes, they've been there for years. We operate from a small building in Banda Aceh.'

'Dealing with mentally ill women?'

'Yes, mostly women but some girls and occasionally men.'

'As part of a rehabilitation programme?'

'Yes. Some of the women claimed they had been raped and others couldn't cope with the loss of their boyfriends and husbands killed in the fighting. Many people don't come forward either because they are either ashamed, scared or will not admit to having mental depression. People here don't rely on Prozac like they do back home.'

'How big is this problem here?'

'Out of a population of about three and a half million people in Aceh province, I would say only a few thousand are affected but we don't know the true scale of the problem. Some people won't adhere to the dictates of Jakarta. Everybody knows there is a lot of natural gas and oil up there,' Halcyon explained.

'Hence the trouble,' Nick replied.

'Maybe. Politics often goes deeper than that. It has been estimated that ten thousand people may have been killed by the Indonesian security forces over the past ten years.'

'I just had no idea it was on such a large scale.'

'Not many people do. It's a small number compared to East Timor. A lot of it gets hushed up as the foreign press are often denied access. Our charity keeps a low profile. I think our office there has been destroyed by the tsunami.'

'That's not good. Will you order the food?'

'Yes sure,' Halcyon said, noticing the waitress standing next to them. She ordered without looking at the menu.

'Tell me more about the charity,' Nick asked.

'Mercy Aid International is based in Edinburgh but our recruiting office is in London. We mostly use female psychologists with language skills to go anywhere in the world. I helped to run the London office but also travelled around to set up bases for our people to work from. To give you an example, we have a unit working in Cambodia to help children involved with the sex industry. In India, many young girls are sent down from Nepal to work in the brothels of Bombay and other places because their parents can't support them. Many catch AIDS within a year and once that happens, they are worthless. Young girls go back to Nepal to die. Some are not even fifteen. We do what we can to help but this is only a small outfit,' Halcyon explained.

'Who are these perpetrators?'

'Almost anybody you can think of. In India, many long-distance lorry drivers park up by the roadside and the girls hop in to do their business. AIDS is spreading fast all over India but also in countries like Malawi, Botswana and South Africa. There is a huge demand for very young girls because men think they won't catch AIDS from them.'

'And the Pope tells people not to wear condoms!'

'European sex tourists also come over to abuse boys and girls all over the Far East where sex is cheap. The authorities usually turn a blind eye until somebody makes a big fuss. Usually after a farcical court case, the foreigner pays a fee or gets a mild sentence.'

'Not much of a deterrent then,' Nick mused.

'No, wherever poverty exists, women and children will be abused. They are also raped in many parts of the world where armies and militias operate. In many places in Africa, young girls are abducted from their villages to act as cooks and sex slaves but that sort of thing can happen anywhere.'

'Can it possibly get any worse?'

'Oh yes. In the Balkans, women have been raped to death and then thrown out into the streets to be eaten by dogs. The level of hatred in the world is frightening. Even hardened soldiers sent by the UN to these trouble spots never recover from seeing these things. Many British troops were sickened by what they saw in Kosovo.'

'What is the current political situation in Aceh just now?' Nick asked, feeling nauseated by what he had just heard.

'There is supposedly a temporary truce between the GAM guerrillas and the Indonesian security forces whilst the tsunami relief is going on. Under the eyes of the world, the Indonesian government does not want to be seen conducting an internal war at this time.'

'It may actually be a good time to get rid of your enemy when there are so many bodies lying around,' Nick said with black humour.

'Except tsunami victims are usually killed by drowning, not shot or bludgeoned to death,' Halcyon replied.

'Yes, I know. I'm sorry for trying to be glib. What is GAM?'

'They are the Free Aceh Movement, calling for an independent Islamic state. They've been at it since the 1970s but armed insurrection only started in the 1980s when the government refused to allow Aceh to keep the profits from its oil and gas reserves. That is roughly it. The people wanted political autonomy, something the Suharto government would not agree to. It remains to be seen if the current government will cave in but I suspect it will be back to business as usual once the tsunami crisis is over.'

'I didn't consider the civil war when I decided to come out here,' Nick replied.

'It's mostly confined to the country areas and there is no fighting in the streets. You'll be fine! We don't run any medical facilities but I suspect we'll get you over to the Red Cross or some other medical outfit quite soon.'

'When can we head up north? Surely, the longer we stay here, the more hopeless it will be for these people,' Nick said logically.

'The situation seems very chaotic just now. Once the road has reopened, we'll get to Aceh but our first mission is to find out what has happened to our team there.'

'That sounds logical,' Nick agreed.

'Welcome to Sumatra!' Halcyon replied.

The food arrived just as Nick finished his first Tiger beer. He felt a mixture of tiredness and excitement, now slightly more apprehensive in the knowledge that people were being killed for political reasons. Sumatra seemed like a disturbed and exotic country with a massive natural disaster on its hands. He had already learnt a lot in a short space of time, despite having just arrived. His taste buds also learnt the meaning of spice as he started on the sambal ikan bilis. It was an enjoyable but fiery welcome. Halcyon tucked into the food like a seasoned professional.

CHAPTER 23

BANDA ACEH

THE RAIN HAD PETERED OUT AS THE traffic trickled its way up north to Aceh. The trunk road from Medan groaned under the heavy trucks as the improvised stretches took the strain. The convoy snaked its way slowly but made steady progress. Halcyon had finally received word from the aid coordinator to head north. The nervous wait had been replaced with a sense of urgency. Rami filled the little Honda with fuel and topped up some jerry cans. They could only pray that some big truck didn't drive into the back of them. Being lightweight and thin-walled, the vehicle wouldn't stand much of a chance in a crash. The charitable organisation couldn't stretch to a cheap off-roader let alone a pukka Land Rover. The vehicle was loaded to the max with food, water and other equipment including a mini gas fired stove. In a worst case scenario, they would have to sleep in the van, as there wasn't room to carry a tent. Their first mission was to find the four missing staff members. After that, they were free to help with the disaster relief.

The slow progress of following the back of one lorry had become tiresome, subduing Rami into uttering monosyllabic curses in Malay as the van was too underpowered to overtake. He had lost his chirpiness not long after leaving Medan, concentrating on the road. It was too easy to become mesmerised by the same rear end for hours on end. Nick suggested having a break, knowing that tiredness could kill.

'Rami, why don't we pull up for a bit?'

'OK, good idea,' he agreed.

At a suitable moment, he disengaged from the convoy and pulled off the road. The east coast of Sumatra had taken less of a battering from the tsunami compared to the west. Even so, the damage could be seen as 500 kilometres of coastline lay devastated. Where they were travelling, the area still looked reasonably intact, with the full scale of the disaster only becoming more apparent further north. The little van came to a standstill in a small clearing beside the main road. With the afternoon sun beating down mercilessly, the tropical vegetation quickly dried out. The fauna didn't care as it had adapted well over the centuries.

'Why don't I make some food for you?' Rami suggested.

'No, you have a rest. You've done all the driving,' Nick replied.

'No problem, I cook you egg and chips.'

'Just show me what you have in the van,' Nick asked politely.

'You no like local food, lah. I have salty fish and kangkung. Nice to eat with rice,' Rami giggled.

He proceeded to show Nick and Halcyon what was in the back of the van. Before setting off, they had suggested buying a limited number of things, not forgetting the Nescafe and milk powder. Having no idea what food or drink would be available, the large sack of rice would keep them going for a while but the fresh eggs and vegetables were quickly perishable in the heat. The remainder came in tins, such as sardines, baked beans and spam. Rami had also brought several jars of salted fish for his own use, which would keep indefinitely in oil. It was extremely smelly when fried but tasted sublime. The salty tang of the firm fish complimented the blandness of freshly cooked rice. Kangkung provided a cheap and nutritious meal, being a variety of spinach found in many local ponds. Nick felt sure he could rattle something up.

'Rami, set the stove up and then you sit down. Let me do the cooking,' he offered.

'But you orang puteh! How you learn to cook?' Rami laughed at the thought of Nick's suggestion.

'Orang puteh?' Nick asked quizzically.

'Yes, you white man. White man don't cook, lah!' Rami fell into hysterics. It was infectious. Halcyon had started to giggle.

'Rami, please set up the stove,' Nick said with a straight face.

'OK, lah.'

He was going to milk the situation for what it was worth, determined to string out the humour. Rami contemplated whether Nick was being serious about doing the cooking. He saw him unscrewing the jar of salty fish, smelling the content. He then picked up a block of hardened paste wrapped in greaseproof paper before asking Rami what it was. It smelt even worse than the salty fish.

'That is blachan! You no like it! Very smelly but good to eat!' Rami laughed again.

'It does remind me of something.'

'What?' Rami asked curiously.

'Like dead fish.'

'Very good! It's made from shrimp. We use it for sambal.'

'I've tried it.'

'So you like Indonesian food?'

'Yes. I'll cook it for you.'

'Only use a little bit of blachan, OK?' Rami implored, intrigued to see what Nick was going to do.

He set up the small propane-powered stove on the ground as Nick rummaged around the back of the van for a medium-sized saucepan and frying pan. He scooped three handfuls of rice into the saucepan and washed it with a small amount of water to remove the starch before cooking. Finding some garlic and fresh red chillies, he quickly prepared these on the small chopping board. He rinsed the kangkung with some of the bottled water before shredding them. It was then a simple matter of frying the garlic, chilli and blachan in oil before adding several pieces of the salted fish. The kangkung was added last, to prevent overcooking.

With two burners on the stove, it was possible to cook the rice and the fish at the same time. Nick served the spicy fish and spinach concoction with fluffy steamed rice. Rami and Halcyon watched in awed silence. It was a simple dish, but sharing their first meal together had been a bonding session. Rami sat on the floor of the van by the sliding door. He felt totally bemused, amazed that an 'orang puteh' could actually cook local food so well. A sense of quiet glee washed over him, having had a wonderful meal cooked for him by a foreigner. Already the tedium of the drive had deserted him.

They packed away the things before heading off. The convoy had become interspersed with military vehicles. Trucks full of soldiers treated the civilian convoy with impunity, frequently swinging out to overtake in an arrogant manner. No objections were raised. It was better not to argue with men armed with automatic weapons. Nick sat at the front with Rami to lend him moral support as Halcyon dozed in the back.

'These soldiers don't look very friendly,' Nick said in a matter-of-fact way.

'I think there is going to be plenty trouble,' Rami replied softly, as if scared of being heard.

'They must be going to help with the relief effort, surely?'

'Maybe, but I think they go fight with GAM,' Rami replied, keeping his eyes on the road and deliberately avoided eye contact with the soldiers.

'Are they good fighters?' Nick asked, trying to get an insider's angle after accepting Halcyon's explanation.

'Yes, but they don't have many weapons.'

'Why are they fighting the government?'

'These people don't want to be Indonesian. You know about Suharto?'

'Vaguely, He was the president for many years.'

'Yes, correct. Some people in Aceh think he was strong man fighting with the Dutch but you know how many people he killed afterwards?'

'Do you mean local people?'

'Yes, Chinese people. He killed over one million,' Rami replied.

'That must be an exaggeration, surely.'

'Nobody knows for sure.'

'Don't you have a new president?'

'Yes, but they all the same. They come and tell Aceh people they can have more freedom but all the time they kill the GAM fighters.'

'What about the ceasefire?'

'Maybe for now but when the tsunami disaster is over the army will take over again,' Rami said convincingly.

'Tell me about the people of Aceh,' Nick gently probed.

'They are very proud people. First, they fight the Dutch for thirty years from 1873 and got beaten. Now they fight the Indonesian government. The people only want to fish and be happy, but they will fight back when the soldiers come.'

'I can see how these abuses fuel the separatist movement but surely the army hierarchy must see this and discipline the soldiers?' Nick asked.

'Nick, your English is too much for me!' Rami protested passively.

'Sorry. Why can't the generals control the soldiers?'

'The generals only want to win this war to get oil money. They don't care about the people. In Lhokseumawe, some soldier rape a young girl and he got only little punishment.'

'Can't they go to the police?'

'It's the same thing. Many people are scared of them also. Now you understand the problem?'

'Yes. How many people have died in the troubles?' Nick asked.

'We don't know, maybe over nine or ten thousand.'

'That's a lot. Why has the United Nations done nothing about this?'

'United Nations? They are like lions with no teeth! They cannot stop the government. Nobody can save the Aceh people, not even America.'

'Then why won't the Aceh people just be happy to be part of Indonesia?'

'Aceh don't need Jakarta! The people here are different to Jarkarta people. Your people and Australia people the same but also different.

'Yes, I can see where you're coming from,' Nick replied, having tuned in quickly to Rami's style of speaking.

'Maybe now you know why there is so much trouble in Aceh.'

Nick finally understood why the Acehnese didn't want to dance to Jakarta's tune but there was still something he couldn't quite understand. He had noticed from the day he set foot at the airport in Medan the hostility from the immigrations officer. Now the soldiers were glaring at him from the back of the trucks rather than giving friendly waves.

'Rami, tell me something. I get the feeling that the authorities don't want people like me to be here. Why is that?'

'Indonesian people don't want to lose face but the government knows they need help from outside. If this happen in your country, do you want help from Indonesia?'

'Yes, why not? Offering humanitarian aid is the job of any civilised country. We all live on the same planet. What is there to feel shameful about?' Nick asked.

'This is also Muslim country, Nick. People hate Britain and America for the war in Afghanistan and Iraq. They think it is shameful to take help from the countries of the infidels,' Rami replied.

'I am here to help your people with no political motives.'

'Some people here don't think like that. Think about the Aceh people. If you think these soldiers don't like you, then what about them?'

'Point taken,' Nick replied.

'All I can say is be careful.' It was good advice.

They journeyed for mile after mile with ever changing scenery. The land facing out towards the coast now resembled a vast expense of emptiness, with solitary trees sticking out from the middle of nowhere. It was like some forlorn reminder of what had once been a lush green tropical paradise, swept aside by the rushing sea. The land was now the colour of mud grey. What had once been a vibrant ecosystem was nothing more than a dead swamp. The detritus of civilisation lay in the stinking piles of rubbish. Even fishing boats were now marooned miles inland, having been swept in by the gigantic waves. It was unlikely they'd ever get back to sea again.

Night-time approached rapidly, signified by the glow of the tail lights in front of them. They had been on the road for over fourteen hours, and were just reaching the outskirts of Banda Aceh. A police cordon stopped the vehicles from proceeding any further, directing them to park for the night. Even in the dark, it was clear how many dispossessed people had congregated together in temporary campsites. There was an air of chaos, with shelters constructed from little more than bits of wood and plastic.

Some sites had proper tents, showing that aid was getting through. Many people were cooking on portable stoves, courtesy of the UNHCR. It being too dark to see, Halcyon knew they needed to find a spot to bed down for the night.

Rami drove slowly into an area containing several erected tents laid out in neat rows. At least that signified some sort of organisation. The weary travellers set out to find where they were first, then looked for a source of clean water. They had come to the right place. The facilities had been provided by the Indonesian government. The latrines were simple holes in the ground, treated with chemicals as septic tanks had not been installed yet. It was basic, but better than nothing as the potential for spreading disease would be higher without it. The tents were already filled with the injured and traumatised.

Halcyon knew there was no option but to sleep in the van that night, despite the heat and discomfort. Rami had brought mosquito netting to cover the windows, which had to be left open for ventilation. They badly needed the rest but also knew that mosquitoes would be eating them alive. Being stuck in the cramped confines of a small van would be a night of purgatory. Nick could already hear the incessant noise of the mosquitoes fighting to get inside. Hell awaited them.

Chapter 24

Field Aid Post

A FTER A FITFUL NIGHT'S SLEEP, THE THREE of them came to in the light of dawn, scarcely believing they had just spent it in a tin can. The tiny ill-fitting seats had not been designed for sleeping in, made worse by the persistent mosquito attacks. It was something only a monk could have endured with equanimity but even they would have slapped the pests into oblivion, blowing their chances of reaching nirvana.

Feeling justifiably stiff and sore, they got out of the van. The vista spread out before them like some silent movie reel. The van had been parked in an area near to twenty blue tents, pitched in five rows of four, with three bigger tents set to one side. The smaller ablution tents were set a short distance away, leaving no doubt as to one's intention when heading out that way. Already the restless natives had stirred from their slumber, scurrying about. Mornings were usually the best part of the day before the fug of civilisation spewed out the hydrocarbons. Despite the freshness of a new morning, the air was noticeably putrid. It was coming from the dead in Banda Aceh, just a few miles away.

The colossal destruction of the whole area was obvious to see, as if the gods had wreaked havoc in a moment of madness. Remnants of an odd building or two still remained but the general area resembled a pile of rubble. Crushed cars, fridges and damaged furniture were strewn across the apocalyptic landscape. Thousands of decaying bodies lay in the rubble as the maggots writhed amidst the liquefying flesh. It was nature's way of cleaning up.

'Christ, it's awful,' Nick muttered, surveying the scene through binoculars.

'It usually is. How are you feeling?' Halcyon asked, watching him closely.

'Bloody stiff.'

'No, I mean mentally?'

'Holding up,' Nick replied.

'I wasn't sure if you were prepared for this. Some people don't cope very well at all.'

'That's reassuring.'

'I've seen worse.'

'Such as?'

'Rwanda and Sierra Leone.'

'In what way?'

'They were butchered by other human beings there. In Sierra Leone, people had their arms and legs chopped off by the crazed militia. It was also common practice to eat the enemy, usually the livers, which were cut out when they were still alive,' she replied.

'What fine young cannibals,' Nick muttered quietly.

'Fancy some breakfast?' Halcyon asked.

'Not really. Any idea where we could find the nearest Hilton?' Nick asked wryly.

'Why don't you make us some coffee? I'll find out what's going on,' Halcyon suggested.

'Milk and sugar?'

'No, just black,' she replied, before heading off towards the tents.

The refugee centre had been set up by the Indonesian government to serve as a field aid post. Halcyon quickly found the administration tent, which was already in a state of muted activity. Her presence had been noticed but nobody rushed forward to engage in a conversation. They probably wondered what a Westerner was doing there. With many aid organisations milling around in Medan, they could only presume the cavalry had arrived. They on the other hand had been out there for over two weeks already, being the very first to arrive. A man stepped forward, seeing her ill at ease.

'Hello Miss. What can I do for you?' he asked politely.

'Good morning. My name is Halcyon Cooper from Mercy Aid International. We arrived in the area last night,' she replied, smiling at the man.

'I am Bambang Ruswiati. I'm in charge of this government medical aid post,' he replied.

'Can you tell me how we could get some accommodation around here?' Halcyon asked.

'We only have places for the injured people. Maybe some other organisation can help you. Don't you have your own supplies?'

'We had our own premises in Aceh which presumably has been destroyed. I'll need to confirm that.'

'You had an office in Aceh before the tsunami?' Bambang asked.

'Yes. Our charity has been there for over a year.'

'Doing what?'

'Helping some of the local women.'

'I didn't know the government allowed foreign people to work there.'

'It was a special situation. We were there to offer psychological support just as we are now. We also have a surgeon with us, so let us know if there is any way we can help.'

'Thank you for the offer but be careful, this is a dangerous area.'

'I have been to other disaster areas before.'

'Where did you sleep last night?'

'In our small van over there,' Halcyon pointed out.

'How many of you?' Bambang asked.

'Three.'

'Not very comfortable then,' Bambang laughed out of sympathy.

'I've been in worse conditions but we could do with somewhere to stay.'

'I will see if I can find you some space here. We have tents for the workers.'

'Thank you. Do you have any fresh water to spare?'

'Yes, of course. There is a water tank at the back but only for drinking and cooking. More supplies are coming in but the roads are bad. You know that already.'

'Yes, we do. Is there any way to get into Banda Aceh?' Halcyon asked.

'The place is closed to everybody except for the people clearing up the area. It is very bad, many, many bodies there,' Bambang explained.

'My charity needs to know what has happened to our workers. Could we go there?'

'I will think about it. We have a kitchen tent next door so why don't you get some food first.'

'Thanks for the hospitality,' Halcyon smiled gratefully, wondering if Nick was up for eating yet.

'OK, no problem. I will come and speak to you soon.'

She ambled back to the van to find Nick making some coffee and fried eggs, despite his poor appetite. He and Rami had considered their meagre breakfast whilst waiting for Halcyon to return although Nick still wasn't sure if the eggs would stay down.

'There's breakfast over there in the food tent if you want it,' she informed them.

'Thanks. How did you get on?' Nick asked.

'These people are from the government. They'll put us up if they can. Apparently Banda Aceh is closed to everyone except for the clear-up team. There're getting all the dead bodies out first.'

'Nice job,' Nick said with little enthusiasm, handing her the coffee and eggs.

'I also told them what you did. Perhaps you could help out here.'

'How many bodies do you reckon are in Banda Aceh?' Nick asked, sipping his coffee.

'No idea. What do you reckon, Rami?' Halcyon asked.

'I think maybe eighty thousand but I don't know,' he replied.

With the death toll unknown, there would be many dead amongst the estimated 450,000 people missing. The body count in Aceh had risen quickly as more were pulled from the rubble. The psychological trauma of working there had already taken its toll. Recovery teams were only allowed to work for ten days at a time before taking an enforced break. Psychological counselling was paramount as the bulk of the manpower had come from local volunteers. Many had lost loved ones. Their personal grief had to be held in check as they worked quickly to prevent a major health crisis. Local custom dictated that the dead had to be buried as soon as possible but many would never be buried, having turned into fish food already. Halcyon saw Bambang striding up to them.

'Hello, hello, how are you? I am Bambang,' he said cheerfully with a warm welcome, offering his hand to Nick, and nodding to Rami.

'Hi, I'm Nick Forbes. I believe this is a medical aid post,' Nick replied, shaking his hand.

'That's right. You are a surgeon?'

'Yes, an orthopaedic surgeon. Halcyon has told you about our mission here?'

'Only a little bit,' Bambang replied with a nervous giggle.

'Our first mission is to find out about some missing people working for this organisation. We need to go to Banda Aceh but after that, I would be happy to help in any way.'

'You know everything there is gone, except the mosque?'

'Yes, but we would still like to go and see for ourselves. Is that possible?'

'Of course, I can arrange it but I warn you now it is not very nice there.'

'We need to go,' Halcyon added.

'OK, no problem.'

'What sort of medical facilities do you have here?' Nick asked.

'We have a doctor and three nurses. We can only do some simple operations but if somebody needs to go to hospital, we can arrange for a helicopter evacuation. We try to do what we can first.'

'I'd be happy to tend to any simple fractures but let me know if any hospital needs my services,' Nick added.

'Thank you for the kind offer. We have found some space for you to stay. There are separate tents for the men and women.'

'It'll be greatly appreciated. When can we get to Banda Aceh?' Halcyon asked.

'You can go today but are you really sure you want to do this?' Bambang asked again.

'Yes, very much.'When can we head off?' she asked.

'The truck is already waiting,' Bambang replied, indicating the spot where people were already congregating to board the vehicle.

'I guess there is no time for a quick wash and shave,' Nick replied.

'You can have five minutes, OK? We cannot wait too long.'

'That'll be fine,' Halcyon smiled, badly needing the toilet.

'OK, get to that truck when you are ready,' Bambang said, walking off.

'We won't be long.'

Neither she nor Nick had noticed the increased level of activity down one end of the tented complex. A small throng of men were already climbing into the back of an open truck, armed with crowbars and lengths of rope. Nick gulped down the last of his coffee, before heading off to the ablutions area. Halcyon followed after grabbing her sunhat from the van. It was a super-quick visit. Rami stood by to see them off.

'Nick, selamat siang,' Rami said.

'What?'

'Good day, lah. I teach you some Malay later.'

'Thank you, Rami,'

'You say terima kasih,' Rami replied.

'Terima kasih,' Nick replied, having picked that up at the airport.

'You speak good Malay already!' Rami laughed.

There had been no time to wash nor was it necessary where they were going. It was already crowded when they climbed on board, helped up by eager hands. People smiled but wondered who the hell they were. Being too polite to ask, they kept quiet. It didn't matter anyway as they were all heading in the same direction. The veterans were already smoking for what they were worth. It helped to mask the smell.

The truck rumbled off towards the devastated city. From the vantage point on top of the truck Nick could see just how much destruction had happened there. Huge swathes of ground had simply been washed up, leaving nothing but an unimaginable tangle of steel coils, concrete and wood from the shattered houses. The whole place was eerily quiet, adding to the sombre mood of the morning. It was only just after seven in the morning but the early start was important before the midday sun scorched down on them. Rather stupidly, he had forgotten to bring a hat.

Large numbers of soldiers and police were in strong evidence as they neared Banda Aceh. The truck rumbled to a halt at the designated location but it could have been anywhere as far as Nick was concerned. The men jumped off at the back, keen to get going as they braced themselves for another gruelling day. Bambang climbed out of the cab at the front and approached Nick and Halcyon.

'I have some gloves and masks for you. Look around but take care. It is very dangerous here. Some of these buildings can fall down.'

'There isn't much left to fall down,' Nick muttered, surveying the scene.

'Still, you take care, OK?' Bambang asked out of concern.

'Do you know roughly where Jalan Ahmad Yani is?' Halcyon suddenly asked.

'Is that where you had your office?' he replied.

'Yes.'

'OK, Banda Aceh is like this. It is split into two parts by the Kreung Aceh river. You can still see the Mesjid Raya Baiturrahman, or the Great Mosque over there. That is on the south side. Behind the mosque is the Pasar Aceh central market. Jalan Ahmad Yani is on the north side, over there. That is where a lot of the hotels were, also your office, I think. As you can see, everything is gone.'

'We'll head in that direction,' she replied.

What Bambang had said was only too obvious. Thankfully the mosque had survived but everything else around it had gone. There would be little point in trying to get to Jalan Ahmad Yani. Other recovery teams had probably combed the area already. Halcyon needed to get a mental picture of the site, as if it was something important. She may never know what had happened to the Mercy Aid team but at least she could say she had been there. The whereabouts of the Swiss psychologist and the three local helpers may always remain a mystery.

She knew that even before the tsunami some of the bolder women had turned up to seek help. Many had been beaten up in an effort to get information, some even raped by the security forces. Many pro-Jakarta Acehnese had sided with the security forces, feeding information about the freedom fighters and the Mercy Aid International office. Fearing reports of atrocities in Aceh province leaking out, the building had been under surveillance. No military dominated government would ever take kindly to bad publicity. Now all the evidence was gone, there was nothing left to note the charity's presence there.

The sense of foreboding had permeated the atmosphere all around them. Sniffer dogs were not needed as the human nose could do the job well enough. Sensing the futility of being there, they could only give moral support to the recovery team as they worked. The harrowing task continued relentlessly but they had seen for themselves at first hand the utter madness of the place. Instinctively, they knew the Mercy Aid team had perished. Their job there was done. With great relief, they finally arrived back at the tent site.

The emotionally gruelling day had given Nick a good insight of a disaster area. Helicopters scouted the area, searching for pockets of survivors in desperate need of supplies. Many of the badly injured people had already been airlifted out to Medan but it was not possible to evacuate everybody by helicopter. The only other option had been to set up local medical facilities and temporary shelters. The infrastructure had been totally destroyed, and only time and money could rebuild it. That needed government resolve and help from the UN.

Their new accommodation was luxurious in comparison with sleeping in the van. Nick met some of his tent mates but Rami opted to stay in the van, finding the confined space suitable for his small frame. Power came from a petrol-fired generator, providing enough energy for the communications equipment and lights. After a much-needed wash with just a basin of water, they sat in the food tent eating vegetable curry and rice. Halcyon started the conversation.

'What do you think? Is there is any way the team could have survived the disaster?'

'No.' Nick replied quickly.

'Any thoughts about what we can do to find out?'

'Have the authorities been able to compile a list of the dead and missing?'

'I don't know. Maybe Bambang can tell us.'

'That's our only hope.'

'There seems to be an awful lot of children here, don't you think?' Halcyon asked.

'Perhaps their parents died when out working.'

'Our next job would be to ask what plans have been made to look after them. Priority should go to any orphans.'

'You have a good point there.'

'If only there was an abandoned school or some other building we could use. They need something to rebuild their lives. Do you think Bambang could help us?'

'He's probably got his hands full already but it's worth a try. There must be some municipal building further inland we could use,' Nick suggested.

'I'll ask him tomorrow. What did you think about today?'

'It was just awful.'

'It's always the same, you know. Will you cope?'

'Don't fuss, I am a big boy now,' Nick replied, eating his curry tentatively.

'I know that but I have to ask. It's my job to look after the team.'

'Cut the crap. You sound like some kindergarten Fraulein.'

'Did you notice there were more soldiers around today?' Halcyon asked.

'Yes. They're not the happiest bunch, are they?'

'Did you know they butchered two hundred and fifty thousand people in East Timor?'

'What?' Nick asked with a start.

'That's what happens when soldiers run amok.'

'Is that for real? I can hardly believe all this has been going on without me knowing about it. Why has so little been said in the press?'

'That was thirty years ago. A million people were killed recently in Rwanda.'

'But it is still going on here in Aceh?'

'To a smaller extent. The press don't get a look in.'

'Did Mercy Aid know about this before they sent people out?'

'Yes, that's why we're here.'

'Tell me, where does your name come from?'

'That would depend on which version you believe.'

'I only asked a simple question,' Nick said, feigning exasperation.

'Well, Halcyon was apparently a Greek girl who fell in love with King Ceyx. When he died at sea, she complained to the gods who then turned them both into kingfishers. The other version relates to kingfishers who build their nests on the calm sunny seas during the 'halcyon days', with nostalgic connotations.'

'So glad I asked!'

'Is there anything else you want to ask about me, Nick?'

'No. I was just curious about your name. Where is Rami? I've not seen him since we got back,' Nick asked, noticing he wasn't with them.

'He's probably chatting with the locals.'

'How many girls are you sharing with in your tent?'

'About six others. Why, do you want to come and join us?' Halcyon asked cheekily.

'No, I'm busy enough with the boys. One of them is a medic called Jusuf.'

'Have you met him?'

'Just briefly.'

'What's he like?'

'Stiff and formal, almost unfriendly.'

'Lucky you. I'm going to get my head down now.'

'OK. See you in the morning.'

'Sleep well and make sure the bugs don't bite,' she reminded him, using the hackneyed phrase.

'There's nothing left to bite.'

'Oh, I'm sure you're just as tasty tonight,' she said affectionately.

Nick smiled as she walked off, realising the importance of a good sense of humour.

He liked her positive attitude. As a team leader, she seemed perfect for the role.

When he had struggled to eat that evening after seeing the day's horrors, she had eaten without a care in the world. It had more to do with fortitude than callousness. She was definitely a woman of substance.

Chapter 25

Tent City

I T WOULD HAVE BEEN A WONDERFUL NIGHT'S sleep had it not been for the horrible images. Compared to the previous night, the sleeping arrangement was almost luxurious on the campbeds. His tent companions had also snored badly but expedience told him to say nothing. He was there as their guest. It was just before 6 a.m. on his watch. Sensing rather than seeing Jusuf staring at him, Nick realized that the man was naturally curious about his presence.

'Good morning, Jusuf,' Nick greeted him with a friendly wave.

'Yes, good morning,' Jusuf replied, almost inaudibly.

'These beds are very comfortable.'

'Not really.'

'Well, they're not bad,' Nick replied, wondering why the man was so grumpy.

'You can go makan before starting work.'

'Makan?' Nick asked, wondering at the message behind the bilingualism.

'Yes, eat breakfast. Maybe you need to learn some Malay.'

'Yes, of course.'

'We have to get up,' Jusuf said, making it sound like an order.

Nick felt better for the rest but wondered what was eating at the man he had only met last night. It didn't bode well. Slinging his legs off the campbed, he got up and headed out for a wash. He met up with Halcyon, who was looking remarkably fresh, ten minutes later in the food tent. Breakfast was nasi goreng, the Indonesian staple of fried rice. The black coffee with condensed milk didn't taste bad either. Bambang joined them at the table.

'Did you both sleep well?' he asked.

'Yes thanks,' Halcyon answered, presuming Nick had too.

'So, Nick, are you OK to help Jusuf today?'

'Yes, I'd be glad to.'

'No Banda Aceh for you today, ah?' Bambang asked with wry humour, slurping his coffee noisily.

'No, I don't think so,' Nick replied gracefully.

'Good thing too.'

'Bambang, could I ask you something?' Halcyon said.

'Of course.'

'Do you know how many orphans there are in Aceh province because of the tsunami?'

'You mean children with no father or mother?'

'Yes, that's right.'

'We don't know but I think very many. Even here there are a few.'

'Who is looking after them just now?'

'We do, or the people here.'

'Will they eventually go to one special place?'

'Maybe, but the local government has to decide. Why are you asking?'

'I know there are many priorities like the work you're currently doing here but I'm concerned about the long-term mental health of these kids. They need some rehabilitation to start soon.'

'And how do you plan to do this?' Bambang asked.

'I propose to put them up in a secure building and start by making sure they are well looked after.'

'Of course, and where will you find this building?' Bambang asked with candour.

'That's what I want to ask you. Are there any buildings which have not been damaged that we could use?'

'All I can say is that any building not already destroyed will be used for the refugees. There is nothing specifically for the children at the moment, but that will come later.'

'Could they go to Medan or some other big town?' Halcyon persisted.

'They cannot cope with such huge numbers of children. Perhaps you could ask the UNHCR to help,' Bambang suggested thoughtfully.

'I was really meaning just the children without any parents or relatives.'

'At the moment we are still busy trying to stop an epidemic. I don't know of any suitable building for what you suggest. The hospitals and refugee camps are full. Many people still don't have food or water so I cannot help you.'

'Are you in touch with the UNHCR?'

'Of course. We have a satellite phone here.'

'Could I use it?' Halcyon asked.

'Yes, no problem. Just go to the radio tent. Tell the communications man I said you can call UNHCR.'

'Thank you.'

'OK, I have to go to Banda Aceh now. I will see you later. Nick, you have to speak to Jusuf and see what he wants you to do,' Bambang said, rising from the chair.

'Yes, I'll do that.'

They presumed nobody hung around as the tent quickly emptied. Nick finished the last of his coffee and went off in search of Jusuf.

Halcyon wondered if anybody was up yet from their beds at the UNHCR headquarters in Medan. Deciding that it was too early, she hung back for a short while.

Nick found his man in discussion with the three nurses in the medical tent. Jusuf clearly started early and immediately suggested they did a brief tour of the facilities. He was much more serious than the approachable Bambang. The main treatment tents were similar in size to the dining tent except there was a medical couch, a couple of halogen lamps, drip stands, metal instrument trays and a basic anaesthetic machine. Assorted tables held various bits and pieces including a sterilising bath for the surgical instruments. The floor was pure muddy grass. The next tent contained more equipment, dressings and medicines. It looked like a reasonably well-equipped mobile field hospital, adequate if not palatial. Jusuf seemed justifiably proud of his little empire, even becoming slightly animated for the first time when he boasted about the facilities. The nurses followed behind like obedient dogs, avoiding eye contact with Nick for some unfathomable reason.

'What do you think of the equipment?' Jusuf asked.

'You're very well equipped.'

'This is all supplied by the government.'

'Excellent.'

'You know we are trying to do everything we can for our people. This disaster is even too big for your country to deal with if it happened in the UK.'

'I am aware of that,' Nick said sympathetically.

'We can only do basic operations here but already you can see how busy this place is. More people are coming all the time but we only send the very sick to hospital by helicopter. Everything else, we try to do. Come and see some of the patients.'

The tent next door contained some very ill people. Most had

hacking coughs from swallowing dirty water. The nurses went quietly to their aid. They turned to look at Nick.

'Selamat pagi, doktor,' one of the patients said to Jusuf, wondering who Nick was.

'Selamat pagi,' Jusuf replied, with an air of authority.

'What is the most common problem here?' Nick asked.

'A lot of them swallow the infected water. They mostly get diarrhoea but we also have a condition called mucormycosis. This is a fungus infection which can infect the brain, lungs, kidneys, skin. It usually starts in the nasal turbinates. Have you heard of this condition?' Jusuf asked knowledgeably.

'No, I haven't,' Nick replied, feeling a little ashamed of his ignorance. It was something he had not seen in the UK.

'People who get this usually die within a few days from the necrotising sinusitis, before the fungus invades the cribriform plate and causes a menigo-encephalitis,' Jusuf added, sounding off arrogantly.

'Nasty,' Nick muttered.

He was impressed with Jusuf's grasp of medical terminology. He wondered if the man had trained in the UK. He wanted to ask him but Jusuf carried on.

'There is cholera and other forms of dysentery. As you can see, we can treat all these problems. I also try to fix broken bones,' Jusuf said proudly.

'Do you have a portable X-ray here?'

'No, but when it is obvious if somebody has a broken arm or leg, I just put them in plaster.'

'How would you know if bones are properly aligned?'

'I can't. All I can do is give them some anaesthetic and then I reset the bone until it looks straight. After that we put on the plaster. They are happy if they can use the arm or leg again. Of course I cannot treat major fractures.'

'I see,' Nick replied, feeling suitably apprehensive at the John Wayne approach.

'You are an orthopaedic surgeon, yes?' Jusuf asked.

'Yes, that's correct.'

'Tell me, why you are with Mercy Aid International and not with the Red Cross or *Médecins Sans Frontières*?' Jusuf asked directly.

'This was the quickest way I could think of getting out here. They agreed I could come,' Nick explained.

'Well, I have to tell you something. Many Indonesian doctors and nurses have been killed by the tsunami. Many people here don't trust foreign doctors coming from America or the UK.'

'Because of Iraq?' Nick asked, remembering his previous conversation with Rami.

'You people don't speak our language and don't understand our culture. For now, we need you but more doctors are coming from our neighbours in Malaysia. There are temporary hospitals set up in Lambaro and Pidie with many more mobile aid centres like this one. Hopefully you can go home soon.'

'Jusuf, I am just a little confused by your attitude. I volunteered to come to Sumatra to help with a humanitarian cause,' Nick protested.

'OK, don't worry about it. Come with me,' Jusuf said, walking quickly out of the tent.

'Whatever you say,' Nick replied in a vague attempt to mock the man, still pondering what all the jingoistic claptrap was about.

The world had rallied to Indonesia's cause because of the magnitude of the disaster. Doctors shouldn't differentiate between people of different races but Jusuf seemed to have a big chip on his shoulder. It wasn't a case of Western nations trying to colonize the Far East again. Those days had gone for ever. No, there was something more fundamental with Jusuf, which Nick couldn't figure out. They walked into the next tent, housing more sick people. He could immediately see one young woman lying on a mattress in a supine position, drenched with sweat. She was delirious with pain.

'What you think is wrong with her?' Jusuf asked without giving any history.

'How long has she been like this?' Nick replied, not knowing if Jusuf was challenging his clinical skills.

'She was brought in yesterday, saying her stomach pain is bad. I think she has appendicitis. Can you do this operation?'

'Is it OK for me to examine her?' Nick asked.

'Of course, go ahead,' Jusuf replied, as he waved the woman's female companion aside.

Nick knelt down at the right side of the patient, knowing she was oblivious to his presence there. Despite the fact she was sweating, she didn't feel particularly hot. Nick pulled one of her eyelids down and could see it was pale. Her pulse felt very fast. He gently pressed on her abdomen, working his way from the left lower part in an anticlockwise direction until he returned to the same spot. The spleen under the left ribcage could not be felt, nor could the liver on the opposite side. He braced himself for any signs of pain when he pressed the right lower side containing the appendix. She remained much the same. He quickly moved his fingers away to check for any rebound tenderness but couldn't detect any sudden increase in her pain. The abdomen didn't feel rigid enough to indicate the presence of peritonitis. Nick gently slid his left hand in the small of her back and gently pressed with his right hand over her abdomen to check the kidneys. The woman groaned a little. He thought he could feel a little movement in her pelvis. He checked the other kidney. Again the woman moaned at being moved slightly. He was at the disadvantage of not knowing the full history.

'Jusuf, ask the patient's friend what happened,' Nick asked.

'She said this woman was found trapped in the rubble by the

rescue workers. She had gone back to the house after the tsunami to look for her parents. Maybe she fell down through a hole or something. This was only yesterday, not when the tsunami happened. Do you agree she has appendicitis?' Jusuf asked again.

'I'm not so sure. She is certainly very pale with a fast heart rate. I couldn't detect any signs of peritonitis. There is one more thing I need to do.'

Nick bent over the patient again. This time he placed the palms of both his hands over the two bony prominences on the pelvis. Very gently, he pressed down. The springy sensation was there as the woman moaned. The pelvis felt unstable. It was most likely she had suffered from a fractured pelvis and was bleeding internally.

'I think she has a fractured pelvis with a retroperitoneal haemorrhage. Cold you run a drip into her, Jusuf?' Nick asked, surprised this had not been done already.

'Yes, of course. She only arrived when you were having breakfast,' Jusuf replied, trying to mitigate his error.

'She needs to go to hospital immediately. Can you arrange an evacuation?'

'I will have to speak to the main hospital in Medan. A nurse will come back with a drip,' Jusuf said, before promptly leaving the tent.

A nurse quickly arrived with the intravenous needle and a bag of saline. Nick knew better than to tread on Jusuf's toes, not wanting to aggravate the situation by taking over., The woman looked too ill to wait. He inserted the drip and started to run the bag of saline in. He also gave her a shot of pethidine for the pain just as Jusuf strode in.

'The hospital in Medan is full but there is an American hospital ship not far from here. The US Navy will send a helicopter,' Jusuf informed him quickly.

'I've just given her some pethidine. I hope that was OK with you.'

'Why don't you look after her?' Jusuf suggested.

'Fine,' Nick replied, as if he needed the permission.

He watched the man go out of the tent, knowing that something was eating away at him. Perhaps he was just stressed and overworked like everybody else there, dealing with the harrowing conditions. Doctors needed a thick skin to cope but Jusuf seemed rankled by an inferiority complex. He had made a blunder and it showed.

CHAPTER 26
MEDEVAC

THE MORNING WAS STILL CRISP AND FRESH when Halcyon went to the communications tent. She saw Jusuf was there with a scowl on his face. He was clearly exasperated in trying to make some kind of arrangement. She listened to the conversation in Malay. The only word she heard in English was 'helicopter', equivalent to the Malay of 'kapalterbang yang dapat naik tegak'. Clearly it was easier to use the English equivalent. It was only after Jusuf had left the tent that she was informed about the medevac request. Somebody had obviously required an emergency evacuation by helicopter. As no Indonesian Army helicopter was available and the hospital in Medan was full, the US Navy had offered to help. There was a fully-equipped hospital ship standing by just offshore but that piece of news had obviously dented Jusuf's patriotic sentiments. The aid worker translated for Halcyon's sake but the people had seemed wary of Jusuf.

Brushing it aside, she decided to ask one of the English-speaking men to show her how to use the satellite phone. She managed to get through to the UNHCR headquarters in Medan without difficulty. The official there was quite clear about her request. Whilst in agreement with the need to rehabilitate the children, the official denied it on the grounds of priority. Hospitals and houses had to be built first.

144

Halcyon knew that well enough. However, the children were also at risk of suffering from huge long-term psychological damage if the rehabilitation programme didn't start soon. They agreed to keep in contact.

She went for a walkabout. The children were curious to see a foreigner there. Few travellers bothered to venture north unlike the tourist haven of Bali. Initially, the children shied away but still poked their heads out of the tents to look at her. The bolder ones hung around saying the only words they knew like 'Hello' and 'Miss'. Halcyon noticed several had remained unnaturally quiet, even unanimated, as if their brains had been switched off. She felt like an intruder looking in, somehow invading their privacy. Surprisingly, the people welcomed her in to the tents. It showed how little they had. Everything they had once owned was lost. Amongst the gossiping women, she noticed how quiet the men were. Women were better at surviving because they talked. Sharing a problem was better than not doing so. One little girl remained very quiet, showing no interest at Halcyon's presence. Apparently both her parents had died in the tsunami and there were no known relatives around. She had refused to speak with anybody, which was a worrying sign.

Instinctively, Halcyon knew this child was vulnerable. She was exactly the sort of child who needed protection. Without loving care, she and many others like her would be lost to the world. The girl had probably witnessed too much already and her brain refused to work normally. Halcyon had seen this often before, in places such as Rwanda and Sierra Leone. The children had to erase the horrors from their minds. Simply by being children again would help them recover. Her work here would be difficult, made worse without immediate resources. Mercy Aid could provide some of the manpower but it was only the UNHCR who could provide the accommodation she needed. Thanking the local women for showing her around, she vowed to come back to see the girl. Nick and Rami were by the van, engrossed in a conversation.

'Hi guys. What's up?' she asked.

'How did you get on with the UNHCR?' Nick replied without answering her question.

'I got through but they couldn't promise anything just now. I just met some of the kids.'

'What did you think?' Nick asked.

'They seemed pretty wiped out.'

'In what way?'

'Mentally. Their behaviour is not right.'

'That's hardly surprising. What are you going to do?'

'We could start by playing games I suppose. It always helps. Jusuf was in a bad mood.'

'Yeah, he screwed up a diagnosis.'

'Oh, was that all? He seemed pretty hacked off. What's wrong with the patient?'

'Some woman was pulled out of the rubble early this morning and he thought she had appendicitis.'

'Except she didn't?'

'No, she has a broken pelvis after falling through a hole. That's why we're waiting on a helicopter.'

'There's a US navy ship standing by.'

'How do you know?' Nick asked.

'I was in the communications tent. Somebody translated.'

'He didn't seem to take it too well when I corrected his diagnosis. I spoke to Rami about it. He agreed that some of the doctors here don't like westerners.'

'That's just tough. Don't get sentimental about it,' Halcyon advised.

'I think that's the helicopter coming.'

The unmistakable beat of a helicopter quickly filled the air as the large MH-60S Seahawk circled the site. It came in from the west before setting down several hundred metres away. It was the US Navy's equivalent to the Black Hawk. Tents fluttered gently by the draft as the rotors slowed to idle. They saw two crew members jumping out, carrying a stretcher between them. Nick felt obliged to meet them, to explain the woman's injuries. The navy personnel looked professional, except they were not the smiling type.

'What's the situation here?' the big Texan asked abruptly, judging by his drawl.

'Hi, I'm one of the volunteer doctors out here. The casualty has a suspected broken pelvis from a fall. She was pulled out from the rubble this morning. Her condition is critical,' Nick shouted, to make himself heard above the noise from the helicopter.

'OK, lead on,' the crew member shouted back.

'She's in the third tent, second row. There is a local nurse with her.'

'OK, we'll handle this.'

'You'll need to stabilise her pelvis first,' he shouted after them.

'Sure thing,' the Texan replied.

Nick knew the American hospital ship would be fully kitted out. It was designed to handle the most serious kinds of battlefield injuries. The medics on board were probably some of the best trained trauma surgeons around. He watched the helicopter crew stabilising the patient before carrying her out. The female companion tried to go along but she was stopped by a burly man dressed in a batik shirt. Nick could see the fear etched on her face as she remained behind. The Americans ignored the matter and got on with their job. Nick saw the woman pulling out a red and white identity card from her purse as the burly man examined it. He refused to let her get onboard the helicopter with her friend. The Texan returned to Nick for a quick update.

'What medicines has she had?' he asked.

'She's had a shot of pethidine plus a bag of saline.'

'OK. I guess her friend won't be coming with us.'

'Thanks for the help. I'm Nick.'

'Be seeing you, Nick. It's Charlie. Call anytime you need us.'

'Thanks,' Nick replied.

The crew gave a thumbs up from the side door before lifting off. Nick waved to acknowledge them. He was conscious that neither Jusuf nor the Indonesian official had bothered to do so. The children waved enthusiastically at the huge machine. Nick was puzzled by the sudden appearance of the burly official. He looked more like a thug than a policeman. Something about him spelled trouble.

CHAPTER 27

RELOCATION

THE AUTHORITIES HAD DECIDED TO RELOCATE THE dispossessed into semi-permanent camps until new houses could be built. It was a logical but temporary solution to the housing crisis. Many wondered if it was a convenient excuse for the government to exert their control over the local population. If so, it would be a devious way of fighting the separatist movement. Tactically, it would mirror the methods used by the British during the Malayan Emergency to fight the communist uprising in the 1950s. When the Chinese rubber workers living on the edges of the jungle had been coerced to help the communists, they were moved to military-run camps. Deprived of logistical support, the communists lost the war. It was a simple but brilliant idea. Similarly, the GAM guerrilla movement in Sumatra could suffer the same fate.

Bambang had indicated that the fitter refugees would be moved to a freshly constructed camp further inland, away from the tsunami-prone coastline. Three large army trucks lumbered their way up the dusty track the following day and the people were given little warning. There were no objections as the tent site was no place for a long stay.

Nick watched the people moved out. Sitting next to the van in a portable chair, he knew they would be better off sleeping under a solid roof rather than in a tent. Rebuilding their homes by the sea didn't seem a realistic possibility right then. With the army in control, people had to do as they were told. Moving inland would deprive the fishermen of their livelihood although nobody would be eating fish for a while with numerous bodies still floating about in the sea.

Halcyon remained concerned about the children, especially the orphans who had gone away in the trucks. Bambang assured her they would be safe, even suggesting she could set up a children's centre at the new camp. It sounded like a good idea. She asked Nick about it.

'What did you think about Bambang's idea of following these people to the new camp site? There must be more facilities there.'

'To set up your children's centre?'

'Yes. That actually has a nice ring to it.'

'It seems like the most logical thing to do.'

'I somehow doubt if they would give us the facilities.'

'You'll have to persevere with the UNHCR,' Nick suggested.

'I was thinking on the same lines. These kids will be at the bottom of the heap when everybody is fighting for themselves.'

'I think you have already decided to make it your job to look after these kids, haven't you?'

'I have. And what will you do?'

'Stay here and keep fixing the injured until Jusuf decides otherwise.'

'Sounds like we both have a job, then.'

'Happy?' Nick asked.

'I am, but can you work with Jusuf?'

'I can handle him. It won't be for ever,' Nick replied.

'Just don't annoy him any more.'

'I wouldn't do that to idiots.'

'Nick! That kind of attitude will certainly not endear you to Jusuf.'

'I don't care. He's an arrogant bully. People here may be scared of him but I'm not. He's very friendly with that police official who looks like the Indonesian version of the Gestapo.'

'Just keep your mouth shut. Minor officials with big ideas are often dangerous people,' Halcyon advised.

'Rami said his name was Susanto.'

'I've been around long enough to know you either play their game or not at all, especially in dangerous areas like this. I'm going to find out where those people have gone to,' Halcyon said, rising from the chair and walking over to the communications tent.

Nick knew from his own experience that she was right. He wasn't afraid of Jusuf, who seemed like an incompetent medic trying to bluff his way into a position of authority, but Susanto was a different animal. He had a menacing presence about him. Being in the police also meant he had the power to arrest people. In certain situations it could also mean an unofficial death warrant. Nick knew to tread carefully with that man. He could now understand why the people were afraid of the regime. The politicians had distanced themselves from the troubles by allowing the local authorities to take control as they saw fit. Even with the presence of foreign news teams roaming the country, a person could easily disappear without trace.

CHAPTER 28

THE ORPHAN GIRL

THE REFUGEE CAMP HAD BEEN SET UP some ten miles inland from where they were. As they approached, they could see the hastily constructed wooden buildings which bore a striking resemblance to a German POW camp, complete with a guardhouse. Since there was no fence to keep people in or out, it did seem somewhat superfluous. They stated their business to the solitary army sentry before being told to park in front of the administrative building. Halcyon could already recognise some of the children from the tent site. They waved to her.

A red and white Indonesian flag hung limply from the flagpole outside the administrative building, indicating the lack of wind movement. It was oppressively still in the hinterland, unlike the coast where gentle breezes blew. Rami stayed on the veranda as they went in, politely acknowledging his status as a driver. Nick thought it was odd for him to be so subservient. His services as an interpreter could be required. The floor-standing fans circulated cool air around as a fat, balding man looked up from his desk. He was intrigued by the presence of foreigners there.

'Hello, we're from Mercy Aid International,' Halcyon announced with a smile.

'Are you Australian?' The man asked, as if expecting somebody from the outback.

'No, we're actually from the UK. My name is Halcyon and this is Nick,' she replied.

'I am Topo Sutadi, manager of this development. What can I do for you?' he asked with a heavy accent, standing up reluctantly.

'We were told this is a long-term refugee camp. On behalf of the charity we work for, we would like to offer our services.'

'And what is that?' the man asked curiously.

'We are keen to help the children,' Halcyon said simply.

'The children? Please tell me your plan.'

'We thought of setting up a special school to help the children recover from the tsunami.'

'A school? This is a very bad time for everybody,' Topo replied, seemingly confused by the proposal.

'Perhaps I should explain things a bit more. In my experience, children who have suffered from a disaster need to get their life back quickly. We can help you with this.'

'I'm sure the government already knows that. Sure, we can talk about it but first, can I offer you a drink? Maybe a cola or coffee?'

'Cola would be nice,' Halcyon replied.

'That's fine for me and our driver outside,' Nick added.

'No problem. Please sit down. I will get my houseboy to get this.'

Topo summoned a young boy to fetch the drinks immediately. They came with drinking straws sticking out from the bottles. It was their first chilled drink since leaving Medan and Cola had never tasted better. Topo indicated for them to sit on some rattan chairs.

'Thank you for your hospitality,' Halcyon said appreciatively.

'Tell me exactly what you want to do here,' Topo inquired politely.

'Can I ask how many people you are expecting in this camp?' Halcyon asked.

'Maybe five or six thousand. There are many people in Aceh with no home. Yes, big, big problem. The government is very good because they build camps like this one,' Topo said proudly.

'You will surely need many more camps like this to put all these people in?' Halcyon asked.

'Yes, of course, but the problem is not only in Banda Aceh, but also in Meulaboh and Calang further down the coast. They also need shelter and we are building them as fast as we can,' Topo replied.

'How many children do you have here?'

'About four hundred already.'

'Do you have any extra space for a school here?' Halcyon asked.

'Of course, we have plenty of space but where are you going to get this building?'

'Hopefully from the UNHCR. I have spoken to them already. They will try to send us a prefabricated building at sometime but we have to find a site first,' Halcyon replied.

'That is a good idea but I have to speak to the area chief first. He decides about everything that goes on here but don't worry, everything will be OK. Leave it to me,' the man said smugly.

Halcyon almost felt comforted by the man's geniality but he had small shady eyes. If the man was true to his word, she may have found somewhere to start her work. The UNHCR had been positive enough about her idea and this place was ideal. With foreign aid pouring into the country the reconstruction work had already started but the pace was frustratingly slow. The refugee camp so far contained only twenty prefabricated buildings with many more planned for construction. Permanent homes had not been started yet.

'Who is this chief you mentioned?' Nick chipped in.

'He is the head of the police in this area, a good friend of mine. I'm sure he will give his permission for this to go ahead.'

'And how long would that take?' Halcyon wanted to know.

'Well, he is very busy man. Maybe he will need to talk to the UNHCR first and then afterwards if everything is OK, things can happen very quickly. The chief can get the local people to build the school so it may be quicker if you can ask the UNHCR to send him the money.'

'I have no power to ask for anything other than what our own charity can provide,' Halcyon said.

'Of course. I will talk to him. We are always grateful for your assistance.'

'No, thank you for your help. I hope we can work together on this project. May I have your permission to go and see the children?'

'Yes, of course you can. My houseboy can take you around.'

'That would be very good of him.'

'Please feel free to do what you want here,' Topo beamed.

'Thank you very much, Mr Sutadi.'

'It is my pleasure. Just ask me anything you need to know.'

'Shall we go?' Halcyon said to Nick, as the houseboy waited patiently to lead them around the camp.

'Sure. Lead on.'

Feeling suitably positive about the outcome, they shook hands with the fat man. The houseboy showed them around the site, which was far bigger than the medical aid post. They headed away from the administrative building and immediately noticed how it resembled an army barrack. Neat rows of wooden prefabricated buildings lined up next to each other in an orderly fashion. The ground had already been prepared for more buildings to go up, clearly indicating the eventual size. Even the communal eating area could accommodate a thousand people at any one time. It was a basic open-aired structure with a kitchen area to the rear. Nick could detect the heady smell of exotic spices pervading the air.

155

'Why do I feel so self-conscious here? Nick suddenly asked.

'Perhaps you're quite a hunk,' Halcyon jested.

'Cut it out. Great time for Rami to bugger off,' Nick muttered, noticing that the houseboy didn't speak any English apart from saying 'hello'.

'Talk of the devil, I think he is over there,' Halcyon said, pointing to a small crowd.

Rami was speaking to a group of people outside one of the wooden buildings with a half drunk bottle of coke in his hand. He already knew them from the medical aid post. Nick and Halcyon made their way slowly towards him, observing the subdued nature of the people around him. Rami saw them coming and gave a small wave and a smile.

'I see you've made some new friends Rami,' Halcyon said, on catching up with him.

'I already know some of these people from the other place,' he replied.

'So it appears. Ask them how they like it here.'

Rami translated the question, which prompted several replies. He struggled to listen to them all at once, holding up his hands to slow them down.

'They say they are happy here but many want to go home.'

'Home to where?' Halcyon asked out of surprise.

'Where they were before, to build their houses again.'

'Even with the risk of another tsunami?'

'Yes, they know that is possible but it is their choice. They don't want to stay here.'

'Why not? Don't they know this is just a temporary measure?'

'They think the government want to keep them here all the time.'

'Is there a deliberate government policy?'

'Come, we cannot talk about this here,' Rami said, glancing at the houseboy.

'Why, is he a spy or something?' Nick asked with a laugh.

'He will listen to what we are asking and tell the manager. Many people here are fishermen so they want to go back to the sea. There is nothing to do here.'

'Ask them if there are any children here with no parents,' Halcyon suggested.

'Yes, I already know there are some. They live here and these people look after them. You can come and see inside this building if you want,' Rami said, knowing no objections would be raised.

It would have been impolite to refuse the offer but as charity workers they were there to help, not intrude. The crowd made way for them to enter. The rectangular structure had been subdivided into sections where family members could stay together. Simple mattresses covered the floor. Most people had very few personal possessions apart from some clothing and toiletries. It was all pretty stark. Certainly this was no substitute for their previous life and it was obvious why they wanted to go and rebuild their old homes. As they wandered through the building, most of the faces appeared familiar. The people there had come from the tent site, having elected to stay together. Halcyon caught sight of the little girl again, the quiet one who hadn't spoken at all. She sat alone in a corner and stared at the unpainted wooden wall, showing no interest in her surroundings. Halcyon detached herself and went across, squatting down next to the child. She stroked the child's head, noting how unwashed it was.

'Hello, darling. What's the matter? You look very sad. Come and walk around with us,' Halcyon muttered in her most caring English voice, knowing full well the girl didn't understand a word. Rami tried to translate but there was not a flicker of response. Her dark eyes remained blank. The emptiness was disturbing.

'The people say she is 'gila', you know, mad. No mother, no father. She sit like this all day and when people try to take her outside, she scream. They don't know what to do with her,' Rami explained.

'Do they know her name?' Halcyon asked.

'No.'

'Why don't we call her Annie, after the musical,' Nick suggested usefully.

'After the musical?' Rami repeated, seemingly confused.

'She's an orphan but don't worry about it. Just tell her we have decided to call her Annie,' Nick said, cutting short the explanation.

'Lu nama Annie, nama Annie,' Rami tried to tell her, but in vain.

'I think this is going to be hard work,' Halcyon muttered, knowing too well the situation.

It was Nick's first sight of the little girl Halcyon had spoken about. The crowd looked on impassively at their forlorn attempts to get her to speak. Halcyon knew it was even more imperative to get her mission underway, realising just how difficult the task ahead would be. Nick looked at the little girl and felt totally inept as he bent down to examine her, to make sure she didn't have any obvious physical injuries. Convinced there was nothing broken or physically wrong with her, he searched in his pockets to see if he could give her something. Finding his wallet, he knew money would be useless. Instead, he found an old passport photograph of himself. As an instinctive gesture, he placed it in her dress pocket. There was no acknowledgement of the present. At least it was an attempt to communicate. With a resigned smile, he stood up and headed for the door. He felt emotionally more troubled by the girl than seeing the countless bodies.

The bright sunlight outside reminded him how near it was to the equator. He was now preoccupied by the stupendous heat, grateful the walkabout had reached its natural conclusion. It was time to return to the medical aid post. He had learnt another Malay word, 'bodoh'. Several people had said it. Rami explained it meant stupid. He now understood what Mercy Aid International stood for. Little girls like Annie would stand no chance of a decent life in this world unless somebody cared.

They walked back to the van accompanied by some of the locals, who chatted with Rami. Amidst the 'terima kasih's' and 'salamat jalan's' they climbed into the van, promising to be back. Rami tooted as they left the camp. The van was baking hot, which added to Halcyon's perspiration.

Nick had been aware of Rami's relative silence ever since they got there. 'What's up, Rami?' he asked without ceremony.

'I'm scared to tell you,' Rami replied, looking straight ahead at the road.

'You're safe with us. We need to know what's going on.'

'The people told me something.'

'Go on.'

'The chief of police here is a man called Anzala. He is a bad man.'

'Topo talked about him.'

'He controls everything here. You cannot do anything without permission.'

'Even building a school?' Halcyon asked.

'Yes, everything.'

'Topo said the school could be built if the UNHCR paid for it,' she continued.

'Yes, he wants the money. You see the ground for the other buildings?' Rami asked.

'You mean the bulldozed area?' Nick replied.

'Yes. More buildings are supposed to go there.'

'So what are you saying?'

'Anzala says the money has already run out and he wants more from the UN.'

'Make hay when the sun is shining,' Nick said.

'I know that is meant to say something. Better to ask UN to build the school itself.'

'There must be some local corruption going on.'

'The tsunami is very good excuse to make money,' Rami answered ruefully.

'Obviously. What else can you tell us about Anzala?'

'He is looking for any GAM people at the camp.'

'And what would happen if he found them?'

'They get taken away.'

'Where to?'

'We don't know for sure, maybe to prison.'

'Here in Aceh province?'

'Yes, but they have found some bodies in Nissam.'

'Do you mean they have been deliberately killed?' Nick asked.

'Yes, but they are only rumours, lah.'

'Where is Nissam?'

'Not far from here. People say many bad things already happened there.'

'Are these people scared?' Nick probed.

'Of course. They want the foreign governments to help but they are afraid nobody will listen. Some women also get raped. Some get cut up.'

'Cut up? Do you mean mutilated?'

'Yes. I don't want to tell you everything. It's not nice.'

'That is horrible. Has anybody tried to get this information out?' Nick asked.

'No, the press is not allowed to go to Nissam. Just like in East

Timor before, the government will stop them.'

'Because people are getting killed?'

'Yes. Many British and Australian journalists got shot then to stop them from telling the world. The army said they died in crossfire.'

'Except it wasn't?'

'Yes. This is why people tell your government don't sell weapons to Indonesia. The air force will use your Hawk jet from British Aerospace to bomb the GAM people. You understand the problem now?'

'I didn't realise things were that bad.'

'Please don't talk to anybody about this. Somebody will tell the police,' Rami begged, needing the reassurance.

'Relax, Rami. This is just between us,' Nick said.

'I also heard about some women from Ulle Kareng who went to the Mercy Aid office in Banda Aceh,' Rami suddenly added.

'How long ago?' Nick asked.

'That I don't know. They wanted to know where their husbands were killed but the police just said the army killed them in a battle. They cannot get a true answer.'

'That's important news,' Halcyon said.

'Yes. Then afterwards, the office got closed down,' Rami replied.

'Closed down? We never heard about that. How long was this before the tsunami?

'Just before Christmas.'

'And when did you know about this?' Halcyon asked.

'Just now.'

'Do these people know what happened to the people from the Aceh office?' Halcyon asked with a sinking feeling.

'No. Some people think they were taken away by some men who don't wear uniforms.'

'You mean some kind of a paramilitary unit? Anzala perhaps?' Halcyon asked.

'Maybe.'

'How can we find out?'

'Maybe you can try at the police headquarters in Lhokseumawe.'

'We drove through there on the way up here but that's miles away. Do you really think they will tell us?' Nick asked.

'I don't know but I don't think so.'

'Don't worry Rami. You've been a big help already. What do you want to do now?' Nick asked Halcyon.

'We have to find out if our people have been arrested. There is no other choice.'

'If we did go to the police, Susanto and Anzala will know we have been asking questions. They must have had a good reason to remove people working for a foreign charity. '

'Maybe our people heard about the killings in Nissam. Anzala wanted them out of the way to shut them up,' Halcyon reasoned.

'You have to speak to UNHCR about this,' Nick decided.

'I agree but what if they ask Anzala about this? We could all end up being targets as you have already pointed out.'

'We're back to square one, aren't we? How else can we find out about the missing workers?'

'Let me think about it.'

'Don't take too long because there's a roadblock up ahead,' Nick said from the front seat.

'Oh, great,' Halcyon replied, feeling fear for the first time since her arrival.

Rami didn't question the irony this time as he slowed the van down. The single line of traffic inched forward when they were ordered to. Two army jeeps were parked opposite each other in a staggered fashion, creating a deliberate zigzag. Each had a mounted machine gun, manned by two surly looking soldiers. Other soldiers checked the identity of each occupant in the vehicle. Every trunk was also searched before the cars were waved through. The Mercy Aid van crawled slowly forward and stopped when indicated to do so by a soldier carrying a reflective baton. Rami already had the window open, ready to explain their mission. The soldier looked long and hard at Nick and Halcyon, checking their identity papers with care. He finally seemed satisfied enough to wave them through. Clearly the military presence had been stepped up. Rami was keen to get going quickly as he cast a furtive look in the mirror, but resisted pressing the accelerator pedal too hard. Heavily armed soldiers looked for tiny excuses to open fire.

Nick felt uneasy for Halcyon's sake. Finding out that the missing women could have been abducted had made their mission even more dangerous now. The tsunami could have been a blessing for Anzala if he had been responsible for their disappearance. Bodies were turning up all the time in the fetid waters. Nick wondered if Susanto had taken a sudden interest in the medical aid post when he learnt of the presence of Mercy Aid International there. Certainly the local woman he had stopped from boarding the helicopter seemed totally afraid of him. This was definitely the wrong time to ask questions at the local police station.

'I think we should keep quiet until we are out of here,' Nick suggested.

'But what if our women are languishing in some godforsaken place on some trumped up charge?' Halcyon replied.

'They could already be dead for all we know. Anzala is not going to tell us that over a cup of tea, is he? All it will achieve is to warn him we're onto him.'

'We can't just leave the matter, Nick.'

'Aren't you afraid of jeopardising our mission here?' Nick asked.

'Our first mission is to find out about them and yes, our second mission is to help these kids. The fact remains we have a duty to find out what has happened to our own people. We owe them that much.'

'It's your call.'

'You should know that before we embark on any charity mission, we always look at the political situation in that country first. We knew about the civil war here in Aceh and decided the risk was acceptable. We are a female-orientated non-political organisation so, on balance, we shouldn't have any enemies. Since having a presence here, our charity has been made more aware of the local issues.'

'What else other than abductions and killings?' Nick asked.

'OK, this is what I think is going on. There is probably bribery going on in Anzala's favour from somebody in the government, who in turn is receiving a kickback from the oil companies. The separatist movement wants to take control of the oil from the central government to stop the money from going to Jakarta. They need an independent state to achieve this but the government won't allow it because some people could lose a lot of money. Therefore, the GAM guerrilla movement has to be eliminated. The authorities just need to make sure the rest of the world doesn't know about what is going on here.'

'And you think that's where the missing women come in? They had some proof of the killings that were going on?'

'Well, why not? People couldn't exactly make a complaint to the authorities. They came to our organisation instead, in the hope we could help them,' Halcyon said.

'I agree with your take on the situation but I suggest we keep quiet about this until we have more information. Do you agree?'

'OK, I agree but we can't keep quiet for ever,' Halcyon replied.

They stopped speaking for the rest of the journey when each

person became lost in their own thoughts. The situation had become dangerous and Nick was acutely aware of their vulnerability. He knew that being a charity worker offered little immunity from persecution in this situation. Some of these people were murderers seeking to line their own pockets, except they were the law in this part of Sumatra. He now felt acutely concerned just as Rami had done earlier.

CHAPTER 29

THE LIEUTENANT

MORE REFUGEES ARRIVED AT THE FIELD AID post, looking ill and malnourished. They had succumbed to the ravages of neglect, ingesting dirty water when their immune system was already at its lowest ebb. Many had found themselves marooned on rooftops with little to eat or drink for many days, rescued only at the very last moment. Jusuf was secretly glad for Nick's assistance, despite his reticence about foreign doctors. Helicopter crews from various nations continued to scour the land for isolated pockets of survivors.

Nick's role at the field hospital had evolved quickly, finding himself more as a general medical officer than a surgeon. Setting up drips and administering antibiotics had been the mainstay of his job, but some minor surgery broke the tedium. It was essential work, but hardly the complex surgery he was used to doing. He deliberately played the underdog with Jusuf, feeling less stressed by doing so. Occasionally adopting a selective deafness strategy saved several patients from an uncertain outcome, when Jusuf's medical opinion had bordered on the bizarre. The earlier incident of the misdiagnosis still bothered Jusuf. He gave the nurses a hard time. They on the other hand had remained inscrutable, showing no signs of their inner thoughts. Nick did not try to ingratiate himself to them other than to

166

extend his professional courtesy. It could inflame Jusuf's irritation.

Nick reckoned Jusuf was around his mid-thirties, but it was hard to tell with his youthful Asiatic looks. Despite being relatively young, he had the demeanour of a frustrated grizzly bear. The nurses were subservient, too afraid to challenge his decisions. Natural bullies were usually bad at their job.

Nick went over to one of the sick men lying on the campbed, accompanied by an English-speaking nurse. She explained he had stomach pain. Kneeling down, Nick examined the man, pulling up the tee shirt to reveal his abdomen. Nick was convinced it was nothing more than a case of bacterial gastroenteritis, which a short course of antibiotics would cure. It was the look of alarm on the man's face which alerted him to Susanto's presence. Nick turned round and observed the burly man as he asked for identity papers. The new refugees obliged, but the sick man struggled to explain something. Nick glanced at the nurse and raised his eyebrows in a quizzical manner. She remained silent, too scared to intervene. Nick calmly walked up to Susanto and spoke to him.

'You see this man is very sick so I want you to leave him alone.'

'Apa ini? Bercakap Malayu,' the man replied.

'He wants you to speak Malay but I will translate for you,' the nurse offered.

'Ask him what he wants with this man,' Nick said.

'The policeman is asking for the identity card but the man says he has lost it,' the nurse replied.

'There's not much that can be done about that,' Nick said.

'This policeman does not believe him. He could be a terrorist.'

'I don't care. This man is my patient and I don't want him to be disturbed,' Nick said.

The message was translated but the policeman remained uncooperative. Looking carefully at Nick, he muttered something ominous before leaving the tent. Nick felt vindicated but wary.

'What did he say?'

'These people don't like you to tell them what to do. Please be careful.'

'Well, he can bugger off when I'm here.'

'Please, doctor, remember we have to work here too.'

'I'm sorry, I should have thought about that,' Nick replied.

'He has a job to do.'

'And what exactly is that?' Nick asked.

'He is with the special police unit,' the nurse replied.

'I saw him stop a woman from going into the helicopter the other day. Is that what he does?'

'There is a problem with terrorists here, doctor. He has to find and catch them.'

'Do you think they are terrorists or freedom fighters?' Nick posed the question.

'Terrorists. They cause a lot of trouble here.'

'Where are you from?'

'Jakarta.'

'Do you know if that policeman works for Anzala?'

'Who is Anzala?' the nurse asked in ignorance.

'He is the chief of police in this area.'

'Then he must be.'

'Does he go to all the refugee camps?'

'Yes, doctor.'

'Thanks for your help, nurse,' Nick replied.

'Do you want me to do anything else, doctor?'

'Just tell me something. How can he tell if somebody is a terrorist?'

'They live in the jungle and don't have a new identity card. That's how, doctor.'

'Give this man some ciprofloxacin, twice a day for five days. I'm sure he is not the only one without an identity card.'

'Yes, doctor.'

Nick had got used to playing doctors and nurses again. Nobody played like that any more in the UK. He wandered into the communications tent to catch up with Halcyon speaking to the UNHCR in Medan. He heard the one-way conversation immediately, unable to hear what was coming through the earpiece. He froze on seeing Susanto there. Halcyon had obviously not seen him come in but her voice had gone up an octave.

'Yes, they were abducted by the local police and not killed in the tsunami. We heard about it from the local people at a refugee centre. This is important, we're talking about possible abduction and murder here! You must report this matter to somebody!'

Susanto continued to sip his coffee quietly, pretending not to notice. He remained impassive as Halcyon spoke loudly into the satellite phone. Perhaps the man didn't speak English but Halcyon was spouting dangerous talk. Nick caught her eye and mouthed some silent words. He indicated for her to end the conversation but she waved him away, not understanding. It was the final straw as his nerves got the better of him.

'Halcyon, cut the chat now!' he said firmly.

'Excuse me, what is it, Nick?' she replied, putting the UNHCR on hold.

'Outside!' he said angrily.

'I'm sorry, I have to go. I'll call you back,' she said before ending the conversation.

Nick walked out without saying another word. He was mad.

'What was that about?' she asked furiously outside the communications tent.

'Did you see who was in the tent?'

'There were several guys in there. What are you talking about?'

'The one in the fancy shirt is Susanto!'

'Oh, shit! Did he hear me?'

'I could hear you from outside the tent.'

'God, I feel sick. Do you think he speaks English?'

'Even if he doesn't, somebody will tell him what you said. I told you to keep quiet until we were ready to deal with this matter.'

'I'm sorry, Nick. I was talking to the UNHCR about getting that school building and I got carried away. Do you think Susanto will come after us now?'

'What do you think? In fact he is coming this way right now. Just keep quiet and I'll deal with him.'

Nick braced himself for some sort of a confrontation but Susanto called his bluff. He walked straight past to his vehicle, where the driver was waiting. With a final dirty look from Susanto, the four-by-four drove off. Nick wondered how much pleasure Susanto got from his work. If he had been involved with the disappearance of the Mercy Aid workers, Halcyon's little conversation with UNHCR had just sealed their fate. It was time to worry.

CHAPTER 30

ABDUCTION

NICK SLEPT BADLY THAT NIGHT. IN HIS troubled mind, he saw visions of Susanto arriving with a death squad and bundling him away in an unmarked vehicle. Thankfully he was still there in the morning. After breakfast, he tended to more sick people who had arrived yesterday. By mid-morning his work was done which allowed them to head for the refugee camp. Once there, they stopped at Topo Sutadi's office as a matter of courtesy. It was also to find out the latest developments in the camp. Halcyon wanted to start work with the children immediately, which Topo agreed. With the help of his houseboys, the word soon got around that she wanted to play games. The younger children gathered expectantly. Halcyon was delighted at the turnout as the animated children couldn't wait. The quieter ones were more worrying.

Most of the children recognised her immediately. Following her as if she was the Pied Piper of Hamelin, they went along to the large piece of open ground just a short distance away. Despite it being covered in dried mud, they were happy enough to play there. Children from all parts of the camp came running, desperate not to miss out. Nobody had thought of playing games before, something as fundamental to a child as flying is to a bird. Rami became the interpreter. The game of 'it' was simple and fun. The 'its' chased the others until they were caught. The screams of excitement reverberated throughout the camp. Every child wanted a turn at being 'it' so the game continued.

Nick noticed that little Annie wasn't there. He decided to find her, wandering off to her building as the other children played. Not being able to speak Malay, he had trouble asking for her. The closest he could come up with was 'mad child'.

'Anak gila? Anak gila?' he repeated, desperately searching for the right words until somebody finally understood. Rami had used the word 'gila' for describing the madness of the political situation.

'Anak pergi,' a toothless old woman said, making a shooing motion with her hands, to indicate that the girl had gone away.

That was something he had not expected. She had been there only yesterday. Needing to check for himself, he went into the building. The crowd made way without objection. Annie definitely wasn't there. He nodded his thanks before walking over to Topo's office. He saw the fat man by his desk, pretending to be occupied.

'Hi, Topo. I need to ask you about one of the little girls here,' Nick said.

'Of course but first, would you like some Indonesian iced coffee?' he offered.

'Yes, thanks. That's very kind of you.'

'So what do you want to know?' Topo asked, clapping his hands for the houseboy to fetch another coffee.

'There was a little orphan girl here yesterday, in one of the buildings. She was very quiet. People there seem to think she was mad and I'm worried about her. Where has she been taken to?'

'We have many orphans here but I don't know this girl personally. Perhaps some government people have taken her away to a special place.'

'Where exactly?'

'Maybe I can tell you if you give me her name.'

'Nobody knows her name because she wouldn't talk.'

'Then you have a problem.'

'Surely you must have a list of children who were taken away?'

'Maybe somewhere. Anyway, I think these children went to a good government house.'

'Can you tell me where?' Nick asked, as the iced coffee was brought to him.

'You like it?' Topo asked, avoiding the question.

'Yes, it's very sweet,' Nick replied, taking a sip.

'We have very good coffee in Sumatra. Maybe the boy put too much condensed milk in it for you.'

'That's fine. Coming back to this girl, I presume she was taken to a government-run orphanage.'

'Yes, but please don't worry! She will be taken care of,' Topo replied reassuringly.

'We would like to know because the little girl needs help.'

'Well, the social care people will do that. I can see the children are happy today.'

'So, she is with social workers?' Nick persisted.

'Yes, of course. I have also spoken to the chief of police. He will look into getting the school you want,' Topo said, feeling uncomfortable.

'Thank you. I called that little girl Annie. Can you find out where she has gone?'

'You are very worried about her, uh? I have already told you she will be fine. Your charity does not need to get involved with her,' Topo replied.

'How many orphans were taken away yesterday?' Nick persisted.

'I think maybe six.'

'You think? But you should know.'

'Don't tell me what my job is, OK? This is not your business!' Topo replied, suddenly irritated by Nick's line of questioning.

'OK, I'm sorry I asked. Just one more thing. Do you know a policeman called Susanto?'

'Yes. Why do you ask?' Topo asked suspiciously.

'It's just something I need to know. Did he come here yesterday?'

'I don't know. Look, the police don't have to tell me what they are doing. They will come if they think there is a terrorist here.'

'Thanks for the coffee,' Nick said curtly.

Nick left none the wiser about Annie's whereabouts. Clearly, children had been taken away without any official records being kept. Even during a time of crisis, Topo had a duty to keep track of the refugees coming in and going out of there. The displaced orphans may have gone to some government institution for all he knew something was not adding up. Seeing the battered state of the country, he doubted if a functioning social service still existed. He wandered back to the baking hot playground which shimmered under the midday sun. The children seemed happy enough to run around but the iced coffee wouldn't keep him cool for very long. He had to talk to Halcyon about Annie but it would have to wait. There was no point in spoiling the fun for the other kids.

CHAPTER 31

TIDE OF CHANGE

A S THE VAN MADE ITS WAY BACK to the medical aid post, Nick mulled over what he knew of little Annie and her sudden disappearance. There was something wrong about Topo's attitude but Halcyon was too fired up with excitement to talk about anything else. She seemed more determined than ever to get her school building. As soon as they arrived back at the medical aid post she headed for the communications tent to get in touch with UNHCR. By chance, Bambang was there.

'Hi, Bambang. Can I use the satellite phone?' she asked.

'No, you cannot use the equipment any more,' he replied sternly.

'Why, is there a problem with the phone?'

'No, only our people can use it.'

'But I need to get through to UNHCR in Medan,' Halcyon replied, suddenly aware of the tension in the tent.

'We have been asked to tell you to go. I'm sorry.'

'Go? Why? What's happened?'

'I have been given my orders.'

'By Susanto?'

'Yes.'

'Where can we go?' Halcyon asked, out of alarm.

'That is your problem.'

'What about Nick's work here?'

'You can thank him for helping these people.'

'Why this sudden change in attitude?' Halcyon wanted to know.

'I cannot say any more. Please, you have to go tonight.'

'Are we in danger?' Halcyon asked tersely.

'I don't know. This is not my wish, but it is necessary for you to leave this place.'

'OK, I get the picture, Bambang. Thanks for putting us up.'

'You can stay for a meal and take what provisions you need.'

'Thank you. I wish you good luck with the work here.'

'Don't worry about us. You just keep safe.'

She raised her hand in a gesture of goodbye but the pained look on Bambang's face told its own story. It was quite clear this was a consequence of her conversation with the UNHCR yesterday. She found Nick sitting on the portable camp chair, eating some peanuts from their small supply.

'Nick, we've got trouble. They want us off the site,' she informed him quickly.

He continued to eat his peanuts calmly whilst digesting the facts, looking up at her only when he was ready to speak.

'Why?'

'I think Susanto wants us out of here. They won't let me use the satellite phone.'

'Why not?'

'Bambang didn't give any reasons.'

'Susanto must have been listening to your conversation yesterday,' Nick reasoned.

'Look, I'm sorry about that. We're in danger staying here.'

'Where do you suggest we go?' Nick asked calmly.

'I don't know. How about the refugee camp?' she suggested.

'That would be better than sleeping in this van. There's something I wanted to discuss with you earlier.'

'What?' Halcyon asked.

'I looked for Annie when you were playing with the children. I noticed she wasn't there. Topo said she's gone to some orphanage.'

'When?'

'Yesterday, after we left.'

'So why are you worried?'

'He didn't seem to care which children had been taken away.'

'Who took them away? Did he say?'

'Apparently, somebody from the government. It was as vague as that,' Nick said.

'How many children?'

'I asked him if he had a list of the children who had gone away but he failed to respond to that.'

'And you think something is wrong?'

'It's just a gut feeling. He was just too shifty for my liking.'

'Well, we have no choice tonight but to go back there. Bambang said we could have a meal before leaving.'

'In that case, let's go break the news to Rami,' Nick reasoned logically.

'What if Topo refuses to let us stay there?'

'We'll sleep with the refugees if we have to. At least if we're taken away by Susanto, there may be some witnesses around. That could be a deterrent, although I suspect it won't stop him.'

'I don't know how to apologise for the cock up yesterday.'

'It's done. Let's go eat,' Nick said magnanimously, but still rankled by the matter.

Rami was already in the food tent, talking to his countrymen. It was curry and rice again but nobody really cared. Halcyon explained the situation and he understood why they had to leave.

'Susanto was here again today,' he said, just to confirm their suspicions.

'We thought as much,' Nick replied.

'He wanted to know what we were going.'

'Did anybody say anything about where we were?'

'He knows anyway.'

'We thought we would go back to the refugee camp tonight,' Nick informed him.

'I think that is the best place also,' Rami replied.

'In that case, let's eat up and then fetch our things from the tent,' Halcyon said.

It was a quick and undignified meal. The atmosphere was tense as the people knew about the situation. Nobody wanted to linger and make small talk, uncomfortable in the knowledge that Susanto would pay them unwanted attention for fraternising with the foreigners. Nick and Halcyon went to collect their belongings without further ado. Jusuf was in the men's tent lying on his back when Nick arrived.

'We're heading off,' Nick said without ceremony.

'OK,' Jusuf replied simply.

'Hope you'll manage by yourself.'

'I always manage. Anyway, we are now getting enough help from Malaysia and Singapore so you can go back home,' Jusuf replied rudely.

'Thanks for the sentiment. Just tell me something, Jusuf. Where did you do your medical training?' Nick asked in a similar tone.

'St Mary's in London. Why?'

'Because your English is very good.'

'It is unfortunate you don't speak my language when you are in my country.'

'Did you like London?' Nick asked, choosing to ignore the comment.

'No, I thought your people were racist.'

'What, all of them?' Nick asked mockingly.

'Now you're making fun of me.'

'Jusuf, you've not liked me since the first day I arrived. Why is that?'

'Because you think you are clever. I also think you hate Muslims.'

'What?'

'You don't have to bluff with me.'

'I don't differentiate between race and religion nor do I think I'm being clever.'

'Hah! That I find hard to believe. You British and Americans are all the same. Don't you think a good Muslim is a dead one? You only come here to pretend to show some pity for my people but you still want to tell us what to do.'

'You're talking through your arse as usual. Well, you won't have to put up with me sleeping in your tent any more.'

'Did you know that when I was in London, some of the white patients refused to let me examine them? You don't call that racism?' Jusuf went on.

'I can't answer for other people and I'm not in the mood to argue with you. I have to go,' Nick replied, finally understanding what Jusuf's little problem was all about.

'Indonesian hospitality forces me to thank you for your help,' Jusuf said, suddenly sitting up on the campbed.

'Well, that's big of you. Say goodbye to the nurses for me.'

'I should also tell you something before you go,' Jusuf said, changing the subject.

'What?' Nick asked, bracing himself for more embittered diatribe.

'You have to be careful of Susanto.'

'Thanks for the tip. I've already figured that out for myself,' Nick replied.

'Then go back home to Scotland safely.'

'By the way, the people you met in London do not represent the whole country and I'm sorry you had a bad time. Just understand that the whole world is shocked by the tsunami and I came here in good faith.'

'OK, I believe you. Go.'

It wasn't the friendliest of goodbyes and Jusuf didn't extend himself to offering his hand. His misguided pride wouldn't allow it. At least Nick now understood why he had been eaten up by hatred, which ironically had made him a racist himself. The world of medicine should have no boundaries but even in Scotland, he had known of unfortunate incidences where bigots would not allow themselves to be treated by foreign doctors. It had cast an everlasting legacy of hatred. Despite their duty to save lives, some doctors were capable of becoming suicide bombers for the sake of jihad. Right now, it was Susanto who presented the real and immediate danger.

CHAPTER 32

DEN OF HELL

TOPO SUTADI HAD JUST FINISHED HIS MEAL when he heard the vehicle arriving in the dark. His curiousity was soon answered when they explained their story. Groaning inwardly, he thought about citing some bureaucratic reason for turning them away but couldn't find the right excuse. It was too difficult to argue when he was staying in a large building by himself, and unofficially with the boys. Secretly, he swore to himself but kept the smile on for show. His current lifestyle would be compromised but the lizard looking down from the ceiling was less bothered. The boys would have to vacate their rooms and sleep on the floor.

After making some polite conversation, the guests retired to their rooms. Nick couldn't sleep in the stifling heat. A pang of guilt hit him about taking the bed space but the final straw came from the sound of sexual activity coming from Topo's room. He could only imagine what was going on. He knew Halcyon would be angry if she had been awake, even demanding to know what was going on. Starting a fight in the middle of the night over something which had been normal practice in the building was not a good idea. By three o'clock in the morning, he realised sleep was impossible. There was no point in trying any more as he slipped out to the veranda just in boxer shorts. The wooden floor creaked on the way out and he hoped nobody would hear him. He was surprised to find Rami outside smoking a cigar.

'Hey, I didn't expect to see you here,' Nick whispered softly.

'Like you also! Can't sleep, lah,' the little man replied with a low chuckle. He was sitting on the wooden bench with crossed legs.

'This heat is really too much,' Nick said, running his hands over his sweaty brow before sitting down next to Rami.

'Cooler when monsoon come. You want cigar?'

'Yes, why not? It's been a bitch of a day,' Nick replied as a form of self-justification.

'This one is from Sumatra, very good tobacco. Which type of cigar you like to smoke?' Rami asked, handing him a medium-sized cheroot.

'Usually Cohiba, maybe a Fonseca.'

'Wah, you must be rich doctor!' Rami said, giggling away at the thought of reaching cigar heaven by smoking one of those.

'I don't smoke very many,' Nick replied, lighting the cheroot with a match before drawing on the rich, flavoursome tobacco.

'Bad for your health, lah! So, how long we stay here, Nick?'

'I'm not sure. Why?'

'I don't like this place. Something tells me it is bad,' Rami said, trying to explain things in his own unique way.

'You mean Topo?'

'Maybe.'

'Is he abusing these boys?'

'I think so. You have been listening to the noise?'

'Yes. Does that sort of thing happen out here a lot?' Nick asked.

'It can happen anywhere, not just here.'

'So why don't the police do something about it?'

'They get paid to keep quiet, why do you think?' Rami replied, as if it had been that obvious.

Nick took a big puff from his cigar, noting the similar taste to the cheroots he had once bought in Amsterdam. It was from the same type of Sumatran tobacco, a link to the colonial past. A sense of reality crept into his thoughts.

'Have you heard anything about the children being taken away from this camp?' Nick asked.

'Yes. The government people come here all the time to check on the new people coming. Some children go away if they can to make more space.'

'Where do they go?'

'Some stay with relatives.'

'And the others?'

'Don't know. Some people say to go to village near Sigli.'

'What's there?'

'Maybe a place for homeless children.'

'Do you mean an orphanage?'

'Yes.'

'Do you know for sure?'

'No.'

'Where is this place?' Nick asked.

'About one hour from here.'

'Can we go there?'

'What for, Nick?'

'To see if they are in an orphanage.'

'Why don't you ask Topo?' Rami suggested disturbingly.

'I'm not sure that is a good idea.'

'Why, because you think he is a bad man?'

'You tell me,' Nick insisted.

'I think the people here are scared of him. He pretends he works for the government but everybody knows he runs some kind of extra business.'

'What do you mean by that?' Nick asked.

'That is what people don't know for sure. They see children come, children go.'

'You mean there is a child racket going on?'.

'Maybe. There is no proof. We have to be careful talking about this, ah?'

'Is Susanto involved with this?'

'Maybe. He works for Anzala.'

'Do the people tell you all this because you work for a foreign charity?'

'I think so. They cannot trust anybody else around here.'

'Except you?'

'Yes.'

'I think we have to go to Sigli to find out about this orphanage.'

'Nick, we cannot!'

'Why not?'

'Because it's too dangerous. There are many roadblocks and soldiers. The GAM people are still fighting there.'

'They will let us through, surely. We work for a charity organisa-tion,' Nick reasoned.

'No, you don't know these people. They will shoot you if you try to find out too much about them.'

'I need to know if Annie and the other children are there. There is no choice. Give me the keys of the van and I'll go there myself if you want.'

'You have to ask Halcyon first. Also this place is hard to find and you cannot speak Malay. Please Nick, you will only get in trouble if you go,' Rami implored, hoping to dissuade him.

'But do you know where it is?'

'Maybe, but, Nick, this is crazy!'

'We can't go and ask the police can we? We have to go!' Nick whispered loudly.

'OK, I'll take you there,' Rami replied, shaking his head in consternation.

'What time should we go?' Nick asked.

'I think early, before six o'clock. It will take over one hour to drive,' Rami replied.

'OK, let's get ready. It is now 4 a.m. See you back here just before six.'

'You mean today?' Rami asked in horror.

'Yes, why not?'

'Crazy lah! I thought you meant tomorrow!'

'Let's strike while the iron's hot.'

'I don't understand.'

'Don't worry. It means we have to go today.'

'Please, you have to ask Halcyon first.'

'She's asleep. Do you want to wake her up?' Nick replied.

'No! You know what 'mati' means?'

'Go on, tell me.'

'It means we are dead!' Rami informed him with a worried look.

'See you here at six,' Nick said with a smile, recognising the concern on the little man's face.

Rami looked fear-stricken as he went in. Nick remained where he was, the cigar long finished. It was pointless to try and get any sleep now. Sitting out on the veranda, he contemplated the crickets chirping away in the background as the dawn crept up on another day. Sumatra still retained that magical feeling as life blossomed once more over the battered land. He had made up his mind to find little Annie as a personal crusade, despite lurking dangers. He remembered Jusuf's warning about Susanto. He could only hope Halcyon would understand his decision to go. The charity wasn't there for his benefit but he had thought enough about it already. This was a justifiable mission.

He went in to prepare for the day ahead. Suspecting it would be hot and stuffy, he decided to put on his baggy combat trousers and a loose tee shirt. The combats would stop the mosquitoes from biting his legs. He took the aluminium water flask and the old non-digital Canon waterproof camera. The taste of the bitter cheroot still lingered in his mouth as he brushed his teeth. Leaving a note under Halcyon's door, he tiptoed out of the building. The morning dew had thrown some freshness into the air as they both set off in the van. The solitary soldier at the entrance continued to slumber, barely acknowledging as they drove past. Rami was conscious of not drawing attention by driving too fast at that time of the morning but the roads were mostly empty except for the odd scooter going along. Human presence had come alive despite the deceptively quiet houses as people cooked their first meal of the day. Nick could smell the fried bananas and nasi goreng coming through the open window which set off his gastric juices. Rami eventually pulled up outside a snack shop just after 7 a.m. It was breakfast time.

They climbed out of the vehicle and headed towards the small dilapidated building by the roadside. It was no more than a shack. Rami ordered two coffees and some sweet cakes. They ate their breakfast standing up as Rami made some polite conversation with the serving woman. He gently probed about the security situation in the area, and then asked for directions to the orphanage. From the woman's worried expression, Nick knew something was wrong. He would wait for Rami to tell him in good time.

They set off for Sigli again. So far, they had encountered only one set of roadblocks which had presented no difficulty. Being involved in a humanitarian mission had allowed them to go almost anywhere. Rami relayed his conversation with the local woman.

'The woman told me many people have been moved from the villages around here.'

'Why? Because of the anti-terrorist action?' Nick asked knowledgeably.

'Yes, you know about the situation now. I also asked her about the children.'

'What did she say?'

'She thinks they are in one empty village.'

'Thinks or knows?'

'Rumours, lah. Local people talk when they drink coffee.'

'Did she say whether it was an official orphanage?' Nick asked.

'Nothing around here is official.'

'I take it that means it's illegal.'

'Yes, we have to be careful. I can take you to this place but don't do nothing crazy, Nick. You promise ah?' Rami asked for some reassurance.

'Yes, of course. I swear on my life,' he replied, already feeling unnerved.

'I trust you, OK?'

Nick felt too occupied to answer. The small van slowed as it approached a junction, turning left from the main road to head up a smaller, twisty road. Nick could see that there were fewer signs of human habitation as they drove along, just an eerie spectacle of boarded-up houses along the route. Small deserted villages came and went but the village they wanted was still a mile away. Signposts were in short supply and there was no satellite navigation. Rami slowed the van down, unsure which direction to take at a fork junction. Deciding to take the left one, he cautiously drove around one corner before coming to a sudden stop. The village was dead ahead. Quickly reversing back, he swung the van into a shaded area of banana trees. It was a convenient place to hide the van before stopping the engine.

'I think that is the village over there,' Rami said.

'Are you sure?'

'No. I don't know this part of the country. So what do you want to do now?'

'I'll go and take a look first.'

'Maybe it's better from this side,' Rami suggested, pointing to the tree covered hillock in front of them.

'OK. I'll be about half an hour.'

'Be careful.'

Nick got out and headed for the thick shrubbery in front of him beyond the banana trees. As the morning was still cool and damp, he decided to leave his water bottle behind. The small banana area soon gave way to thicker vegetation, slowing his progress as he negotiated his way up the small hill. It was a good call to wear the combat trousers rather than shorts as the mosquitoes stirred into life. Even the small rise of land felt an effort to climb in the high humidity, making him breathless and sweaty already. He could sense rather than see the village as the unmistakable sweet scent of a village reached his nostrils. It was a combination of soot from the wood burning stoves and animal compost.

He approached cautiously, mindful that most of the villages in the area had been evacuated by the security forces. It was designed to stop the GAM guerrillas from getting logistical support. He headed for a large tree silhouetting the skyline. Finding a small clearance beyond it, he crawled like a leopard over the last few yards without making any sudden moves. Peering over the edge, he moved nothing apart from his eyes as he scouted the village. A single road ran through it with several houses on either side. There were three vehicles parked outside one of the houses, including a white SUV with UN lettering on the door.

He carried on watching for twenty minutes as the time flew by without him noticing. Without his big camera and a long telephoto lens, it was difficult to see anything close up. He scanned the area for any signs of activity for a while more. Suddenly a Caucasian man appeared from the big house with a local man. They both seemed very amicable with one another. Nick quickly removed his waterproof camera from the belt holder and fired off a few shots. In the secluded quietness of his hideout, it made an unholy din as the motor winder spun into action. There was no reaction from either men. Being one hundred and fifty metres away, they had not heard the camera. With a fixed 32mm lens, the camera image was small but it was still a picture.

The Caucasian man drove off in the UN vehicle. It made Nick wonder if there was a UN-sanctioned operation going on after all. Reassured by this possibility, he considered his options. Presumably the UN would only have an orphanage in an area safe from guerrilla activity and there was no obvious army presence there. Making up his mind, he decided to descend from cover and head for the village. He was camouflaged against the vegetation of the small hill. Nobody saw him until he was on the road. Three men suddenly decided to appear from the house as they watched him approach. With suspicious looks, they challenged his presence from twenty metres away.

'What do you want?' one of the men asked aggressively in English.

'Is this a UN mission?' Nick asked in return.

'No.'

'I thought I saw a UN vehicle parked here.'

'That is none of your business. Why are you here?'

'I am looking for a girl,' Nick replied as he walked up to them.

'Why?'

'For personal reasons.'

'What exactly do you want?'

'A young girl less than ten years old.'

'Who told you to come here?' the same man asked.

'Susanto,' Nick replied, suddenly sensing the danger he was in.

'Lieutenant Susanto? You know him?'

'Yes, he works for General Anzala. Does that mean anything to you?' Nick bluffed.

'How do you know this man Anzala?'

'I know him through Topo Sutadi. He works at one of the camps. Perhaps you know who he is.'

'Maybe. And these people told you to come here?'

'Yes,' Nick lied.

'They told you we have children here?'

'Yes, they said I can do anything I want.'

'Where is your car?' the man asked suspiciously.

'I told my driver to go away and buy some food. He will come back in one hour,' Nick replied.

'So why were you walking on the road? We didn't see your driver.'

'I asked him to stop a mile away so I can walk and see the area.'

'Did you know it is not safe to walk around here?'

'I was told there are no guerrillas here.'

'Show me your identity card,' the man demanded unbelievingly.

Nick handed over his Mercy Aid International ID as requested. The man gave it a close look. Nick's semi-military outfit made him looked more like some foreign mercenary than an aid worker.

'What exactly do you want?'

'I'm looking for a girl, about nine or ten years old.'

'You want a girl,' the man repeated, digesting his words slowly.

'Yes.'

'And you know what this place is?'

'Yes, of course I do,' Nick said convincingly, having figured it was no ordinary orphanage.

'And you come to do some business?'

190

'Yes,' Nick muttered, feeling nauseated.

'I will talk to Susanto first. You come in and sit down,' the man ordered.

With little option, Nick went in as directed. The man remained outside to get a better reception on his mobile phone. Nick felt trapped. He had got in to a situation in which he was completely out of his depth. The men had made no pretence of hiding the automatics tucked behind their trousers in the waistbands. They looked like rough men who would kill rather than ask too many questions. Once Susanto knew he was there, it was as good as a death warrant. The senior of the three men came back in.

'Susanto said OK, go ahead. You can choose anything you want.'

'Show me what you have,' Nick replied with a false bravado. He had not expected Susanto to be so genial.

'OK, my friend. First I need the money!' the man said with an inviting smile.

'How much?'

'How much do you want to spend?'

'Enough for just one girl.'

'That will cost you two hundred dollars.'

'Let me check how much I have,' Nick replied, removing his wallet.

'That is not much money for a doctor,' the man goaded him.

'Susanto told you what I did?'

'Yes, but don't worry. Many people come here; lawyers, bankers, politicians, everybody. Susanto didn't know you like to have fun,' the man laughed.

The musty smell inside the building accentuated the smell out on the hillock. It was of defunct wood burning kitchen stoves no longer in use, but the smell had been ingrained in the wooden building. Nick doubted if this had been a family home for a while, having been turned into a brothel. The main parlour contained a few easy chairs and a large TV with a satellite box. The DVD player was undoubtedly used for porno movies. He began to observe the men quietly as he counted the money in his wallet. The most effeminate man had his black hair tied in a ponytail with a long manicured nail on his little finger. The second man looked quite ordinary, but the leader, who had done all the talking, had coarse hard set features which was badly scarred by acne. He appeared to be the most threatening of the trio but Nick had no doubts that any of them would be capable of putting holes into him.

'OK, we do business first and then you can enjoy yourself,' the leader said enticingly.

'I only have Indonesian currency or British pounds,' Nick replied.

'Why you don't have US dollars? It is the best.'

'I forgot to get some.'

'OK, how many pounds have you got?'

'One hundred and twenty.'

'That is not enough.'

'Will you give me a discount this time?'

'OK, give me the money. Only this one time,' the man said, concluding the deal suddenly.

'Here, take it,' Nick replied with a mixture of fear and trepidation.

'Come,' the man uttered with a monosyllable.

Nick felt sick to the core as he followed. He presumed he now had to choose someone, giving him an opportunity to look for Annie. Something niggled away in his head. Susanto knew he was there so why did these men appear to be so genial?. Something didn't stack up. He decided to find out more.

'Can you tell me who that man was who came earlier?' Nick asked.

'Hey, you naughty boy! You cannot ask that! This is a professional business!' the man replied, as if confidentiality came as part of the service.

'He must have stopped here before going to work. Do many people from the UN come here?'

'I cannot tell you,' the man chuckled.

'Does Susanto work with these UN people?' Nick persisted.

'You should know,' the man replied with slight irritation.

'Yes, of course I do,' Nick said, realising he had reached the end of the road.

'Susanto wants you to enjoy yourself,' the man said, suddenly breaking out in a broad smile. He had hidden the darker thoughts well behind his murderous eyes.

Nick smiled back at him despite wanting to hit the odious bastard. There was something vaguely threatening about the whole situation. He knew Susanto had not suddenly become his best friend. These men were challenging his resolve to go through with the transaction by calling his bluff. Nick knew they were buying time until Susanto arrived but they also wanted him to sweat for coming here on pretence. Nick looked nervous, not excited by what lay ahead.

The old wooden steps creaked as they went up to the first floor. There were several rooms leading off from the landing with their doors open. He could immediately see various children of all ages either sleeping or staring expectantly at him. The man showed him into the first room which contained some of the older girls.

'Choose, choose,' the man said, waving his hands excitedly.

Nick looked around and saw the children lifting their heads from their beds. Some looked tired despite the false smiley face they had to put on. He looked hard for Annie but couldn't see her.

'Any more?' Nick asked.

'You no like these? OK, come,' the man ordered, looking slightly annoyed.

Nick was shown into the next room where there were even younger girls. Peering in the semi-gloom, he struggled to contain his horror. All but one of the girls looked up at him. It was little Annie. She remained curled up, facing towards the wall. Nick quickly pointed to her. The man shook his head at Nick's poor choice.

'You want her? She's stupid. No good for you,' he informed Nick.

'Well, I want her!' Nick almost shouted back, feeling a mixture of anger and relief at seeing Annie in this filthy place.

'OK, you're the boss. Out, out,' the man shouted to the other children.

The door closed behind him as soon as the other girls had been pushed out of the room. Nick felt devastated, emotionally drained, in the semi-darkened room. It was a nightmare situation, made worse by knowing these men knew he was not a paedophile. He couldn't leave this place without Annie, or indeed any of the other children, but getting them all out would be impossible. He made up his mind quickly. Crouching down next to Annie, he spoke gently to her, knowing full well she wouldn't understand. She lay there like an unresponsive rag doll. He looked around to see if there were any of her possessions. Apart from one or two dolls, there wasn't much else there. He wasn't even sure if they belonged to her or to some other wretched child. She still had the same cheap dress on with two big pockets. Nick noted that the picture he gave her was still there, poking out of the corner. If there were small miracles, that was it. Either nobody had bothered to check her pockets or they had left the photo alone.

He picked her up tenderly and noticed just how little she weighed.

Cradling her in his left arm, he left the room and walked down the stairs with tears welling up in his eyes. The men looked up in surprise on seeing him.

'That was very quick. What happened?' the head man asked, looking concerned as Nick carried the limp girl in his arms.

He didn't bother to reply but carried on walking out of the building. The men got on their feet.

'Hey, hey, where you going?'

'She is no good. She is sick, I'm taking her away!' Nick shouted in a mixture of panic and fear. His self-control had nearly gone, now relying on gut instincts. It was only the adrenalin pumping through his arteries which keep his legs moving. He knew that if he stopped, they would just freeze.

'No, you come back!' the man shouted, as he reached behind his back to pull out the automatic.

Nick sprinted down the road towards Rami and the van, ignoring the furious shouts behind him. He didn't hear the automatics being cocked in his rush to get away. The blast when it came sounded ferocious as something whizzed past his head. The bullet sliced through the air as the enormity of the situation suddenly hit him. These people were obviously very annoyed. More bullets flew around him as he ran off to his left and into the jungle. Most hand guns were only accurate up to fifty metres, and less accurate when fired on the run. He expected hot metal to hit him at any time, pushing his adrenalin levels higher. He heard bullets crashing into the vegetation behind him, forcing him to run deeper into the twilight zone. Small trees whipped by his legs but he felt no pain as the endorphins kicked in. He continued to run, stumbling frequently as Annie clung on to him. Despite weighing very little, it was a big effort to carry another person in the high humidity. With sweat lashing into his tee shirt, he continued to run at speed.

The furious shouts got angrier. He was already lost in the jungle so he presumed the men were the same. His lungs felt like bursting. With his brain screaming for oxygen, dizziness threatened to overcome him. He felt disorientated. The dehydration factor had started to make his head pound away like crazy, wishing he had brought his Sigg flask with him. After running at full speed for twenty minutes, he had to stop. There was no choice. Annie slumped beside him, looking just as confused as before. He listened out for the pursuers, struggling to hear anything above the thumping sounds in his ears. Even the jungle had gone quiet as the animals knew something was afoot. He and Annie were stuck in the Sumatran jungle with no idea of what to do next. It was time to remember his army training. He should head towards a designated reference point when things went wrong. That was the small banana plantation where Rami was but it could be lying in any direction. It was all but impossible to get his bearings under the jungle canopy. The feeling of utter desolation hit him hard.

He had to control his breathing first of all to calm down. Retracing his steps mentally, he remembered running towards the van until he darted off to the left to make use of the jungle cover. By doing so, he had also led the men away from Rami, who must have heard the gunshots and wondered what had happened. If Rami stayed where he was, Nick would have to travel in a clockwise direction to hit the road they came on. Then all he would have to do was to follow it until he got to the banana trees. It was simple in theory. That way, he would get away from the village and avoid the men. He carried on deeper into the jungle, trying to bear right at all times. The monotony of the jungle soon became apparent when the noises started again. At least it was reassuring, unlike the unremitting heat and humidity.

Annie clung on, with beads of sweat running down her forehead. Nick walked silently, putting down one foot carefully and feeling for solid ground before lifting the other foot. The leopard walk was a slow process but it allowed him time to breathe properly, using the oxygen to feed his muscles rather than panic. He carried on for an age, having no idea how far they had covered despite counting his steps. Assuming each stride to be less than a yard, he had probably covered more than a thousand, making it little more than half a mile. In virgin jungle, it was hard work.

He was thirsty and his arms felt like dropping off. Thankfully Annie remained quiet despite the ordeal. Nick now had to let her walk for a little, feeling too tired to carry on as he did. He set her down into the ground and watched her crouch down. It wasn't a good sign. With some perseverance, he managed to stand her up. Appearing unsteady at first, she just managed to carry her own body weight. Nick guided her slowly by the hand. The jungle was no place for a child, let alone a psychologically damaged one.

Approaching a clearing, the gloom suddenly gave way to bright sunshine. He stopped to look ahead, keeping under cover. The clearing was only a few hundred yards long, well cleared of trees but covered in tall elephant grass. He saw a wooden shack towards one end of the clearing, which looked deserted. Hoping there was some drinking water there, he led Annie by hand to the wooden building. It was a basic affair and quite old in appearance. The rickety door was locked and the building looked deserted. He peered in the window but the bright sunshine outside had made it difficult to see in. With hopes dashed of finding any drinking water, he still thought about kicking the door in, just in case there was anything consumable. Just then he heard Annie scream. It caught him by surprise. She had been silent until now. Pulling away from the window, he could now see the reflection on the glass. Several automatic rifles were pointed in his direction. Instinctively, he raised his arms, before turning around. Nobody spoke as the men looked at him. They had covered their faces with coloured handkerchiefs.

'American or Australian?' one of the gunmen asked in perfect English.

'Scottish,' Nick replied.

'What are you doing here?'

'I am a doctor with Mercy Aid International. This is one of the children I have just rescued,' Nick replied calmly, despite facing eight automatic rifles.

He could see the assorted weapons ranging from M16s, AK47s to Heckler and Koch G4 automatic rifles. It must have been a logistical nightmare to keep them all supplied with different types of bullets.

'Why should I believe you?' the leader asked.

'I can show you my identity card.'

'OK. Drop your arms and show me.'

Nick did as he was told and reached into his pocket. The leader looked at the ID card before handing it back. He was the only one now who didn't have his rifle pointed at Nick's head.

'Tell me what you are doing here,' he continued.

'I work for a UK charity. This girl is one of the orphans from a refugee camp near Banda Aceh. She was taken away to work in a child brothel about a mile away from here.'

'How did you find this place?'

'We had a tip-off from some of the refugees.'

'But you came looking by yourself?'

'No. There is a driver working for the same charity who is still near to this village we just came from. I had to run away with this child when people started to shoot at us. And who are you?' Nick asked, curious to know who he was dealing with.

'Resistance fighters,' the man replied.

'I am here on a humanitarian mission and I have no quarrel with your organisation. I demand that you let us go,' Nick said.

'For now you have to come with us. The army is closing in on this area and it's not safe. Do you understand?' the leader asked.

'Yes I do. Will you guarantee our safety?' Nick asked.

'We'll not harm you. I think you and this little girl need a drink,' the leader said, ordering his men to lower their weapons and producing a water bottle.

'Where did you learn to speak English?' Nick wanted to know, taking the water bottle from the guerrilla leader.

'I was a schoolteacher. Have you come to help with the tsunami disaster?'

'Yes, I have. We've heard rumours that GAM is deliberately targeting the relief convoys. Is that true?' Nick asked, giving the girl some water.

'What you heard is all government propaganda. They are only saying that to justify wiping us all out, despite the ceasefire.'

'How do you survive in the jungle?' Nick asked.

'With difficulty.'

'I can see that. Thank you for helping us.'

'We'll make some food before moving on. The little girl does not look well.'

'No. She's an orphan from the disaster. I can't believe these people took her there.'

'You did well to get her out. We know about that place but we don't have the resources to do anything about it. That's what you get with army and police corruption.'

'I'm learning about the situation here all the time.'

'Then this will open your eyes, I hope,' the guerilla leader said with a rueful smile.

'Yes, without any doubt.'

'Good. Just rest for now. We have a long walk ahead of us.'

Nick felt relieved to be in their company. Some of the men lit a small fire just within the jungle in order to disperse the smoke amongst the trees and avoid being spotted. They made a meal of watery rice, adding small pieces of 'bush meat', from animals killed in the jungle. The young men seemed affable enough, especially when they learnt he was a surgeon. Nick offered to look at their wounds but knew it would only be a token gesture without any proper dressings. He had no choice but to receive their protection despite knowing the army was closing in. They handed him a bowl of the rice gruel. Nick was afraid Annie's stomach had shrunk too much to accept the food. If she had to eat anything, that was the best form of carbohydrate to begin with. A couple of spoonfuls was at least a start but the bush meat would have been harder to digest. Nick felt obliged not to ask what it was.

CHAPTER 33

GUERRILLA AMBUSH

A NNIE HAD MANAGED TO REST HER TIRED body and the watery rice had given her some badly needed calories. Much of her muscle mass had broken down due to self starvation because her disturbed mind had stopped her from eating. On seeing the masked men, something in her brain had jolted back to life and there was now some hope. Even the tough jungle fighters had shown their concern but it was time to move on.

Nick realised the abandoned shack served as a useful meeting point for the fighters but it could equally be a death trap if the army knew about it. For that reason, the men had quickly dispersed when Nick approached, warned by the lookouts using short-range radios. After lunch, they gathered their weapons and meagre supplies before heading off, knowing the war was far from being over. With years of jungle living, they were extremely fit and did not carry a spare ounce of fat. Nick suspected he would struggle to keep up with them, being totally unused to walking in the difficult terrain.

They spoke very little on the move, keeping their eyes open instead for a possible ambush. A tripod-mounted machine gun could easily take them out in a single burst. Booby traps were also easy to rig up and almost impossible to see in the poor light. The Indonesian military were only too adept at their job, being utterly ruthless and professional after the killing fields of East Timor.

With no idea of where they were heading, Nick tried to get his bearings. It was all but impossible to navigate in the impenetrable jungle. Everything looked the same. He was grateful to the men for taking turns at carrying Annie. Nick knew enough about standard operating procedures to keep a silent routine and walk without leaving a trail. Regardless of their efforts, a good jungle tracker could easily spot the clues. A broken twig or a bent leaf was enough to give them away. The Indonesian army had by now trained enough jungle warfare specialists to follow the guerrillas in their own back yard.

The walk lasted for over six hours with only short breaks in between. The afternoon heat had eased off when they finally arrived at a small kampong on the fringes of the jungle. It had been risky to use the narrow trail but it was quicker. The villagers showed no telltale signs of nervousness to announce the army was nearby. They were greeted with a muted welcome, the villagers knowing that there would be reprisals if the army knew the guerrillas had been there. One of the local women giggled on seeing Nick and his little follower. With the tension broken, the village chief agreed to let them stay. Wearily, the men slumped down against the brick wall of the village hall, lighting their sweet-smelling cigarettes with relief. Nick was offered one. He accepted, if only to bond with these men. He noticed the slight menthol flavour and gentle popping sounds it made, making him wonder what was in the tobacco. It was certainly pleasant enough, unlike the acrid European cigarettes.

'Local cigarette, you like? We put cloves in it,' the leader asked as he squatted on the floor.

'Not bad but I don't normally smoke,' Nick replied.

'Better for you but my men want to die early!' the man laughed, thinking of their predicament in the one-sided war.

'I don't even know your name,' Nick muttered, blowing off

smoke without inhaling.

'It is better you don't know,' the leader replied frankly.

'How did you come to be a fighter after being a schoolteacher?'

'Because of the war.'

'But why was it so necessary take up arms?' Nick asked.

'How much do you know about the political situation here?' the leader asked.

'A little. I know that you people want to be independent from Jakarta. This is something we never hear about in the UK.'

'That is because your western reporters are not allowed to come here.'

'But surely journalists have the right to report from places they want to.'

'Maybe in most places but not here. Let me tell you something. In 1975, Indonesia invaded East Timor to take the territory from the Portuguese. There was a guerrilla war there until 1999 when a UN referendum said the people can have independence. Some of the soldiers at that time killed several Australian and British journalists to stop them from reporting the atrocities going on there. Now, one of the army officers who did the killing is in the government. Can you see the problem that we have?'

'Our driver did mention something like that. But is it the oil you want?'

'There is oil, but why should the government get it? Our people can use that money to build schools and hospitals.'

'But surely you had these things before the tsunami?'

'Yes, we did but we could have much more. We are also fighting tyranny. The Indonesian army killed over two hundred thousand people in East Timor and over ten thousand people in Aceh. During the time of the communist troubles in the 1960s, many Chinese were also killed in Java by Suharto. By comparison in Northern Ireland, your paratroopers killed thirteen people on Bloody Sunday and there was a big protest about it. In Indonesia, we are talking about hundreds of thousands.'

'I can only imagine the scale. But why don't the UN do something about this?'

'What can they do?' the leader laughed out of despair.

'Perhaps you can tell me.'

'Our people don't matter to them. We are seen as rebels, just like the rebels in Congo or the Tamil Tigers in Sri Lanka, except we don't see ourselves as the aggressors. They would only ask us to give up to avoid further bad publicity for themselves.'

'But you won't let that happen?' Nick asked.

'No. We will never give up our claim to independence. The army won't give up either. If they come here tonight, you must run away. They don't want foreigners to know about this war. Do you understand that?'

'Yes. Which way should I go if that happened?'

'We're heading for the main road due west of here. Follow the sun if you get lost but we'll take you there tomorrow if we can. From there you can get a lift back to Medan with the girl.'

'I am grateful for your help,' Nick thanked him.

'OK, I cannot offer you a comfortable bed but for tonight, it is better if you don't sleep here. You can stay at another place towards the end of the village from where you can run into the jungle if there is an attack. Come, I will show you,' the leader said, picking his rifle as he got up.

Nick raised himself and felt the ache in his legs, realising Annie was already asleep. In the twilight zone of evening, he followed the guerrilla leader through the village, noticing how the wooden houses had been built on stilts. They were designed to escape the floods during the rainy season. The village consisted of about two dozen small houses and a small village hall made from brick. The men had decided to take a chance by sleeping there, keeping at least one guard on duty at all times. A few well-aimed grenades could easily finish them off.

Nick saw the dilapidated shed which was to be his sleeping quarters. At least it was on the edge of the jungle if he had to make a run for it. A space had been created for a simple mattress on the floor, which looked inviting after his tiring day. With his mind and body totally bruised, even this minimal hospitality was truly welcome. Nick already knew he would be bitten alive by the mosquitoes but it was better than being hit by a bullet. A bowl of rice and spicy rendang curry had been left there but the girl was too tired to eat. Nick ate what there was and settled down for the night.

He must have drifted off into a deep sleep as the mosquitoes enjoyed gorging themselves on his arms and face without interruption. Despite the unpleasant swollen bites, he felt better mentally from the decent rest. Annie also came to, appearing to be more animated. She looked around the small shed and then at Nick, no longer staring at a blank wall.

'Hello. Did you sleep well?' he asked, for the sake of saying something.

She didn't answer and stared blankly at him.

'My name is Nick and your name is Annie. That is until you tell me what your proper name is. OK?'

There was still nothing from her. He got up and opened the door in order to let in some fresh air. The enclosed confines of the shed had been claustrophobic. He led Annie into the bushes to relieve herself. The guerrilla leader was there when he returned.

'I thought you had run away. How was your night?' the man asked.

'Itchy,' Nick replied, referring to the bites.

'OK, eat this. After that, we're moving out,' the leader said, handing Nick some fried bananas cooked in batter for the two of them.

Nick noticed how Annie quietly accepted the pisang ambong without any prompting, holding onto the greasy delicacy in her filthy hands. Her fingernails had grown long with caked dirt beneath them but it wasn't the right time to tell her to wash her hands. His were not much cleaner. Nick followed the leader as they ate the delicious fritters.

The guerrillas had packed up and were silently making a beeline for the path leading out of the village. Nick let Annie walk in front of him, still concerned that her legs may be too weak for her to walk any distance. She seemed stronger today and followed without fuss. The leader was doing point again as Nick, Annie and a teenage guerrilla took the rear. The trail snaked its way through the thick vegetation, making it good ambush country. Rather than hacking their way through thick jungle, they had decided to take a calculated risk by using the shortcut. The villagers had reassuringly told them there were no soldiers in the area.

The peaceful monotony had lulled them into a false sense of security as they concentrated on putting one foot down in front of the other. The jungle had even sounded normal as they progressed quietly. However, many pairs of eyes were watching them. Green and black camouflage cream had made the men's faces blend in with the jungle background, giving nothing away. Nick only concerned himself with Annie's pace, which had showed signs of faltering. They were slightly behind the main group as the young guerrilla urged them to keep up. Nick merely nodded and took Annie's hand, gently pulling her along. He then heard plopping sounds coming from one side of the jungle.

The young guerrilla immediately recognised what it was as he shouted in his own language to the rest of the group. Nick also knew instantly it was the sound of grenade launchers. He hit the ground and pulled Annie down with him.

The grenades exploded up ahead. Automatic weapons opened up as bullets tore into the men. A few fired back but it was a one-sided battle. The young guerrilla charged past in a bent posture, firing his weapon as he went. Nick saw him being cut down with spurts of blood popping out from his head and torso. He knew the rest wouldn't stand a chance either.

Keeping low, he pulled Annie into the jungle on the opposite side of the track. They crawled away from the path as the bullets flew overhead, slicing through the branches with deadly effect. The gunfire continued with some intensity until the returning fire from the guerrillas petered out. They were all dead. The noise had allowed Nick to escape into the deep vegetation without being seen. Now desperate for cover, he hid beneath a big leaf and gently placed his hand over Annie's mouth. She trembled as he pressed her close to him. The sudden silence after the gunfire became equally unbearable. He knew the soldiers would soon be coming out to search for survivors. The army would not be taking any prisoners as orders rang out. He froze when a platoon of well-camouflaged soldiers emerged from the opposite side of the track and checked the dead one by one. They fired a shot into each head just to make sure.

With each gunshot, Annie jumped, pushing herself deeper into Nick's chest. He remained still, keeping his eyes and ears alert, conscious of his heartbeat thumping away. The soldiers now advanced in a line towards them, using their boots and rifles to check the undergrowth, ready to shoot at anything which moved. He heard the rustle come closer, knowing the chance of being taken alive was remote. He prayed for the first time in his life, keeping both eyes shut and waited for the inevitable to happen. Suddenly the cover above them was pulled away and a frightened young soldier shouted hysterically, pointing the barrel of the automatic rifle just inches from his face. It was so close he could smell the cordite from the recently fired weapon.

More soldiers rushed over and took aim with murder in their eyes. They were too excited from the heat of battle to control their tempers. It was then when Annie decided to scream. The tension suddenly became unbearable but Nick didn't move an inch. The soldiers only had to move their trigger finger one millimeter and their guns would go off. He clung tightly onto Annie to stop her screams piercing through the jungle. An officer rushed forward to take charge, furious to see survivors there. Seeing that Nick was unarmed, he pulled him onto his feet and brutally punched him at the side of the head. Temporarily disorientated, Nick was barely aware that Annie was still clinging onto his leg, screaming for all she was worth.

'You! What is this? What are you doing here?' the officer asked angrily, correctly presuming that Nick spoke English.

'Please, don't harm us. We are unarmed civilians.'

'You liar!' the man barked back at him, grabbing his tee shirt roughly.

'I can show you my identity card. I work for Mercy Aid International.'

'OK, show me quickly!' he shouted, looking Nick menacingly in the eye.

Nick reached down to his pocket to retrieve the ID card once again, acutely aware that several guns were still pointing at him. The last thing he needed was for some misunderstanding to occur now but the ID card had certainly been a life-saver.

'Take it,' he said to the lieutenant.

The man looked at the card but decided to keep it. Nick thought better than to ask for it back.

'Who is this girl?'

'She is a sick child. I am trying to help help her. I am a doctor,' Nick replied.

'Than why are you in the jungle with these terrorists?'

'We got lost and they were taking us to the main road.'

'You liar! I can kill you here, do you understand?' the man shouted.

'I am telling you the truth. I know it sounds hard to believe.'

'You look like a journalist. Are you trying to write a story against the Indonesian army?'

'No,I'm a doctor, like I told you. I found this girl in a village.'

'Which village?'

'I don't know what it's called. It takes a day to walk from here,' Nick answered.

'Why did you go there?'

'I wanted to see these children. They had been taken from a refugee camp.'

'How did you meet the terrorists?'

'They ambushed us.'

'Where is their base?'

'I cannot tell you because we were not taken there.'

'I know you are lying. One last time, where is their base?' the officer screamed.

'I don't know,' Nick shouted back in desperation.

'OK, you come with me but if you try to run away, you will be shot. Do you understand that?'

'Yes. As civilians and I am claiming a right to your protection.'

'You have no rights in a war zone.'

Nick did not answer but knew that was not true. It hardly mattered as he was at their mercy. The lieutenant gave the order for him to be searched. They emptied his pockets and removed his waterproof camera from the belt case. The lieutenant quickly looked at the few possessions and decided they had no military value, except for the camera. It looked old-fashioned, not something a journalist would use. Nick read his mind and decided to try his luck. He needed the film.

'Please, I am a doctor helping your country with the tsunami. I have been working at a government field hospital near Banda Aceh. I only took some pictures to show the doctors in Scotland how bad some of the injuries were. I have not taken any pictures of the war, I promise you. The camera is of no use to anybody else. You can check who I am with my organisation.'

The lieutenant looked at the camera again and weighed the matter before handing it back. Nick quickly replaced it back in the belt holder. He issued orders for the soldiers to lift their weapons except for Nick's personal guard. Some of them lit up a cigarette to calm their nerves after the battle. Nick walked past the dead men and mercifully noted they had all died quickly. Nobody had been left alive to be interrogated. It was a disturbing experience to have witnessed a massacre. The men stood no chance, and Nick realised his own survival had been due to Annie slowing them down. The young guerrilla behind them had shown no hesitation in rushing forwards and paid the ultimate price for his bravery. A more experienced fighter would have sought cover from the opposite side and picked off the enemy one by one by watching the muzzle flashes. It was too late to learn now. The body of the dead schoolteacher also made everything seem so pointless.

After walking for about an hour, they came out of the jungle into an open area. The little path had taken them to the side of a paddy field, next to a small village which had a proper road. Several army trucks were already waiting there. Nick and Annie were ordered to get into the back of one of them, his guard choosing to remain on the ground to talk with the driver. They too smoked cigarettes, belligerently staring at Nick with menacing intensity. He badly needed a drink of water and no doubt Annie did too. He motioned to the guard for some water. The army driver fetched them a bottle from the cab and threw it into the back. Looking around the truck, Nick noticed the vehicle was pretty much the same as any other regular military transport. The seats were arranged along the sides facing each other, with more space in the centre for the soldiers to sit on the floor. He also caught sight of ammunition boxes, containing 7.62 mm cartridges, M203 grenades and a single box of purple-coloured smoke bombs tucked beneath the seats. They had English writing on them, no doubt supplied by either a British or American company. Several organisations around the world wanted an arms embargo against Indonesia for their human rights abuses but there was certainly no shortage of ammunition here.

He could see a few injured soldiers emerging from the jungle. The guerrilla fighters had not all died in vain as some managed to shoot back. Nick was wondering if the Indonesian military were calling for air support to evacuate their injured when he heard the helicopter. It was flying towards them but sounded familiar, just like the US Navy helicopter taking the injured woman away from the field hospital.

The chopper flew low over their position without showing any signs of landing. Without doubt they had seen the military activity down below but the helicopter belonged to the US Navy. The soldiers looked up and followed it as it went past, not bothering to wave. Neither did the helicopter crew. Nick sat and wondered what the Indonesian military were planning to do with him. The thought of going to prison felt most unappealling. He could be accused of helping the guerrilla movement or even kidnapping a child. With his options limited despite the fact that Mercy Aid International would back up his story, Nick knew that the military's take on the situation mattered greatly, leaving the courts to decide his fate. At least he had not been shot out of hand. With the world's press now covering the tsunami, it might also be a bad time to release him. He could tell the world about what had just happened, drawing the wrong kind of attention to a country seeking international help. Things didn't bode well at all.

The MH-60S Seahawk helicopter flew on until the change of the sound suddenly indicated it had turned around. The clatter of the blades was unmistakable as they cut into the air, making the soldiers look at the sleek machine again. They wondered what the Americans were up to. Seeing the soldiers were preoccupied with the helicopter, Nick suddenly had an idea. He quickly reached down for one of the purple smoke bombs and tucked it in his waistband, covering it up with his tee shirt. He shouted to the guard to catch his attention.

'Kenching, kenching,' Nick shouted, pointing at Annie to indicate that she needed a leak. Thankfully, Rami had taught him some useful words.

The guard waved them off the lorry, as they watched the helicopter return. Once on the ground, Nick pointed to the paddy field to indicate where they were going. It would be in full view of the soldiers so there was no possibility of escaping. Quickly, Nick led the girl to the lush green paddy field and held onto her hand as usual. The guard seemed more engrossed with the helicopter than watching some little girl taking a leak. On reaching the edge of the paddy field, Nick knew the helicopter was almost upon them as he quickly reached for the purple smoke bomb. Pulling the pin, he threw the canister like a hand grenade. Thick purple smoke belched out as the soldiers quickly realised what had happened. They raised their rifles and shouted in a rage. Nick frantically waved at the helicopter, signalling for it to land. The soldiers ran up to him, mouthing obscenities as they pushed him into a kneeling position. He knew he was in big trouble but the soldiers wouldn't shoot in front of American witnesses.

The navy pilot had seen the purple smoke. It meant only one thing: come in and land. The machine circled as the crew assessed the situation, knowing that they could get stuck in the mud if they landed in the paddy field. Instead, the pilot landed next to the paddy field on a more solid piece of ground. The Texan master sergeant jumped out and jogged up to Nick, ignoring the squad of irate soldiers with their raised rifles. The American immediately recognised Nick from the field hospital.

'Hi buddy. We saw smoke. You in some kinda trouble?' the Texan asked.

'Sort of,' Nick replied, shouting to make himself heard.

'Stand up. You're the surgeon guy, right?' the airman asked.

'Yes, that's right. Thanks for stopping by,' Nick replied, noting the soldiers had released their grip on his shoulders so he could stand up.

'They look mighty pissed off. So what have you been doing?'

'I was in the middle of a firefight between these army guys and some freedom fighters back in the jungle. They're all dead,' Nick replied.

'I won't ask too much about it but do you need to get out of here?'

'Yes, we do, me and this little girl here.'

'OK, I'll have to negotiate with these guys first,' the American said.

The soldiers could only speak bad English, making any meaningful discussion impossible. Nick's guard knew his job was to keep Nick there until ordered otherwise, and kept his rifle pointed at him. The American quickly realised that tact and diplomacy was not going to work here. He radioed back to the Seahawk and spoke with his superior officer, explaining the standoff. Nodding his head in agreement with the instructions, the American suddenly looked serious. Nick noticed a sudden change of activity on the helicopter. The door gunner deliberately strapped a fresh belt of ammunition into the machine gun and swung it into position. The situation had changed in a matter of seconds, potentially setting off an international incident. Nick knew that this time when the bullets flew, there would be lots of them and he was in the firing line.

The American shouted an order to him. 'OK, get yourself and the girl onto the chopper, now!'

Nick hesitated, wondering what the odds were of one helicopter beating a squad of soldiers on the ground. He didn't want the responsibility of starting another war but the Americans seemed to know what they were doing. Without saying a word, Nick took his cue and picked Annie up, slowly walking to the helicopter.

He could hear the soldiers protesting loudly behind him, no doubt itching to pull the trigger. The big American told the soldiers to put their weapons down in a loud voice, threatening to shoot the sons of bitches if they didn't. He had no weapon on himself, but relied on the door gunner to watch every move they made. It was quid pro quo. Nobody would be stupid enough to fire the first shot. Now realising they could not detain Nick without starting a fight with the US Navy, the soldiers let him go. The Americans had figured out as much, using machine gun diplomacy to save the day. Nick would never know if the gunner had cocked his weapon or not.

Several hands helped him and the girl to get on board. Once secured, the aircraft lifted off and headed towards the sea. The machine gunner smiled smugly to the troops below and waved, chewing his gum. He saw them sticking their fingers back in return.

The master sergeant plugged in his throat microphone and spoke to the pilot. After exchanging a few words, he gestured to Nick to pick up the spare headset hanging from the ceiling bracket.

'The captain wants to speak to you. Use that,' he indicated.

Nick strapped on the headset and spoke into the stubby mouthpiece.

'Hello, this is Nick Forbes,' he said.

'You OK back there?' the captain asked.

'Yes, thanks. Lucky you came by.'

'What's been going on down below?'

'I've just seen a group of freedom fighters get killed by the army. There's also a child brothel down there somewhere and I have just one of the girls with me. There are more children there,' Nick shouted above the din from the rotor blades.

'Did you say child brothel?'

'Yes, it's run by some kind of an organised paedophile ring. I think the chief of police in the area is involved, possibly somebody in the UN also.'

'Are you kidding me with this? Did you say the UN?' the pilot asked.

'Well, I saw a UN vehicle,' Nick replied.

'Where is this place you talk about?'

'I don't know. We have been walking around the jungle for a couple of days. The driver from my organisation took me somewhere near Sigli.'

'Yep, that's not far from here. How about we do a loop around Sigli? Do you think you can recognise the village from the air?'

'I'll give it a try.'

'OK Nick, get yourself by the door and holler when you see that goddamn place. Those sons of bitches!' the pilot shouted out.

'What do you plan to do if we find it?' Nick asked.

'That's your call, Nick, what do you want us to do?'

'There's no point in calling the police. Can we get the kids out?'

'We can't use the marines for this one as we have no military jurisdiction over here. This is purely a humanitarian mission. I'll talk to the master sergeant.'

'Roger that,' Nick replied, slipping into American easy speak without thinking.

The helicopter suddenly swung towards the right and maintained a height of four hundred metres above sea level. It made a clock-wise circular search pattern as it flew above the green carpet below, covering a three mile radius around Sigli. Nick saw several small empty villages as the 'no go' area became apparent. They were well away from the tsunami-hit areas so it did look like political action rather than a disaster zone evacuation. No doubt, guerrilla activity was still going on down there despite the Army's attempts to flush them out. Nick remained focused on finding the village from the air as the helicopter flew around in a big circle. Trying to get a bearing on where the village was seemed difficult as he had only seen it from the ground. There wasn't a convenient landmark nearby such as a skyscraper. Nick spoke to the pilot again.

'Captain, is there any chance you could fly over the main road? Perhaps I could get my bearings from there. We were heading south from the refugee camp before making a left turn off the road.'

'Sure thing, Nick. Hang on.'

The helicopter swung sharply again until it tracked the main road. Flying above it in a southerly direction, Nick could now get his bearings. He thought he could recognise the small shack by the roadside where he and Rami had stopped for breakfast. Following the road a short distance away was the turn-off they had taken. From the high vantage point, he could see the small twisty road leading to the village with the hillock beside it. From the air, it hardly looked like a mound at all. The vehicles outside the building confirmed the spot.

'Captain, I can see the village at ten o'clock from our position. That small hill is the marker.'

'OK, I see it. Are there any telegraph wires around the place?'

'No, I didn't see any. The target house is the one with the cars outside. It should be safe to land between the hillock and the house.'

'Thanks for that information. OK, we're going in. Here's the plan. As far as these people are concerned, we're on a search and rescue mission for tsunami survivors. How many kids are in that building?'

'Hard to say, probably about twenty.'

'They're probably small and light. We can squeeze them in. Are these guys armed?'

'Yes they are.'

'OK, we'll be ready for that but you just sit tight.'

'I have to go in,' Nick replied.

'No can do, Nick. This is now official navy business.'

'I don't want to argue with you, captain, but I know the layout of the place and I also know what these men look like. The kids will be terrified when we go in but at least they have seen me before. Are you able to lend me a gun?' Nick asked.

'You ever used one?'

'Yes.'

'OK, but we're not responsible if you get hurt. The master sergeant is listening in to this conversation. Once on the ground, he is in charge. You go in with him but do as you're told. Only use the weapon if your life is at risk. Do you understand that?'

'I copy,' Nick replied, seeing the Texan smile at him with steely blue eyes.

'Good, you're beginning to sound like an American. We land in two minutes. Go get your gun,' the captain ordered.

The master sergeant already had the handgun out of the secure locker. There was an assortment of weapons in there, making Nick wonder if they were really just on a humanitarian mission.

'This is a Browning automatic with thirteen rounds in the mag.

Just pull this back to cock it. Take the safety off before firing but hopefully you won't be using that thing,' the sergeant shouted, handing Nick the weapon.

'Thanks. I take it the bullets come out this end?' Nick shouted back, pointing to the barrel.

'Yeah, only when it's working,' the master sergeant replied with a grin. 'The helo is going to drop on the road in front of the house and we're just going to walk straight in. Are you OK with that?'

Nick stuck his thumb up in reply, his throat now dry with nervous anticipation. He noticed the master sergeant had unclipped an M16 rifle from the gun rack and loaded it with a full magazine. He also took another spare magazine with him. Nick seriously began to wonder if this was the right thing to do. He had already cheated death once too often over the past two days.

The helicopter came in fast on its first approach and set down where it was supposed to, blowing off part of the roof from the downdraught. The pilot figured nobody was going to sue for compensation.

They saw several men run out of the building. They jumped into the vehicles and screeched past the helicopter. The master sergeant jumped down, quickly followed by Nick. As they raced to the building with the door gunner covering them, Nick wondered if one of the vehicles had been Susanto's. The sergeant stood with his back against the wall by the door with Nick standing next to him. In true SWAT fashion, he swivelled round and rushed in, M16 at the ready. Nick followed behind him with the safety off on the Browning.

They searched the front room and found it to be empty. Porno was still on the TV as Nick glanced up the stairs. The Texan swept through the kitchen area but Nick had already decided to run up the stairs. As the stairs creaked, the sergeant felt a bolt of fear go through him, thinking there were more bad guys up there waiting for them.

Nick was ready to shoot if necessary, but he knew there were children around. The military training at Fort George near Inverness came flooding back to him. The live firing on the individual battle shooting range was done in training, but now this was for real and somebody could shoot back. He quickly scanned the upper floor but only found the children staring excitedly out of the window towards the helicopter. The master sergeant caught up with him in a flash, angry that Nick had gone up alone.

'Nick, you could have got your head blown off! Next time, you wait!' the airman shouted at him.

'I'm sorry,' he replied, looking at the children.

'Where did you learn that shit from?'

'I use to play soldiers at the weekends.'

'No way!' the master sergeant exclaimed.

Nick applied the safety on the gun and quickly marshalled the children together. He pointed at the helicopter through the window and they soon got the message. With squeals of excitement, they rushed down the stairs and headed for the machine. The master sergeant checked each room to make sure nobody had been left behind as Nick herded the children towards the helicopter. The machine gunner hauled them on board as quickly as he could. The master sergeant walked backwards slowly, covering the area. Once he was in, the door was slammed shut and the machine rose from the ground.

'You OK, buddy?' the master sergeant asked once the guns had been stowed.

'Yes.' It was all he could say, watching the children tightly wedged together.

The sudden flood of relief had been overwhelming, making the tears well up. He hung on and didn't cry. He saw little Annie looking bewildered, thinking of what horrors she must have endured. The other children seemed less traumatised, more excited to be in a helicopter. Annie looked out of the window, as if interested in life once more.

'You did good back there.'

'So did you,' Nick replied.

'Stay with the day job. It's safer.'

'I'll remember that,' Nick said, grinning at the friendly Texan.

'That there is Zack the gunner.'

'Glad the cavalry arrived in time,' Nick replied, shaking the man's hand.

'Just like in the movies, huh?' the man replied.

'Pretty much. Charlie, could you let me know where these children end up, especially that little girl over there?' Nick asked, referring to Annie.

'Sure. We're heading back to the ship right now. Anywhere you want to get off?'

'Could you ask the captain to drop me off at the refugee camp?'

'Done. By the way, your face looks shit.'

'It's the bloody mosquitoes. Drop me an email sometime,' Nick said, passing over his address.

'I will do. You take care and get back home,' Charlie said, offering some friendly advice.

With its massive engines, the helicopter had no trouble in carrying the payload of skinny children. It headed out towards the refugee camp where Nick had asked to be put down, taking hardly any time to reach the site. Nick thanked the crew and patted Annie's head before climbing down. Dust swirled as he ran half bent towards Halcyon. The machine quickly lifted off again, allowing the crowds to surge towards him. They were happy to know he was still alive. No doubt Rami had been telling his stories again in vivid detail. He looked up to see Annie waving to him. She had finally returned to the land of the living.

Chapter 34

Enlightenment

Nick had every right to feel suitably pleased with himself as the crowds clapped. He walked up to Halcyon and prepared himself for a hug but she stood her ground with arms folded.

'Where the hell have you been?' she asked furiously.

'Don't I even get a hug first?' he replied with a smile.

'Damn you, this is not funny, Nick! I need to know what you've been up to. Rami has been sick with worry.'

'Did he tell you that Annie and I were being shot at?'

'No! He heard shots but didn't see a thing. You had no right to go there without my permission.'

'I'm sorry.'

'Is that all you can say! It's just not good enough!'

'Then what is? That helicopter is full of children from that filthy brothel. Even Annie is in there!' Nick replied, losing his patience.

'What brothel?' Halcyon asked.

'Didn't Rami tell you?'

'No, all he knew was that you had gone for over an hour before he heard gunshots. After a while, he saw Susanto drive up in his car. He thought you were either dead or the police had arrested you. Even now, he is in his room feeling full of remorse for not coming to find out what happened. He is totally distressed by all this.'

'It's a long story. I could do with a drink.'

'Unless you have one, I don't think Topo will be too obliging. He seems pretty annoyed about this whole business.'

'That's understandable,' Nick laughed, suddenly seeing the funny side of what he had done.

'Why?'

'Because I've just busted his little enterprise, and Susanto's.'

'You'd better tell me everything before we get into more trouble,' Halcyon insisted.

'Sure, but first I need a beer.'

They walked back to the administration building with the crowd following behind. Topo shied away when he saw Nick, knowing that Nick looked mad enough to hit him. Without asking, Nick searched the fridge and helped himself to a cola. He also got a bottle for Halcyon, disappointed the fat man didn't have any beers. No doubt, he was a devout muslim. The fat man didn't object but seethed within his soul. He knew Susanto would be just as angry but there was nothing they could do to Nick right now without attracting more attention. He melted away and left Nick and Halcyon alone. Rami came out of his room on hearing Nick's voice.

'Nick, I'm sorry. Please forgive me. I didn't come to look for you,' he pleaded.

'That's because I told you to stay put. You have nothing to be ashamed of.'

'I thought you were dead. Maybe they would shoot me too if I went to the house.'

'Hey, relax. We got the job done. All the children are now safe. After all, it was you who found out where they were.'

'I did nothing but you rescued them.'

'Let's call it a team effort. Why don't you go and talk to your friends and tell them about the children?'

'Yes, OK. Please, I'm very sorry, ah?'

'Rami, will you just get out of here and have a chinwag with your friends,' Nick said with a laugh.

'I don't understand,'

'It means go and talk!' Nick replied, encouraging the man to pursue his favorite pastime.

'OK. I'm so happy now!'

They watched as the little man left the building with obvious relief showing on his face. It left Nick alone with Halcyon to explain his story. He felt totally weary, having had very little sleep over the past two nights. Evening had approached again and he badly needed a wash and some food. Before he could switch off, he needed to tell Halcyon something else.

'When I was at the village, there was a UN vehicle there. These people are involved with Susanto.'

'The UN? Susanto knows you know this?' Halcyon asked.

'Unfortunately yes. The men in the village phoned him to check my identity. They knew I wasn't part of the paedophile ring.'

'What did this man from the UN look like?'

'Caucasian, early fifties, average built. I got a photograph,' Nick informed her.

'Good. Keep the camera with you. Do you think we're safe to stay here tonight?'

'It would be better than getting stopped by the army or police in the middle of nowhere.'

'You're right. The UNHCR needs to know about this person. I'll speak to them tomorrow.'

'That'll put Topo and Susanto on the spot. I'm sure they'll be glad to lend you the telephone,' Nick said in jest.

'I can call direct. The mobile network is up and running again.'

'Thank goodness for that. I need a shower.'

'Nick.'

'What?'

'I'm sorry for giving you a hard time when you got back.'

'Forget it.'

'I did worry about you. I was almost sick when Rami told me about the shooting.'

'It's over. I'm back now.'

'OK. We'll have something to eat when you've had your shower.'

'Yes, sure.'

'One more thing.'

'What?'

'You look awful.'

She watched him rise from the chair and walk to his room. Apart from the mosquito bites, he also had a nasty bruise to his face. She cried silently. She should have hugged him when he got off the helicopter.

Chapter 35

Nissam

O N THE FOLLOWING DAY, HALCYON GOT THROUGH to the UNHCR in Medan without difficulty. She had spoken before to Marcello Mione, the UNHCR coordinator in Medan. This time he told her they had received some information from the US Navy about the paedophile ring. It was good to know. The man was Swiss Italian but spoke good English. She was informed they had already dispatched someone from the UNHCR team working in Nissam to speak to Nick. It wasn't long before a UNHCR vehicle appeared at the camp.

Halcyon watched as a middle-aged woman jumped down from the passenger seat. She was strikingly beautiful, in the mould of Grace Kelly. Her blonde hair was bunched up in a purposeful bun behind her head, almost in businesslike fashion. She was somebody who commanded immediate attention as would a famous movie star. Topo shuffled out to greet her and noted the UNHCR vehicle. She asked for Nick, already knowing who the fat man was. Halcyon took the opportunity to introduce herself.

'Hello, I'm Halcyon Cooper from Mercy Aid International.'

'Hi, I'm Sylvie Palla. I believe you spoke to Marcello this morning,' she said, shaking hands with Halcyon.

'Perhaps we should talk somewhere else,' Halcyon suggested,

noting Topo's suspicious presence.

'Where is Nick?'

'He's still sleeping. I didn't want to tell him you were coming until you had arrived.'

'That's fine. And you are the manager of this camp?' she asked Topo coolly.

'Yes, I am. How can I help you?' he replied.

'I'd like to take a look at the facilities here.'

'Yes of course. Please, feel welcome,' Topo replied ingratiatingly.

'Thank you.'

'I will show you around,' he offered.

'No, that won't be necessary. It's just a routine inspection.'

'Of course,' Topo felt obliged to say, slighted by her subtle insult.

'Will you ask Nick to join me when he is ready?' she asked Halcyon.

'Yes, I'll get him for you,' Halcyon replied, impressed by her persona.

'Good, I'll just be walking around.'

Halcyon watched her stride out confidently in her expensive-looking trouser suit and leather shoes. She felt decidedly dowdy in comparison, wishing she had brought more to wear. Topo scowled as he returned to his desk, hating the foreign woman. In his country, men gave the orders. Halcyon noted the simmering hatred in him as she walked past to fetch Nick. After a gentle knock, she went in. Nick was sprawled out on his back, wearing only boxer shorts. She allowed her eyes to roam over his body, noting his athletic physique. She felt a shudder run through her as she lingered a little over the bulge beneath his boxers.

'Nick, wake up.'

'What?'

'Sorry, but I have to wake you.'

'Why?'

'There's someone here from the UNHCR who wants to talk to you called Sylvie. I managed to get through to Medan.'

'Who?'

'Just get up and put some clothes on,' Halcyon said like a mother.

'OK. Give me five minutes.'

'See you outside.'

He had actually been awake for a while but had been mulling over recent events. In a semi-sleepy state, he tried to push the bad things to the back of his mind. Struggling to get up, he still felt physically exhausted. His face hurt. With some reluctance, he got up to wash and shave, before venturing outside. He could see the large four-by-four UNHCR vehicle parked outside. Halcyon was with the other woman. They talked as excited children played nearby. Nick headed out to meet them, noticing the attractive woman.

'Hi, I believe you wanted to see me,' he said.

'You must be Nick. I'm Sylvie,' she replied, holding out her hand.

Nick shook hands and noticed her well-manicured fingernails. He could also smell her perfume.

'You must forgive the way I look,' he replied, his face still marked and itchy.

'You look fine. Halcyon has been telling me about the situation here.'

'So you're up to speed with developments?'

'Nearly. We're obviously busy with the tsunami and other local matters in Nissam. This business has just made our work more challenging.'

'We've heard something about Nissam. Sorry to add to your busy schedule,' Nick replied.

'The situation is becoming more dangerous every day. I suggest you both get back to Medan and then leave Sumatra as soon as possible.'

'What are you able to tell us about Nissam?'

'It's too early to say. It may end up as a war crime investigation.'

'Has the UN actually classified the troubles here as a war?'

'That's a political question. Let us focus on your immediate situation.'

'Sure.'

'This matter with the paedophile ring will escalate. I can imagine some people are very angry at what you have done. That's why I suggest that you leave now.'

'I'd like to say something,' Halcyon interrupted.

'What is it?' Sylvie replied.

'I plan to stay here and run a rehabilitation programme. That's what I came out to do. There are too many traumatised children here to simply do nothing.'

'I fully sympathise with your sentiments but you are in danger. It's your decision to stay but you are very isolated here. The nearest foreign aid camp is fifteen kilometres away.'

'Yes, I know that. I think that Nick should go home because he was directly involved with these people. It would be highly unlikely they would come for me when the UNHCR is already aware of what is going on,' Halcyon argued.

'We can try and give you some support but your safety cannot be guaranteed.'

'I already know that.'

'What would you like to do, Nick?' Sylvie asked.

'I have no choice but to leave. There is a murderous policeman here called Susanto who is on the loose and I'm not his favourite person right now. '

'OK, how will you get back to Medan?'

'We have a van and a driver.'

'I don't think it would be safe to travel by road without an escort. I suggest you come to Nissam with me and we'll find a way of getting you back to Medan,' she offered.

'Thanks. That sounds more sensible. Before we go, is there any more word about the workers from this charity who disappeared before the tsunami?'

'Not at the moment, I've been briefed by Marcello about this matter and it'll be part of our investigation.'

'May I ask what you do exactly?'

'I work for a section of the UNHCR investigating human rights abuses,' Sylvie replied.

'That's wonderful,' Nick replied with a grin.

'Does that amuse you?' Sylvie asked in a cool tone.

'No, not at all. I'm just glad somebody is taking some action over this matter. I know very little about your organisation.'

'You could always look it up on the internet.'

'Yes, I could but that would be a little difficult just now.'

'Not with a satellite link it isn't,' she replied with a haughty look.

'I just need a few minutes to fetch my things. Can you try and persuade Halcyon to leave too?' Nick asked, suddenly annoyed by her apparent arrogance.

'Of course,' Sylvie replied, knowing the answer already.

'I'm staying right here,' Halcyon said, just to confirm the situation.

'Final offer?' Sylvie asked.

'I've made up my mind but thanks for asking.'

'OK, it's your choice. Halcyon won't be coming.'

He didn't need to hear the confirmation. Marching quickly off to the administrative building, he roughly crammed his belongings into the two rucksacks. He wasn't sure if Sylvie was being condescending or just poking fun. Topo happened to be at the main door as he was about to leave. It gave him a chance to vent some of his anger.

'I'm going. The next time you abuse one of these boys, I hope you go blind.'

'Go home, English.'

'I'm Scottish, you twat,' Nick replied, doubting if the man knew the term.

Nick left without any further verbal exchanges with the pervert. Sylvie was waiting by the four-by-four when Nick joined her and Halcyon.

'Did you say goodbye to your friend Topo?' Sylvie asked in her faintly German accent.

'Not exactly. And where are you from?' he asked in turn.

'I come from Basle, the German part of Switzerland.'

'You must be one of these annoying people who can speak different languages,' he said, still irritated from a mixture of tiredness and seeing Topo.

'Oh just some French, Italian, Russian, Mandarin and a little Malay. It's my job,' she smiled.

'It must be a tough job!'

'Shall we go?' Sylvie asked, picking up some of Nick's antagonistic comments.

'Yes, why don't we?' he replied.

Nick said goodbye to Halcyon as she finally hugged him. It felt strange to be leaving her behind, worried she was alone except for Rami. Sylvie told him to join her in the back seat. He wound the window down as the vehicle reversed to leave.

'I'll be in touch. Say hi to Rami for me!'

'Take care, Nick,' Halcyon replied, waving to him.

He saw her cry as they drove away.

CHAPTER 36

EXHUMATION

THEY ARRIVED LATE IN THE AFTERNOON WITHOUT drama, passing through the few roadblocks with ease on the way to Nissam. Apart from being a little tired and slightly irritated, Nick answered most of the questions about his time in Sumatra with civility. He felt Sylvie was probing him, mentally analysing the person he was. She remained pleasant but professionally aloof, introducing him to the team when they got there. The reception was distinctly cool, which made him wonder if he was intruding. There was just a hint of resentment, as if the dynamics within the closely knit team had TO change. The team knew they had to be babysitters again, just because the local police couldn't be trusted to do their job. Sylvie made light of it.

'Relax. They don't bite. Your room is next to the kitchen. I hope you don't mind. The maid doesn't use it as she goes home every day. Our rooms are upstairs.'

'That's perfect,' Nick replied, aware he was the token outsider.

'Any problem, Jacque?' Sylvie asked one of the men.

'Ils ont trouve une grande tombe aujourd'hui,' the Frenchman replied deliberately in French.

'Quand?'

'Juste recemment.'

'They have just found a grave. I have to go. Just ask the maid for anything you need,' Sylvie said.

'Anything?' Nick replied to inject some humour into the tense situation.

'Within reason. Why don't you write me a report on what you told me in the car? You can use my laptop on that desk,' she replied with a slight smile.

'I may take the opportunity to get some sleep. Didn't get very much of that recently.'

'Sure. Suit yourself. We'll be back later.'

Sylvie collected her camera and left with the other people. As team leader, it was her decision to visit the site straight away despite the fact dead people couldn't run away. She wanted to gather the fresh evidence before dark. Nick heard the cars drive off in a hurry, making the house very quiet all of a sudden. Looking around, he saw a modern house built on three floors. It was quite large by local standards. Perhaps it belonged to a property tycoon but the big money was in Bali where property prices were taking off.

The maid's room was obviously the smallest room in the house. It had a single bed and one small cupboard. Most live-in maids had to live in cramped conditions but it was probably better than sharing a room with umpteen siblings at home. The rented property obviously came with a maid, or else they had hired one specifically.

She offered him a coffee and a choice of sticky cakes which came in variety of lurid colours. The local woman didn't speak English, but Nick had learnt enough Malay to say the cakes were delicious. Feeling too tired from his recent ordeal to write a report, he lay on his front and dangled his legs over the edge of the short bed. He dozed off peacefully to the sound of the maid preparing food for the evening meal. The gentle aromas coming from the kitchen took him into another world, a far more pleasant one than guns and death. It was dark by the time the team arrived back, heralded by the slamming of car doors. He heard French voices speaking excitedly. Something told him they had had a bad day out. He walked barefooted into the living room to join them but was largely ignored. They started to work on their laptops, several people chain-smoking between gulps of coffee.

'Did you find much?' Nick asked Sylvie out of curiosity.

'Oh hello, Nick. It wasn't a good day.'

'Perhaps I shouldn't ask any more,' he replied, hoping she would volunteer the information.

'How did you get on with your report?'

'To be honest, I fell asleep.'

'Not with the maid, I hope?' she replied, matching Nick's earlier humour.

'No, she just made me coffee. Can I get you a cup?'

'Yes, that would be good.'

He fetched two cups of the inky black liquid. Surprisingly, the local coffee tasted quite mild despite the appearance. Sylvie sipped away as she walked over to one of the easy chairs.

'Do you mind me asking you about your work?' Nick asked.

'Not at all. What do you want to know?'

'Since you didn't say a great deal when we first met, I'm curious to know how you got involved in all this.'

'Very simply, I am a lawyer. I became interested in gathering the evidence rather than acting as the prosecutor. Very often, it is hard to prove who did what in a war scenario.'

'And you started working in Switzerland for the UNHCR?'

'Yes.'

'Do you have any family?' Nick asked directly.

'That's a personal question.'

'I'm just curious. It can't be easy doing this job if you did have children.'

'No, I don't have any. And what about you? Are you involved with Halcyon?' Sylvie asked, sufficiently intrigued by Nick to follow his line of questioning.

'No, and I don't have children either.'

'You work as a surgeon, yes?' Sylvie asked.

'When I can. I don't have a permanent job.'

'So you volunteered to come to Sumatra?'

'Yes.'

'That's very noble of you.'

'I came here for some adventure but tell me more about your job,' Nick insisted.

'There is not much to it. We monitor human rights abuses and investigate cases of genocide. When necessary, we send in a forensics team and they do all the clever stuff. I just collect all the information and the whole thing goes to the international courts in The Hague for the lawyers to do their work.'

'Where do the forensics team come from?'

'From anywhere. In the UK, there are just four accredited forensic anthropologists who can go to any part of the world to investigate major crime scenes. Each developed country has its own.'

'I just presumed the UNHCR had a dedicated forensics team.'

'We don't have them sitting in one office waiting for a call to come through. They are usually university professors with full-time jobs. If you like, they work for us on the side.'

'Is there a forensics team in Nissam?'

'Yes, they arrived recently. They were working at another site but they have started work at the place we went to today. Why, would you like to see what they do?'

'Is that possible?' Nick replied, intrigued by the offer.

'Yes, of course but it would depend on whether your stomach

is strong enough to cope with what you see. It is different from an operating table.'

'I'm used to it,' Nick replied with a hint of bravado.

'We shall see.'

'The bodies that were found, how were they killed?'

'We don't know as yet but there were signs of torture.'

'How could you tell if the bodies were decomposed?'

'That's what our forensics team are for. It doesn't take much to guess that people with their hands and feet tied up didn't die naturally.'

'How did your team know about this new grave?'

'We were already working in the area but this came from another local source.'

'I've heard that many people have already been killed in Aceh from the troubles. Why has the UN not intervened?'

'I cannot give you the answer because there are too many political considerations. We have been working hard in East Timor and as you know, the UN has taken great efforts to maintain peace over there. Most of the UN troops come from Australia.'

'What about here in Aceh? Did the Indonesian government agree to cooperate with the UN just because international aid is needed for the tsunami?' Nick asked sceptically.

'You can draw your own conclusions on that one,' Sylvie replied.

'It sucks, to coin a phrase.'

'No government will ever admit to having a deliberate policy of killing troublemakers. The Germans may have built efficient concentration camps but it was the British who first thought of it in South Africa when they were fighting the Boers. Thousands died from disease and starvation. It didn't just happen in Belsen or Auschwitz. The local government here will probably say these bodies belong to the terrorists who died in the fighting.'

'Except they were murdered?

'That's what we have to prove.'

'How powerful is the UN?' Nick asked.

'What do you mean?'

'Could they have stopped the killings in Cambodia or Rwanda?'

'I don't know but perhaps the wrong decisions were taken at that time. The UN has a large military force in the Congo right now fighting with the unlawful militia. And yes, the UN is a powerful organisation but it would have been powerless to intervene in Cambodia when the whole country was involved in killing its own population.'

'So why did the UN not intervene earlier in Aceh when there is already plenty of evidence of atrocities?'

'Should the UN have intervened in Northern Ireland when the bombs were going off?'

'Perhaps.'

'Do you really think so?' Sylvie asked.

'I don't know.'

'Sometimes, there are no easy answers. The UN cannot simply march in and take over some country which has not asked for help.'

'I'm learning all the time despite knowing very little about the UN or the UNHCR. Your comment earlier about using the internet was a little irritating.'

'Why, because I'm a lawyer with a probing mind?'

'Are you always so clinical?'

'No, but I like to challenge people's views. You didn't tell me I was annoying you,' Sylvie replied, looking him deep into his eyes.

'Annoy is probably too strong a word. Are you married?'

'What is this? A personal interview?'

'No, just payback time. I didn't get a chance to ask much about you in the car.'

'But I had a good reason to ask you about yourself.'

'Now that you know me, I should know something about you.'

'Well, I'm not the marrying kind. I have a girlfriend in Geneva.'

'Oh,' Nick replied, taken aback by the unexpected answer.

'Does that surprise you?' she asked with a laugh.

'No, not at all. I just hadn't thought of that.'

'I'm going for a shower before dinner.'

'See you when come down.'

Nick watched her go up the stairs, aware that some of the men in the room had turned to watch her too. They appeared to be engrossed with their laptops but he knew his conversation with Sylvie had not gone unnoticed. He wasn't shocked by her relevation. She was evidently intelligent and exuded a natural air of aloofness but her natural beauty had captivated his mind.

Chapter 37

Emotions

THE EVENING HAD TURNED BALMY WITH THE sticky tropical heat. They sat together at the long table, which was covered with a cheap chequered plastic liner. The electric fan overhead stirred the air enthusiastically as the crickets chirped outside. Much of the conversation was in French, making Nick wonder if that had been done deliberately. Occasionally, somebody would bother to translate but Sylvie switched between languages with ease, even chatting to the housekeeper in Malay. He concentrated on the food as nobody else was eating very much. Perhaps what they had seen was too disturbing. He decided to join in the conversation.

'Some of the workers from my organisation may have been abducted and killed. What are the chances they are in that grave?' he asked, causing several heads to turn in his direction.

'Yes, we know about them. When did they disappear?' a thin, balding man called Raymond asked in perfect English.

'Possibly just before the tsunami.'

'How do you know they did not die then?'

'We don't, but some of the local people thought they may have been taken away by the security forces.'

'Who exactly? The army? The police?'

'I don't know.'

'And you think there is some connection with this place?'

'They may have known about these killings. Some of the local people went to see them because the local police wouldn't say much about those who had been killed in the fighting.'

'Sure, we understand what you are saying but sometimes we don't get the answers. The work here in Nissam will take a long time to process, perhaps many months. If the pathologists can establish a DNA data bank of the dead people and link them to the living relatives, maybe we can get to know who the victims are, even your people.'

'One of the missing women is a Swiss national,' Nick said.

'Then we will need to get some DNA material from her relatives.'

'What if she is still alive? Won't her family be upset?' another worker asked.

'That will be your job then, Rolf, to break the news gently,' Raymond answered, causing a small ripple of laughter.

'It must have been something really important if they killed her. Killing a foreigner usually brings unwanted publicity,' Rolf concluded.

'Rolfy, you are surpassing yourself with some brilliant logic today,' Raymond answered, to more laughter.

'I do have my moments, even if I say so,' the man answered, playing to his audience.

'Nick, ignore these idiots. If these women are here, we will find out,' Sylvie said, watching Nick carefully, in case he thought the men were mocking him.

'What they say say makes good sense. I know they are only joking.'

The conversation fragmented into several smaller ones as the meal ended. Nick left the table and walked out to the garden. He noted that light pollution had not blighted this dark corner of Sumatra, making the stars above look very clear. He felt a presence next to him and recognised the perfume.

'I hope you were not too surprised by the conversation,' she said.

'No, I'm used to alternative humour in the medical profession.'

'Is that what you call it?'

'Some may call them sick jokes.'

'We're actually quite restrained with telling crude jokes because you're here. It's important for us to be able to laugh at death. Otherwise, the job is too unbearable. Can you understand that?'

'There's no need to worry. I apologise for asking you about your personal life earlier.'

'What, about not being married and having a girlfriend?'

'Yes.'

'Are you bothered about that?' she asked.

'No. It's just a waste for some lucky man.'

'Why is that?'

'Because you are very attractive.'

'Oh come on. I must be at least fifteen years older than you.'

'Perhaps age does not matter so much these days.'

'Thank you, Nick. I'm sure you'll find the perfect woman someday.'

'Perhaps I already have.'

'Well that's wonderful. You still haven't told me about Halcyon. Is she just somebody you work with or do you have feelings for her? I saw her cry when you left.'

'She's a good work colleague. What about the guys you work with here? Do they know about your life?'

'No, they don't. I suppose they look after me because I'm the boss.'

'It's obvious they don't like me being here.'

'Rubbish. They have a lot of work to do. Some of them have not seen their families for months. Honestly, they're nice people really.'

'I believe you. It must be great to have a family.'

'Why, don't you have one?'

'Not really.'

'Are your parents dead?'

'My father is.'

'And your mother?'

'She's alive but she has her own problems.'

'Is there something missing in your life Nick?'

'Like what?'

'Like somebody who really means something to you. I don't know, but I think there is something very sad about you.'

'Maybe you're right.'

'Is that why you came to Sumatra?' she asked, looking at him.

'Perhaps.'

'One day you will find what you are looking for. I know this.'

'Thanks for the vote of confidence.'

'What about tomorrow? Are you mentally fit to come with us?'

'Of course. Seeing dead bodies won't be a problem.'

'So long as you're sure.'

'Yes, I am.'

'In that case, get some sleep.'

'You too. Good night,' Nick said.

She walked in without turning around. He didn't feel tired as the afternoon nap had obviously recharged his batteries. He wondered if Sylvie was trying to make a point by what she said. People like her and Halcyon were psychologically strong enough to cope with scenes of mass murder. He had seen the numerous bodies in Banda Aceh but they had been killed in an act of God. This was different.

It would be a crime site where people had either been killed on the spot or their bodies taken there. He knew he couldn't afford to crack mentally despite feeling the strain. Perhaps agreeing to go wasn't the best decision he had made. He could always change his mind tomorrow.

CHAPTER 38

THE PROFESSOR

NICK GOT UP BEFORE 5 A.M. AND fired up Sylvie's laptop. He couldn't sleep any more. The screen crackled into life as he thought about writing his report. It would be in a chronological order of events, starting with his first encounter with the refugees at the aid camp. The words rattled off easily enough without him having to think too hard. He heard the maid arrive just after 6 a.m. She merely acknowledged his presence before busying herself in the kitchen. He took the coffee on offer and continued with the report. It was ready just after 7 a.m. when he made a copy onto a fresh CDR. He stretched and went for a shower.

Breakfast was ready by the time he dressed. The others came down with muted giggles, raising his suspicions that they were poking fun at him. However, unlike the previous day, there was a sense of camaraderie. Just like a bunch of school boys about to go on an outing, they teased each other. The excitement of the forthcoming day had now taken over his thoughts.

'Ah, Nick! How are you today, my friend?' Raymond asked.

'I'm very well, thanks.'

'Good. Make sure you have a good breakfast,' Raymond said, raising a few more giggles.

'Why, in case I lose my appetite later?' Nick replied.

'Maybe, or perhaps the maid is having a bad day.'

'Don't worry, I'll eat yours too.'

'Oh, very strong words! I hope your stomach is not as delicate as mine!'

'OK, come on. Stop this, let's get on,' Sylvie said, sitting down to her breakfast.

'I've done your report,' Nick said.

'You've been up early?'

'It only took a couple of hours.'

'Good. I'll look forward to reading it. Are you ready to leave?'

'Yes.'

'This is just some advice for you. Being with us means you are representing the UNHCR. I suggest you say nothing to anybody and just keep your eyes open. It will not be pleasant.'

'I understand.'

'Good. We will give you one of these passes,' Sylvie said, referring to his new ID card. It looked good enough.

They ate their breakfast without ceremony but Nick felt like a bundle of knots, unsure what lay ahead. He deliberately did not take a camera along but perched a set of sunglasses on his head in case he needed them. It was more of a case of concealing his thoughts in case his eyes showed the horror of what he was about to see. He went in Sylvie's car as the others got in another vehicle. On the way to the site, the soldiers made a big show of checking their identity badges before letting them through. They eventually stopped at the designated area, alongside several military Land Rovers. It seemed incongruous for the military to be there when the UN was effectively investigating a crime scene committed by the security forces.

The village was deserted but otherwise looked like any one of the many thousands across the country. Mango trees lay between some of the houses made from wood and corrugated zinc. Special areas of interest had been marked out with plastic taping as the unmistakable sound of shovels working the earth filled the air. Sylvie and the team headed for the area, walking down the side of one house into a dark bamboo area. Beyond the thicket of trees, a clearing suddenly appeared with a hive of activity. They could see several people shovelling earth in a newly created rectangle trench. The evil within the place was palpable just as the overpowering stench from the rotting corpses took their breath away. Flies buzzed as Nick watched in fascination at the forensic work taking place. People were suited up in white overalls, kneeling down and observing the ground closely. He could see them gently pulling away at bits of clothing material but nothing there resembled an identifiable body. The team clearly knew that each pile of rags contained a decomposing body, usually just skin and bones. They continued with their painstaking work, careful to preserve the evidence. From one corner, he could hear a Scottish accent.

A diminutive woman in overalls and wellington boots hovered around the site as if it were some archaeological dig. She was clearly in charge, directing the efforts of the team. She seemed indifferent to the task ahead as Nick diverted his gaze from the trench to look around. There were many other observers there, which made Nick feel less redundant as a bystander. Sylvie's team busied themselves with getting photographic evidence. He remembered her advice to look but keep his mouth shut. In morbid fascination, he edged closer to the pit which was covered in soft, freshly dug earth. Then, with a sliding sensation, he could feel his foot losing its grip until it gave way beneath him. Some of the earth tumbled back into the pit as he fell in. He tried to keep upright and landed on a jelly-like pile of material. It lay just beneath a thin layer of soil. A putrid stench hit him immediately as the gasses exploded from the decaying body. He choked. A shrill voice shouted out from the other end of the trench.

246

Nick instantly knew he was in trouble, adding to the nausea which had threatened to overcome him. He tried hard not to throw up, lest he contaminate the site even further.

'You there! What the hell do you think you are doing? You have just stuck your dirty big feet in my graveyard!' the woman screamed, marching smartly up to him.

'I'm extremely sorry. I seem to have slipped on the loose soil,' Nick muttered, feeling like a fool.

'Which bloody outfit are you with?'

'I'm here with the UNHCR.'

'Don't they teach you to keep out of crime sites?'

'Yes, this is totally my fault.'

'Well, don't jump into my pit again!'

'Are you Scottish?' Nick asked to diffuse the growing tension between them.

'What of it?' she replied, sounding totally irritated.

'I'm from Edinburgh.'

'And I'm the professor of anatomy from Dundee. From your accent, you do sound like some pompous ass from Edinburgh,' she said belligerently, standing with her hands on her hips.

'I trained in Dundee.'

'Doing what?'

'Medicine.'

'Then you should know who I am unless you didn't bother turning up to your lectures! When did you graduate?'

'Eight years ago.'

'Well, that was before I came. What's the connection with the UNHCR?'

'I haven't told you the whole truth.'

'Now may be a good time before I throw you out.'

'I'm not actually with the UNHCR but with an organisation

helping out with the tsunami. We believe some of our workers may be lying in this pit.'

'Oh, don't be silly. These bodies have been here since long before that.'

'Can I get out and explain the whole situation to you?'

'Yes, before you decide to muck things up even more.'

'Once again, I'm really sorry,' Nick apologised, aware of the great commotion he was causing.

'Stop snivelling and come with me,' the professor ordered.

They climbed out of the trench and Nick could see how furious Sylvie was with him. He made an apologetic grimace as he followed behind the professor. They walked past the house into another part of the village where several tents had been erected. The professor sat down on a foldable chair and beckoned Nick to do the same. He meekly complied.

'Tell me who you are and what exactly are you doing here,' she asked, crossing one leg over the other with her oversized boot dangling down.

'I'm Nick Forbes. It's a long story as to why I'm here.'

'Just keep it short. I don't have much time,' the professor said without smiling.

'Our organisation helps women caught up in the local conflict. The four women working for our charity had disappeared just shortly before the tsunami.'

'Go on, tell me more.'

'They were working in Banda Aceh when contact was suddenly lost.'

'Were they helping people who had been abused by the security forces?'

'Yes, we think so.'

'And what's your involvement with the UNHCR?'

'They are merely keeping me safe until I can get back to Medan. I was involved in disrupting a paedophile ring run by the security forces. These people may also be involved in the abduction of our workers.'

'My, you've been busy. What specialty are you in?'

'Orthopaedics.'

'So instead of hacking off limbs, you're now trampling on dead bodies.'

'That's hardly fair. Look, I've apologised already.'

'*Mors tua vita mea.*'

'I'm sorry?' Nick asked.

'It means your death is my life. Don't they teach you young people Latin any more?'

'Sadly no,' Nick replied.

'Now tell me exactly who is missing from your team?'

'Four women. A Swiss psychologist and three local women acting as helpers and interpreters.'

'I shall keep my eye out for them but you may be barking up the wrong tree. So far we have only uncovered young men believed to be guerrilla fighters,' the professor said.

'Just for my own information, how could you tell the difference between a Caucasian and an Asiatic body?' Nick asked out of curiosity.

'Right, come with me,' the professor uttered with relish, jumping up from her stool. She had switched over to teaching mode.

They strode into another tent full of human remains, contained in various cardboard boxes. The diminutive professor was no more than five feet tall but her commanding presence made up for her size. She slipped on a fresh pair of latex gloves and removed a soil-encrusted skull out of one of the boxes. Forgetting the horrific circumstances from where it had come, the professor gave Nick a lecture.

'Right, look at this skull. You can tell immediately this is an Asiatic person. The orbital ridge here is thicker in appearance and the facial dimensions are also different, being wider across the face. The skull is also generally smaller for age and sex matched comparisons but this is getting more difficult to tell nowadays. Even Japanese children are much bigger now compared to their ancestors because they eat western food high in calcium, as found in milk and other dairy products. I could also tell the height of this person just by examining one of the finger bones because they correlate well to the person's height. The pelvic bone can tell you which sex you are looking at because the female pelvis is broader.'

'So junk food is not all bad then?' Nick replied with some candour.

'Come over here,' the professor ordered, without bothering to reply.

She reached into another cardboard box containing an assortment of bones. She picked up a small fragment and showed it to Nick.

'Where is this from?'

Even as a surgeon, he struggled to identify the piece. 'I really couldn't say,' he finally admitted.

'Well, it's a piece of the sphenoidal bone. We found it amongst a pile of other shattered bones. The sphenoid bone lies deep within the skull and this piece has been forcibly broken. It would imply that the person had suffered a massive blow to the front of the face, caving the whole structure. And what is this piece?' she asked, holding up a vertebra.

'That looks like a cervical spine vertebra,' Nick answered.

'Yes. They are anatomically different from the thoracic and lumbar vertebrae due to the presence of the foramen transversarium. As you know, the vertebral arteries go through these foramina to supply blood to the back of the head. What else do you see?'

'There is an unusual line cut into the bone.'

'Correct. It shows a sharp blade of some kind has entered the neck, leaving an indent on the bone. This person probably had his throat cut.'

'Fascinating.'

'Well, I would love to continue but I need to get on with the work.'

'Thanks for the anatomy lesson,' Nick replied.

'You had obviously left medical school before I arrived. Our students get a proper education now.'

'Yes, naturally.'

'There's nothing natural about it, just good old fashioned teaching. I'll let the UNHCR people know if we find anything,' the professor said.

'I'll mention you to the prof in Edinburgh when I next see him at a meeting.'

'Yes, ask him to stand on a soapbox. You might be able to see him then. Give him my regards.'

'Sure,' Nick laughed, knowing the forensics professor wasn't the tallest man in the world.

He watched her walk away. She raised her hand in a friendly gesture and he could only presume she had forgiven him for blundering into the pit. He liked her dry sense of humour, even the impromptu short introduction into forensic pathology. He admired what she and her team did. The smell and heat alone was not for the faint-hearted. He caught up with Sylvie by the pit side, careful not to fall in again.

'How was the professor?' she asked.

'Absolutely tore me apart,' Nick replied with a straight face.

'That was a stupid thing to do.'

'Please, just don't say any more.'

'Did you mention about your missing women to her?'

'Yes, they haven't found them. There are only men in this grave.'

'Let's take a walk,' Sylvie suggested quietly.

'Sure.'

'Don't turn around but there are two Indonesian men who have been looking at you very closely.'

'Are they behind us?'

'Yes.'

'We'll stop in the shade by that abandoned house and I'll try to have a look,' Nick said.

They casually strolled up to the house before sitting down on the step, shaded by the roof extension hanging over the entrance. Nick made a play of wiping the sweat from his forehead before lowering the wraparound Oakley sunglasses on his head. Without turning his head, he could now swivel his eyes to look at the two men whilst pretending to look directly ahead. He muttered quietly to Sylvie.

'I see them now. That's Susanto on the left.'

'He is the policeman you think is involved with the children?'

'Yes, and maybe for our missing women also.'

'I don't think it's safe for you to be here any more.'

'Could you arrange for me to get back to Medan today?'

'It shouldn't be a problem but I'll have to clear it with Marcello first.'

'Thanks.'

'I need to tell my team we are going back to the house to make the necessary arrangements. Give me a minute.'

She raised Raymond on the mobile phone and spoke in French. After telling Raymond her plan, she and Nick headed for the vehicle. Sylvie's personal driver flashed a quick smile when he saw her coming. The return journey was more eventful as Susanto had decided to follow behind. The other four-by-four vehicle parked up less than a hundred metres away when they reached the house.

Nick stank badly. He stripped off and threw away his old boots which would never smell the same again. The small shower room next to the kitchen had an open grill at the top for natural ventilation. It was basic, something for the maid to use, but the shower felt great. The afternoon heat had warmed up the water tank on the roof so there was plenty of warm water. He noticed the beads of water trickling down the tiled wall due to the humidity. With the water gushing out of the large shower head above, he didn't hear the door open as Sylvie slipped in beside him.

'Do you mind if I join you?' she asked, removing her silk dressing gown.

'No,' Nick replied, strangely surprised but not fazed to see her there.

'I have spoken to Marcello and it is OK for you to go to Medan. My driver will take you.'

'Thanks. Is this what Swiss women do?' he asked.

'Just don't speak, Nick,' she replied, placing her hand at the back of his head and pulling him towards her.

Perhaps it was a Swiss custom but it would have been impolite to ask her to leave. He saw her alluring figure only too briefly before her shapely breasts pressed into him. Her blonde hair tumbled as she released it with one hand. It soon became wet under the shower. Their tongues met as she kissed him passionately, her fingers also eagerly searching out for something she had not felt in a long time.

He needed no encouragement as he pushed her gently against the wall, feeling her legs fall apart. He entered her easily and continued to jack her up with powerful strokes. She clung onto his back, digging her manicured nails into his flesh. They made love in complete silence with water cascading down from above. Sylvie eventually let out several little moans as Nick remained conscious that the maid was doing her chores outside. He even wondered if the maid could see them making love from the open grill above, but it only heightened the intensity. Sylvie could not have cared less, perhaps even wishing she was in there with them. The pleasurable sensations seemed to go for ever, until he felt her shudder several times in quick succession. It was his turn before they finished the brief liaison with a lingering kiss. She left without saying a word, leaving him to stand beneath the shower. He braced himself with both hands against the wall as the water continued to pummel his head. Perhaps it was her way of saying goodbye.

After dressing, he packed up and went into the lobby. Sylvie came downstairs, wearing a fresh dress with her hair wrapped up in a towel. If the maid had known about it, she didn't show any signs. The driver carried the rucksacks into the vehicle as Nick took the chance of saying a few last words. It was an emotional moment.

'What was that all about?' he asked.

'Just something we both needed,' she replied.

'I take it we won't be exchanging addresses,' he added.

'No. It's better if we didn't.'

'I understand.'

'Have a safe journey. We have diplomatic status so you'll be OK.'

'Thanks.'

He gave her hand a quick squeeze before leaving the house. She looked on as they drove off, knowing that Susanto would be following. Despite the diplomatic status of the vehicle, Nick would need a lot of luck to get to Medan. She still felt flushed from their recent encounter, enjoying the intimacy for what it was. Nick had made an impact on her in a way other men couldn't.

CHAPTER 39

LONG ROAD TO MEDAN

THE BLUE TOYOTA FOUR-BY-FOUR TAILING THEM KEPT a steady pace as they made their way south. Unlike Rami, the driver couldn't speak much English, which made talking difficult. Being followed by the police had made him anxious. Nick couldn't relax either. Susanto knew Nick was not working for the UNHCR and therefore had no diplomatic immunity. He could easily be arrested on trumped up charges and Nick knew that.

Frequently looking behind in the mirror, the driver hoped the police were only following them for a short while until they were out of their jurisdiction. The road had got quieter on leaving the Nissam district, passing by isolated houses along the route. Nick prayed Susanto would just turn around and go away but there was no such luck. The vehicle behind had started to flash its headlights as the driver looked behind nervously. He slowed the vehicle down as if ready to pull up. Nick glanced over his shoulder and decided they mustn't stop.

'No, no. Don't stop! Drive on! Jalan, jalan!' he shouted to the driver, pointing forwards with his index finger.

The driver felt torn with indecision. He knew the vehicle behind was the police and failing to stop was an offence, regardless if he was with the UNHCR. Nick must be in some kind of trouble because

Sylvie had told him to head for Medan as quickly as possible. He guessed it had something to do with the present investigation going on in Nissam. Choosing to ignore the Toyota behind them, he pressed down the accelerator. Nick looked behind again and could see Susanto shouting obscenities. The Toyota had sped up to overtake, running alongside their vehicle. Susanto looked intently at Nick, indicating with his hand for them to pull aside. The driver panicked, unsure what to do. Nick knew it would all be over if Susanto arrested him. Somebody obviously didn't want him to be a witness when the court case started. The message had to get across to the driver.

'These people will kill you also! Do you understand?' Nick shouted.

'Saya tak faham! Tak faham!'

'Awak mati if you stop,' Nick replied in combo language.

'OK, OK,' the driver said, as the penny finally dropped.

Essentially, they would both be dead if Susanto got to them. The vehicle sped up and pulled away from the Toyota, reaching over ninety miles an hour. Nick held on to the grip handles and prayed Susanto didn't start shooting from his vehicle.

So far, no bullets had headed their way. Even Susanto would know that a UNHCR vehicle filled with bullet holes was not a good thing to have around. Nick remained worried. Medan was still a long way off and they would have to stop for petrol at some stage. He had to think of something fast.

Both vehicles had backed off as the quality of the road was now too poor to be driven on at any great speed. Crashing at ninety miles an hour would be fatal no matter how good the airbags were. Nick felt confident that Susanto could not stop them unless he radioed up ahead for a police roadblock. With that possibility in mind, he needed to speak to UNHCR in Medan before it happened. He looked for a car phone.

'I want to speak to Medan. Is there a car phone I can borrow?' he said.

'Tak cakap,' the driver replied.

'Phone?' Nick asked, indicating with his fingers.

The driver reached into his pocket and pulled out his mobile. Nick now had a phone but no contact number. He wished he had asked Halcyon earlier on, or even Sylvie. Knowing there was no point in even trying to ask the driver for the number, he looked around the vehicle. He opened the glove compartment box to look at some UNHCR correspondence. Quickly finding a number, he prayed it was the right one. He eventually spoke to Marcello.

'Hello, this is Nick Forbes calling from one of your UN vehicles. Sylvie Palla spoke to you earlier.'

'Yes, Nick. What is the situation?'

'We are being followed.'

'By whom?'

'A rogue policeman called Susanto. Sylvie must have mentioned him to you.'

'Yes she did. Where are you?' Marcello asked.

'I would say about one hundred and eighty kilometres out of Nissam. Susanto has already tried to stop us.'

'You can't let that happen,'

'I've gathered that. What should we do?' Nick asked.

'You're still very far from Medan. I'll despatch a couple of vehicles in your direction but it may be several hours before they reach you. Do you want me to speak to the police over here?'

'No. I have no idea how far this thing goes. Susanto may have a contact there.'

'OK, I understand. Make your way down to us but try not to run out of fuel.'

'What if Susanto sets up a roadblock up ahead?'

'Call me if that happens.'

'Thanks for the reassuring advice,' Nick replied, unconvincingly.

'You should also know about something else.'

'What?'

'They have found four female bodies in Banda Aceh.'

'What, our people?'

'Possibly, but we have to check it out.'

'Where exactly were they found?'

'In the centre of Banda Aceh itself.'

'So they did die in the flood, then?'

'We don't know at this stage. Their bodies look different.'

'How you mean?' Nick asked, sounding confused.

'They may have been deliberately placed in the rubble. There was evidence of fresh soil on their clothes. Flood victims don't have that.'

'Have they been dug up from somewhere?'

'That's the working assumption. Somebody is trying to pass them off as tsunami victims.'

'How soon can you make the identification?'

'No idea. I'll ask Sylvie if she can get the professor to go there as soon as possible.'

'Let me know as soon as you have the news.'

'I'll do that, Nick. The cars will be leaving here shortly. They'll flash their lights when they see you so make sure you keep your lights on. One of the guys is ex-South African special forces working for us, called Piet. They are all unarmed but I'm sure they can handle the situation.'

'Thanks for the help, Marcello. I appreciate it.'

Nick handed the phone back to the driver. They had now been on the road for over two hours with the Toyota still following them. Nick felt better for letting Medan know the current situation. The interspersed traffic had allowed them to carve their way through the vehicles, reminding Nick just how slowly they had gone on the way to Aceh in the little Honda van. The area they were driving through had suffered less destruction from the tsunami. Even so, many rivers had burst their banks from the tidal wave but thankfully most bridges had remained intact. The roads had been patched up quickly to allow aid to get through.

They continued south for several more hours as the fuel gauge started to run dangerously low. It was now less than a quarter full. Nick doubted the vehicle had enough diesel to reach Medan. All he could do was hope the UNHCR vehicles found them before they spluttered to a halt. Stopping at a petrol station would give Susanto all the chance he needed.

Both vehicles raced on for another hour as people made way on seeing the blue lights on the police vehicle. The fuel gauge was now at the reserve level. Nick could see another bridge looming up as the driver slowed down fractionally to negotiate the single lane. With no other vehicles around, the Toyota four-by-four did the opposite. It gathered more speed and bore down on them. They had reached the halfway point when they felt a sudden thud from behind. Nick was thrown forwards by the impact, held back only by the seat belt. Their vehicle quickly careered off to the left, hitting the bridge superstructure. It was met with a mighty crash as the vehicle collided with it, crushing Nick's side. It knocked the wind out of him. The vehicle came to a sudden stop and hung dangerously over the side. Nick sat back and surveyed the windscreen, frosted from a thousand cracks. He made a quick check of his arms and legs, which seemed to be working. The driver looked equally intact and managed to make his way out of the vehicle. Nick could see his door was jammed stuck against the bridge metalwork. He would have to make it out on the driver's side. Suddenly he was aware of the Toyota reversing past them. The driver screamed a warning to him but before he could disentangle himself from the seat belt, he felt another thump at the back. The Toyota had deliberately rammed him again.

This time, there was a wrenching sound. The vehicle ripped itself from the superstructure and plunged forwards, heading straight for the water. Panic quickly filled his mind. With a sudden realisation, he knew Susanto had chosen this bridge to send him into the murky water below. Through the side window, he could see the dark water approaching. There was nothing else to do but to brace himself. He was thrown forwards again, this time registering a shattering pain in his left shoulder on impact. Acutely aware that the vehicle was going down, he felt the cold water engulf him. The driver's door had slammed shut on impact and his door was too buckled to open.

With brackish water now filling the cabin, all available light had been snuffed out by the swirling mud as the vehicle hit the bottom. He tried to move but was trapped by the seat belt. Fighting hard, it eventually came away. He kicked out forcefully to free his legs from the crushed dashboard but the inflated airbags had added to the nuisance by getting in the way. Once freed within the vehicle, he tried to push either door open. Neither budged. He could feel the windscreen, shattered but still in one piece. Swinging his legs around, he kicked out. The toughened glass give way just as his lungs were ready to explode. His brain had started to run out of oxygen. The initial fear and panic had given way to a pleasant sensation. He was now in a multicoloured, magical world where time had slowed down. He even considered staying in the vehicle until an imaginary fish beckoned to him to swim through the gap. He followed. It was a tight squeeze but suddenly he was free.

A kaleidoscope of bright emeralds and turquoise appeared as he swam up with the fish. This world remained very pleasant as he made for a lighter patch of water up ahead. He swam casually towards it, remembering to thank the fish. It became brighter when he neared the surface. Suddenly he was through and the reality hit him as he breathed for all he was worth. Oxygen came flooding back into his brain, setting off the panic again. He submerged involuntarily, this time drinking the muddy water. Flailing with his arms and legs, he struggled to tread water. He could see the bridge above him and knew he had to swim before he was swept out to sea. Feeling totally disorientated, he struck out towards one of the banks. Nauseated and breathless, he half swam and half doggy paddled to the bank. Thankfully, he had surfaced nearer to the far bank. He finally made it, retching as he crawled out. The stinking mud felt wonderful as he collapsed on his back. He could see the blue sky and the bridge above. The feeling of relief was short lived when a shadow fell across him. It was Susanto, standing above him with a gun.

'Why don't you just shoot?' Nick cried out in exasperation.

'Do you want me to?' Susanto replied menacingly.

'You speak English after all.'

'And you have been causing people a lot of trouble.'

'Is every policeman as corrupt as you?'

'You should not come here and get involved with things you don't understand.'

'So what are you going to do now?'

'You will come with me.'

'To end up in Nissam like the others?'

'They are terrorists.'

'Do you kill women too?'

'Get up.'

'They have found our people in Aceh.'

'I am arresting you for being a terrorist,' Susanto said coldly.

'The UNHCR already knows about you and they are on the way here.'

'They cannot do anything to save you. This is Indonesia. Now get up.'

Nick felt sick and tired. This was no time to argue with the man. His lungs felt raw as he coughed up more filthy water. Susanto pulled him up and reached for his handcuffs. People had started to arrive on the river bank.

'There are witnesses here. Your time is up, Susanto. It's not me who should be in jail.'

'Put up your hands.'

'Murdering perverts like you should be hung.'

'Maybe we will put you in the cells with the Muslim fanatics. They don't like westerners like you. They will probably cut your throat.'

'Just get on with it,' Nick replied, holding out his hands.

Susanto had got the handcuffs out when Nick saw a group of tough-looking men approach them. The UNHCR vehicles had arrived. They knew a major incident had occurred from looking at the damaged bridge. Piet de Heus quickly assessed the situation and had come to the conclusion that Nick was either dead or injured. He had quickly ordered the team down to the river bank.

'Are you Nick?' he asked.

'Yes.'

'I'm Piet de Heus. You're OK now. It's over.'

'Who are you?' Susanto asked.

'UNHCR. This man is coming with us,' he informed the Indonesian policeman.

'No, he is not. He is under arrest.'

'I'm not going to argue with you. Take the cuffs off,' Piet replied casually with determined authority.

'The UNHCR has no power in this country.'

'What are you arresting him for?'

'He is a terrorist.'

'And you're a murderer and child kidnapper. Am I right?' Piet asked.

'You do not say that to a policeman,' Susanto replied with venom.

'Get those handcuffs off and go away.'

The South African accent had never sounded more reassuring just then. He expected Susanto to draw his weapon but instead he just stood there, unsure what to do. Eventually, he released the hand cuffs. Nick gave Susanto a final look to show his contempt but knew he wasn't out of Sumatra yet. Checking his pockets, he could feel his wallet and passport. Hopefully the laminated photo page wasn't too badly damaged by the water. His waterproof Canon camera was still in its belt holder. He had lost his rucksacks but everything in them was replaceable.

The vehicles sped off towards Medan. He thought about Sylvie to ease the pain. She must have known there was a chance Susanto would try to get him. It didn't matter now. He had the full protection of the UNHCR.

CHAPTER 40

REHAB

HE WAS CHECKED INTO A PRIVATE MEDICAL facility in Medan but Nick had only suffered from multiple lacerations to his legs and a non-displaced fracture to his left collarbone. It could have been worse. The minor cuts and bruises would heal easily, even the fracture. He needed a course of ciprofloxacin to take care of any gut infections but it was the mental scars which scared him. He could remember the cold water rushing in. The experience of cerebral hypoxia was quite pleasant and he now knew what near-death felt like. It had transported him to another world, seeing his life flashed back quickly. Everything had appeared to be very real, even talking to the imaginary fish. He had been in the water for less than four minutes but the whole experience had felt like hours. He shuddered involuntarily at the thought of drowning. Many dead mariners must have learnt what it was like to swim with the mermaids.

He was fit enough to leave the next day. Mercy Aid International still had an account at the hotel. Once in the privacy of his room he took stock of the situation. He knew that, physically, the broken collarbone was not an issue. No lungs had been punctured and even the moderate level of pain was bearable. However, it was the mental scars which bothered him the most. He thought about the bodies in Banda Aceh, the child brothel, the GAM guerrillas, Nissam, and now

Susanto's attempt to kill him. The man had obviously tried to make it look like an accident and nobody would ever question a policeman. The stress of recent events suddenly hit him like an express train, making him think he was heading for a nervous breakdown. He badly needed a whisky but resisted the urge to use alcohol as a quick fix. The UNHCR had advised him to stay put until they knew more about the incident. Leaving Sumatra had been put on hold.

Most of what he had was now at the bottom of the river. Essentially, his passport, wallet and camera were there. He checked the camera. The spool had wound back automatically when the roll of film was used up. He removed it and noted it was completely dry. His clothes had been laundered at the hospital but he needed a new set. Pocketing the film, he decided to head into town.

There was a taxi waiting at the hotel lobby. The largest shopping area was in Jalan Ahmad Yani, the main street which ran in a north-south direction. Everything seemed reasonably cheap but no doubt the locals had their own special price. With several photo shops available he walked into the nearest one. The film would be processed in an hour. With time to kill, he bought another rucksack and some new clothes. He returned to the hotel after collecting the photographs, glad to get away from the madding crowd. The sprawling city wasn't the prettiest in the world although the black-domed Mesjid Raya looked impressive.

He looked at the photographs over a cup of coffee and a sticky bun. The captured images of the refugees reflected the scale of the disaster with some poignancy. He now pondered over the photograph of the man from the UN leaving the child brothel.

The images taken from the hillock were small but seemed perfectly clear. Nick wrote a short letter using the hotel stationery. He enclosed the relevant photographs and addressed it to Glampic, the paparazzi agency in London. He decided to send it by snail mail rather than bother with scanning and email, knowing it would take a few days longer to arrive in England. Hopefully, he would be out of the country by then. He attacked the sticky bun, relishing its deliciously sweet coconut filling. There had to be some justice in the world.

With the hotel still busy with other aid organisations, he didn't see somebody making a beeline for him. The hub of activity had masked the approach until a familiar face suddenly materialised.

'Hello, Nick,' she said, standing next to him.

'Halcyon! What are you doing here?' he replied.

'I came as soon as I could,' she said, hugging him.

'Oh, careful,' he grimaced with pain.

'What's up with the sling?'

'I cracked my collarbone. It's nothing serious. Sit down. Do you want some coffee?'

'Yes please. I'm starving. Could you get me one of those buns too?'

'No problem,' Nick replied, waving to the waitress.

'What did Susanto do to you?'

'He drove us into a bridge. Thankfully the driver got out but I didn't.'

'I saw the damage on the way here. Are you OK?'

'Just a little shaken but otherwise in one piece. What's happening at the refugee camp?'

'The school building should be arriving soon and Topo will be removed from his post.'

'That's good news. Sounds like Marcello has got his act togother,' Nick said, ordering the coffee and bun when the waitress appeared.

'Tell me what happened when you got to Nissam.'

'It was a dumping ground for dead bodies. I met the forensic pathologist doing the site investigation.'

'You heard they found the bodies of our women?'

'Yes, Marcello told me.'

'I hope they'll catch Susanto. How did you get on with Sylvie?'

'She was hospitable.'

'I'm glad she looked after you.'

'She did,' Nick replied without showing any emotions.

'What are your plans now?'

'Head back to Scotland I suppose, but the UNHCR people want me to hang on for a few more days. They need more information.'

'I have to head back up north tomorrow. Why don't we go to town for some fun?'

'I've just been there.'

'We have to do something. You look like you could do with a drink.'

'Shall we just forget about your coffee?'

'Why not? Let's go now,' Halcyon suggested.

'The town is on me,' Nick replied, cancelling the coffee on the way out.

They took another taxi into town along the familiar route. He felt happy she was there, especially after his sudden departure from the refugee camp. Since then, things had happened rapidly. Now that the UNHCR had started their investigations, Nick could relax and forget about Susanto.

For a change, they decided to have something other than Indonesian food. They found a restaurant where steaks were served. The Johnnie Walker whisky helped to ease Nick's sore shoulder as the evening slowly melted away. Halcyon seemed more relaxed than he had ever seen her before, no longer the frumpy thing in combat trousers. Her bobbed hair had grown slightly too long at the front, making it necessary for her to push it aside from time to time. Nick didn't bother with pudding as he watched her eat the cheesecake. No doubt, it was imported frozen from Australia too, just like the steak. It seemed like a long time ago since they first sat down to eat sambal ikan bilis. They walked arm in arm through the streets after the meal, observing the night stalls. Despite the persistent efforts of the vendors, they declined the various offers. Nick didn't need any more cheap tee shirts.

The relative normality of Aceh and the effects of the whisky helped him to relax, blunting the sharp edge of reality. He enjoyed Halcyon's company more than usual. Despite the bright lights of the bustling city, he hankered after the relative quiet of the hotel bar. Halcyon agreed to go back. They took a taxi for the short drive back and once there, Nick ordered two whiskies from the small selection.

'What do you think of the Laphroaig?' he asked.

'It's pretty potent,' Halcyon replied, sniffing the drink.

'They managed to sell it in America during the prohibition by calling it medicine. You're probably smelling the peat.'

'I'm not sure I like it.'

'Keep trying,' Nick replied in amusement.

'It's too strong for me.'

'I'll get you something else if you want.'

'Will you keep in touch?' she suddenly asked, not caring about the drink.

'Yes, of course.'

'I'll miss you,' she said, with a tearful look.

'No you won't. I'm just a big idiot.'

'Why don't you go to somewhere nice like Bali before you go home?'

'Maybe, if you really recommend it'

'The beaches may be slightly messy right now but they need the income. It'll be a different experience from Aceh. I don't want you to go away with just negative memories.'

'I might take your advice. What about you? When will you head home?'

'When the school is up and running and the children don't need me any more.'

'Then you'll move on to another sorry part of the world?'

'It's just a job. Try and get over what's happened over here, OK?'

'I will. I'm fine, really.'

'Make sure that you do because I worry about you.'

'Please don't do that,' Nick laughed.

'I can't help it Nick,' she replied, gently looking at him with affection.

'Look, do you want something different?' he asked, seeing that she was struggling with the whisky.

'No, you have it. I've had enough.'

'Are you sure?' he replied.

'I'd like to have an early night. Why don't you come back to my room?'

'Is that a proposal?' Nick asked in a light-hearted manner.

'Yes,' Halcyon replied.

'Are you being serious?'

'Why don't you come and see?'

He secretly hoped she wasn't. After finishing and signing for the drinks, he walked her back to her room. He deliberately lingered as she opened the door.

'Aren't you coming in?' she asked.

'Halcyon, look, I've had a wonderful night but I don't want to spoil things between us.'

'Why would you?'

'I'm a little messed up about my own feelings.'

'You don't find me attractive, do you?' she asked.

'It's not that at all. Come here,' Nick said.

She went to him as he hugged her. She let out a sob.

'Nick, why won't you come in?' she asked again.

'I love you for who you are but I can't let you get emotionally involved with me.'

'Why not? I don't understand. What's to stop us?'

'I'm already involved with somebody else,' he muttered.

'It doesn't matter, Nick. I want you to stay tonight.'

'It'll make things harder for both of us. I think we should just say goodbye now.'

'You know how I feel about you, don't you?'

'Yes, I know. That's why I cannot stay.'

'Are you in love with somebody else?'

'Yes.'

'I'm glad you told me but for what it's worth, I'll always love you.'

'I think I should go now Halcyon.'

'Will you kiss me properly at least?'

'Sure.'

He kissed her long and hard, noting how enthusiastic the response was. He felt tempted to stay but it was no use. Halcyon may be a strong headed woman but he knew she was hopelessly in love with him. The situation would only get worse if he stayed. As there was little point in prolonging the moment, he decided to break off and walk away. She stood by the door and watched him go until he was out of sight. He would have spent the night with her if she had been Sylvie. It wasn't just a matter of physical attraction because Halcyon was pretty enough but it was the emotional baggage which would come with sleeping with her. Sylvie had a need which he could satisfy but she would never fall in love with him. Feeling emotionally bruised already, he couldn't cope with any further complications in his life despite caring very much for her. The time they had spent together would always be special to him and coming to Sumatra had already changed his life.

Chapter 41

Bali

ALCYON HAD LEFT WITHOUT KNOCKING ON HIS door. He wasn't sure what they would have said to each other if they had met at breakfast but Medan now felt too monotonous. He had heeded her suggestion and made some inquires about going to Bali. With the tourist trade all but gone they needed the business. The helpful hotel staff knew of a good travel agency which arranged the trip for him. The flight had gone smoothly and he could see Bali as the jet came in to land from over the sea. It looked beautiful even from the air. Shielded as it was by the land masses of Sumatra and Java, it had been left relatively untouched by the tsunami. Even so, the airport was nearly empty when Nick arrived.

After decades of booming tourism, the creeping influence of western decadence had changed the local culture. Scantily dressed girls arriving from Australia had adhered more to the dress code of Bondi Beach than that of a Muslim country. It disturbed local sensibilities and the puritanical mullahs had taken note. The numerous disco-bars had made the once quiet island into a Mecca for the hedonists. They had gyrated to the beats of the Kuta-Legian district until the Bali bombers sent their own message of hate. They blew the place up and Bali was no longer the paradise it had once been.

271

The hotel was located across the road from Kuta Beach, on the Jalan Raya Pantai Kuta. It was only fifteen years old but had a tired look about it. The minibus dropped him off by the reception area. The hotel complex consisted of many small buildings within the grounds. They each contained four bedrooms, dotted around in a seemingly confused layout. Despite the numerous signposts people still got lost. Some novice architect had tried to impress with his crass design but Nick wasn't bothered. He was there for a break. The air conditioning units rattled away as he was shown to his room. After settling in, he took a cool shower before heading out to the town centre.

Most of the restaurants were situated along Jalan Legian, running parallel to the beach road. The Hard Rock Café was nestled amongst dozens of other bars and clubs. After the mediocre steak in Medan he was keen for a better one. At least the food at the Hard Rock Cafe was predictable if uninspiring. The music was loud enough to drown any meaningful conversation but the couple at the bar smiled when he appeared.

'Hi. How is the food in this place?' Nick asked, speaking up.

'It's OK,' the girl replied.

'You sound French.'

'We are. I am Lilian, this is my boyfriend, Serge.'

'I'm Nick,' he said shaking hands with the couple.

'Are you here on holiday or business?' Serge asked.

'Holiday. And you?'

'Same. We came here for Christmas and the New Year. Now we feel we cannot leave.'

'Why? There are still plenty of flights out.'

'We are trying to help the economy.'

'By spending money?'

'Yes, we are trying to drink the place dry,' Serge replied with a wink.

'What is there to do here apart from the beach?' Nick asked.

'You could go inland and see the paddy fields.'

'Wow, I'll look forward to doing that,' Nick replied, keeping his tongue in cheek.

'There's really very little to do. Where are you from?' Serge asked.

'Scotland.'

'How come you are in Bali?'

'I was doing some work in Sumatra. This is just a short holiday before I go home.'

'So what is it like over there?'

'Total disaster.'

'It must be really bad, huh?'

'Yes, but things are getting better.'

'What is your job?'

'I work for a charity,' Nick replied, keeping things simple.

'That's cool. We have been travelling in Indo-China and Thailand.'

'It must have been some trip.'

'It was. This was the last place to come before we went back to France,' Serge said.

'What's your job?'

'Me? I am an actor.'

'An out-of-work actor. He doesn't do a lot,' Lilian chipped in.

'She's funny, huh?' Serge replied.

'Is it stage work or movies that you do?'

'I do mostly films.'

'I watch some French films on TV.'

'That's good. I will tell you when I make my next one,' Serge said, making Lilian giggle.

'Yes, do that.'

'Listen, we are going to another bar. So maybe we see you later?' Serge asked.

'Sure. I'm going to grab something to eat in here,' Nick replied.

'OK, au revoir, Nick,' Serge said, shaking his hand.

'See you later,' he replied, having no clue where they would be.

Lilian smiled and wiggled her fingers to say goodbye without actually saying anything. Nick enjoyed the brief chat but now felt conscious of being alone. He ordered a Miller. It was the closest thing they had to a decent beer. He suddenly longed to be back in Edinburgh. Coming to Bali alone was a mistake as he watched Serge and Lilian leave. It made him think of Meg.

Apart from calling her when he had first arrived in Medan, a stubborn irrationality had prevented him from calling her again when he returned there. Perhaps too much had happened in a short space of time, creating an imaginary gulf between them. She couldn't possibly understand what he had been through nor would it be fair to burden her with his tales. It was easier to concentrate on the food instead. The New York strip looked inviting but he hated eating alone.

After a soulless dinner, he made his way back to the hotel. Making friends with inconsequential people had seemed rather pointless and he felt no urge to find the French couple. The streets looked almost deserted, bereft of tourists but the shopkeepers still tried to do business, clearly hoping for better times. They chatted to Nick in a vain attempt to sell him something.

Beyond the main street, the smaller ones were poorly lit. Many shadows lurked amidst the gloom. A few local people sat chatting amongst themselves whilst others hustled the odd passing tourist. The parade of shops came to an end as he turned left to head back to the hotel. He heard the gentle swish of the tide rolling ashore as he walked towards the beach. Despite the gentle sea breeze, he could smell the same clove-infused cigarette like the one he tried in

Sumatra. He was now aware of somebody watching him. A local man was resting against a low wall, smoking a cigarette. The stranger eyed him up with a friendly smile.

'Hello, John, how are you?' the man asked in a friendly way.

'I'm good. How about you?' Nick replied.

'Very well, my friend. Are you on holiday?'

'It must be obvious,' Nick bantered.

'You like Bali?'

'Yes, it's very nice.'

'Maybe too quiet for you,' the man replied, stating the obvious.

'I like it that way.'

'Business is very bad right now but you must come back when it is busy.'

'I may just do that.'

'You come to Bali by yourself?'

'Yes.'

'What, no wife, no girlfriend?'

'No,' Nick replied, smiling at the man.

'Maybe you are running away from a bad wife?' the man joked.

'No. I wanted to see your beautiful island.'

'Even after the tsunami? You must be crazy,' the man laughed again.

'I was in Sumatra so it wasn't too far to come.'

'You were there on business?'

'That's right.'

'You must be in the oil business.'

'No, nothing as exciting as that.'

'Do you want to do something really exciting?'

'What do you have in mind?'

'I can get you a beautiful lady,' the man answered.

'No thanks,' Nick replied, walking away from the pimp, suddenly realizing what he was.

'Hey, John. Wait a minute, tell me what you want.'

'I don't want anything from you' Nick replied in a neutral tone, not wanting to upset the man in case he pulled out a knife on him.

'Hey, I can get you a boy or girl if you don't want a woman. No problem!'

'No!'

Nick felt a sense of danger as he walked away but knew the man would persist in touting for business.

'Hey, come to my village and see for yourself. I can send somebody to your hotel if you want,' the man shouted after him.

'Go away.'

'It's only a few dollars. Come on. You can have a nice time. Hey, John, come back!'

Nick walked away as he heard the mocking laughter behind him. Another local had turned up on his scooter. He felt sickened by them. The thought of selling sex disgusted him. His pace quickened until he reached the hotel, relieved to get there. The hotel receptionist greeted him pleasantly. At least here was a semblance of normality with some good old-fashioned Balinese hospitality. He entered his room and felt the despair hit him. Even here in Bali, the picture postcard beauty was spoilt by the sex trade. He had no doubt that children were involved as the scourge had spread globally.

He couldn't put off phoning Meg any longer. He desperately needed to tell her everything as the memories came flooding back. His head felt like a nuclear reactor fast approaching meltdown. He fought back the panic as he dialled the international number. A familiar voice answered much to his relief.

'Hello?'

'Meg, it's Nick.'

'How are you?'

'Not good.'

'Where are you phoning from?' she asked.

'Bali.'

'What are you doing there?'

'I don't know. I just came here on a whim.'

'What's happened? You sound dreadful.'

'A lot has happened. I still have to go back to Sumatra before going home.'

'Why have you not called before?'

'Communications were down in Aceh. I'm coming back to the UK as soon as the UNHCR are done with me.'

'I've been waiting for your call.'

'Can I come and see you when I return?'

'Where, in London?'

'Yes.'

'Nick, I have something to tell you.'

'What?' he replied with a sinking feeling.

'I want to end our relationship.'

'Why?'

'I just think it would be best for both of us.'

'Has something happened?'

'Yes, you. I can't cope with your life anymore.'

'Are you seeing somebody else?'

'Yes.'

'Are you sleeping with him?' It was all he could think of asking at that moment.

'Yes, I am.'

'Can we talk about this when I get back?' Nick asked, feeling a sudden pang of desperation spear through him.

'There is no point, Nick.'

'Meg, I have to talk to you. Tell me this isn't happening.'

'It's over, Nick.'

'I'll make things up to you.'

'When are you ever going to change Nick? I can't cope with you getting into trouble all the time.'

'I just need another chance. I've changed.'

'Maybe you have but I'm moving on.'

'Meg, you know I love you.'

'Please, Nick, don't say that. I have to go now.'

'Don't hang up!'

'Look after yourself, OK?'

He heard the phone go down. The void of total emptiness had really hit home at that moment. He slumped onto the floor, this time with tears in his eyes. He could no longer stop them from falling. He replaced the receiver and buried his hands in his face. It wasn't supposed to end this way. None of this seemed real anymore.

Chapter 42

Day of the Komodo

THE ENDLESS NIGHT WENT ON FOR EVER. He tried to convince himself that things always happened for a reason but the sudden demise of his relationship came as a shock. He had never knowingly ingratiated himself with a woman and most of his encounters had always happened by chance. More often than not, it was often initiated by the other party, just as Sylvie or even Halcyon had done. Meg had walked into his life when he finished with Emma and now she was gone too. Meg had always been brutally honest with herself and knew he could never settle down. Nick was a lost soul searching for his own salvation.

After a disturbed night, he knew that moping around was pointless. He decided to do a tour of the island, just as Serge and Lilian had suggested. With no other tourists around, there was no need to book ahead. The half-day tour started when he was ready, with his personal guide and driver. They set off into the countryside and passed by many beautiful temples. The paddy fields were there too but he had already seen them in Sumatra. Before long, even the temples looked similar and his enthusiasm waned quickly, especially after visiting several gift shops. He bought a wooden carving as a souvenir from an enthusiastic salesman. The little minivan dropped him off at the hotel just after one o'clock.

He didn't feel hungry and set off for the beach across the road. The sand felt hot under his feet as he walked towards the water, having removed his shoes. A few windsurfers made use of the crashing waves. He sat down to watch them as they tumbled into the white water with impunity, bouncing back to ride the waves again. He bought a fresh coconut from a local vendor, watching the local man chop the top off with a machete. The juice was refreshingly cool but the man also showed him how to scoop out the white flesh using a piece of coconut shell. They made some friendly chat before the loneliness of beach watching took over again.

He could think about nothing apart from Meg. Several hours had passed by as he mulled over his thoughts. The sun had beaten a slow retreat towards the horizon, casting a glorious crimson colour across the blue sky. It was a photographer's delight, except he couldn't shake off his stupor. The joy of life had deserted him as darkness started to close in.

The beach was by now nearly deserted. What few revellers there were had gone in to prepare for another night of subdued drinking. His thoughts were interrupted by the sound of excited voices coming from down the beach. He could see half a dozen local children pointing and squealing at some animated object moving slowly. The gaggle moved closer but his view of the object remained obscured. Finally, he could make out the reptilian shape, about a metre long. The creature ambled towards him, pausing for brief moments to stare at its young tormentors. One brave child even goaded it with a stick before scampering off to a safe distance, squealing with delight.

The creature carried on, coming ever closer, as if drawn to Nick. It stopped a few metres from him and looked him straight in the eye. It was similar to a monitor lizard but scarier. The children spoke excitedly to him.

'Komodo! Komodo!' one of them shouted.

Nick stood his ground as the creature continued towards him. He knew that Komodo dragons came from a group of islands south of Bali. Being good swimmers, they could swim from island to island but this creature was far from home, perhaps swept out to sea by the tsunami. It was a juvenile, still dangerous but unlike the fearsome adults that killed by using the toxic bacteria from their saliva. The small Komodo looked lost, desperately seeking protection from the noisy boys. It was also tired and weak. Nick stared at the creature and noted its blank eyes, as if its soul had died too. The creature knew that without finding a mate, its life was worthless. It should be home with the other komodos, just like Nick should be home in Edinburgh. He felt an immediate bond with the creature, sharing its sadness. He asked the kids to leave it alone but even if they had understood, they ignored him. They continued to harass the creature as it walked down the beach. It turned its head and gave Nick one last look, as if asking for salvation. In the mini drama, he hadn't heard the gentle footsteps walking up to him.

'It is beautiful, no?' a French voice said.

Nick turned around and saw the woman he had met at the Hard Rock Cafe.

'That's a Komodo dragon, apparently,' he replied.

'Yes, I know. These children are crazy. That animal is very dangerous!' she said, emphasising the last sentence in a very Gallic way.

'You know what kids are like. Sorry, I've forgotten your name,' Nick said, struggling to switch his brain back on.

'I'm Lilian. You remember me from the bar last night?'

'Yes, of course. Your boyfriend is called Serge?'

'Bravo, at least you remembered one name!'

'Where is he?'

'He is sleeping.'

'What, at this time?'

'Yes, Serge always sleeps until the evening.'

'You must eat late.'

'Of course. We are French. How was your meal yesterday?'

'Not bad.'

'When do you go home?'

'Day after tomorrow.'

'That is not very long.'

'What about you?' Nick asked.

'Soon, but it is up to Serge. He cannot make up his mind.'

'How long have you been travelling together?'

'Six months.'

'That's a long time.'

'It's not such a big problem for us.'

'I'm glad to hear that.'

'We live in the south of France. Have you been to Cannes? It is on the Riviera.'

'No.'

'You must go there. It's very beautiful.'

'I'd like to. You must come to Edinburgh.'

'Do you have an email address?' she asked.

'Yes, of course.'

'Here, write it in my notebook.'

'Sure.' Nick replied, taking the pen and notebook.

'I will email you.'

'Say hi to Serge for me.'

'When he wakes up! Have a good trip back to Scotland,' Lilian said with a small laugh.

'Same to you.'

With that, she walked off into the twilight, as Nick contemplated the dusk.

Chapter 43

Home Run

THE TAXI PICKED HIM UP FROM THE hotel for the short trip to the airport. He wasn't sorry to leave as Bali had lost its charms. Marcello Mione from the UNHCR wanted to see him when he got back to Medan. With some time to browse at the shops, he searched for a copy of the London Times but the magazine store had the New York Times instead. He bought a copy and unfolded the newspaper. The lower front half ran an article he immediately recognised, showing a blown up image of the photograph he had taken. The paparazzi agency had done its job by selling it to the newspaper. With the UN headquarters set in New York, they had clearly hit the bull's-eye. The article headlined:

UN Deputy General of Finance Involved In Sumatran
Paedophile Ring

Feeling vindicated at last, he bought a coffee and sticky bun to celebrate. He had become addicted to them. There was no mention of Susanto or Anzala but predatory foreigners had been blamed for abusing the poor children, even a highly respected UN official. Nick heard his flight being called for boarding. He thought about the Komodo and hoped it was safe, knowing the locals would probably kill it before it bit any of the children. Now, he was just another passenger, trusting his own life to the competence of the pilot. The aircraft took off smoothly and landed in Medan on time.

Despite being on an internal flight he had to pass through the customs area. Several customs officers looked at him but one came forward. He was asked about his stay in Bali and asked to show his rucksack. Despite having nothing to declare, he was taken to one side.

'Please follow me,' the officer said.

'Is there something wrong?' Nick asked, wondering why he had been stopped.

'No, just a minor problem. Come,' he ordered in a harsh tone of voice.

'I've only been to Bali for a few days and there is nothing illegal in my bag.'

'This way,' the man said, ushering Nick through a door.

He found himself being almost frogmarched down an empty corridor. After turning down a few more passages, he was taken to a room. Once inside, Nick noted the single desk and two chairs. It looked like an interview room.

'Sit down. Somebody will come and see you soon,' the officer instructed.

'Can you tell me what is going on?'

'You will find out soon.'

Nick did as he was told and sat with the door to his back. The officer left the room without being overtly threatening nor pleasant either. Presumably, a more senior officer would come to search his rucksack but nothing was adding up. His mind started to play tricks. Perhaps somebody had planted drugs in his rucksack and he was acting as a mule. Knowing he could be watched on a TV monitor, he left it well alone. If there was an illegal package in his rucksack, his fingerprints wouldn't be on them. The minutes ticked away until finally, he heard the door open.

Half expecting to see a jovial customs officer making an apology for their mistake, he suddenly found his face being slammed into the table. It caught him by total surprise. His left arm was pinned against the table whilst a vice-like grip squeezed the back of his neck. His collar bone exploded with pain and stars swam in front of his eyes. He then heard the familiar voice. Through the corner of his eye, he could see the batik shirt. The man was mouthing obscenities at him, pushing his head harder into the table. Nick tried to say something but it was a one-way conversation with Susanto.

'You think you're clever? You think you can get away from me?' he said.

'Arggh,' Nick growled.

'So you think you can come back to Medan and I will not know about it?'

'No,' Nick managed to utter.

'Do you see the problem you have caused for everybody?'

'No.'

'No?' Susanto asked, shoving Nick's face against the hard surface.

'How did you find me?'

'We have police computers here. Maybe you think I am stupid? I am still a policeman. I can shoot you for resisting arrest.'

'What do you want?'

'I am going to take you to see some people.'

'Who?' Nick asked.

'These people want to have some fun with you.'

'Can we talk about this?'

'You want to talk now? It's too late for that,' Susanto sneered.

'Please,' Nick replied softly.

'No!' Susanto shouted, lifting his right hand from Nick's neck to aim a punch at his head.

Nick felt the pressure lift off momentarily. Much of his upper body was still pinned down by Susanto's own body but there was enough leverage to push up with his right hand. Thankfully his broken collar bone was on the other side, otherwise it would have been impossible to do that. The movement caught Susanto by surprise, taking him off balance. Nick also pushed up with his legs and turned his body around, slipping out from beneath the man. He drove his right elbow into the man's side and pulled his other arm free. Susanto staggered back a short distance.

They sized each other up as Susanto threw the chair out of the way. He adopted a martial art fighting posture. Nick knew he was now in real trouble if the man was any good. There was no option but to lose his arm sling. His shoulder ached as he focused on his karate training. Susanto watched him like a hawk as he bounced up and down on the balls of his feet, feigning several punches before trying a roundhouse kick to Nick's head. Nick dodged that easily, watching the man's eyes closely. Susanto stared at him with hatred, before aiming a kick at Nick's abdomen. He failed to contact. He tried again with his right foot. This time Nick's training came in automatically. He swivelled on his right foot and turned to one side, catching Susanto's lower leg as it went past. With his right hand Nick grabbed Susanto's batik shirt and tucked his right leg behind the man's left leg. With a hefty shove he pushed the man backwards. Susanto landed heavily on his back as the wind was knocked from him. Nick now had to disable Susanto by ramming his foot between his legs. It was Susanto's turn to feel pain as his testicles took the brunt of the hit. He curled up into a ball and felt like dying. Nick saw his chance and grabbed his rucksack, heading out of the door and doubled back up the corridor.

Quickly making his way back to the main area, he followed

the exit signs to the main concourse. Half-expecting to see Susanto coming after him, he headed to the Air Malaysia desk. Thankfully there were plenty of flights to Kuala Lumpur. He would not be seeing Marcello as he had decided to leave the country straight away. Going through the usual security check-in, he prayed nobody would stop him this time. The adrenaline surged through him as he tried to remain calm. If anybody had thought he was nervous, thankfully they didn't bother to ask him why.

He tried to become a grey man in the departure lounge, not drawing any attention to himself by sitting in a quiet corner. He had visions of Susanto rushing there with his gun raised and shooting him for being a terrorist. Various other thoughts crossed his mind even as he boarded the plane. The police could stop the flight at any time and even call it back after it had left the ground. His prayers were finally answered when the plane landed at Kuala Lumpur without a hitch. He could finally relax with a large whisky before his transfer back to the UK. Kicking Susanto between the legs had felt very satisfying. The smug grin on his face came easily as he contemplated the utter look of shock on the other man's face. At least he had said a proper goodbye to Susanto.

CHAPTER 44
THE MAELSTROM

I N NEW YORK, MICHAEL TURNER KNEW THERE was big trouble as soon as the newspaper article came out. The Englishman had done his best to do the housekeeping at the UN but this was totally unexpected. He didn't need the hassle, not after Oil-for-Food. The Secretary-General was livid and demanded a full report. Turner's job at internal affairs was to know about this sort of thing and to stop it from coming out. The suave Dutchman was even married to a respectable pearl twinset-type, giving no clue at all about his dark life. As the financial director, he was highly involved in the rebuilding contract and it would take months to investigate in case he had been compromised. The whole thing was a shambles.

Emails came in thick and fast. Turner's secretary worked feverishly to field all the incoming calls. People around the world were very concerned. The UN had taken another battering but the financial director himself was nowhere to be found. He didn't respond to his emails or phone calls so Turner had no way of speaking to him. The Secretary-General was spitting nails right then, putting him under pressure. The UN was going down with another big scandal and Turner had to contain it. His own reputation was at stake. He remembered the Potomac Two-Step vividly.

The New York Times story had to be verified first, in case the paparazzi were playing their usual tricks. They would sell their photographs to anybody. Even the most respected newspaper could be fooled into buying them. One bad photo of their man standing next to a UN vehicle meant zilch until proven otherwise. He would need a report from the UN team out there to confirm the allegations. He knew the financial director had gone out there to assess the level of funding required to rebuild the devastated province. With so much effort going towards tsunami relief, he had to make sure this unsavoury business didn't go any further.

He considered his options. It would be a simple case of denial if the paparazzi photo was a fake. If it were true, the financial director had to be distanced from the organisation. The fact he was not contactable was significant. Turner had to speak to Marcello Mione out in Medan.

'This is Mike Turner from New York. Internal affairs,' he said clearly, introducing himself.

'Hello, Mike. We've not met. I'm Marcello Mione,' the Swiss national said.

'Good to talk to you. I need to know a few things.'

'Go ahead.'

'Can you confirm the story?'

'Yes, we can. I'm afraid it's true. We had confirmation from the US Navy, who were involved in saving these kids.'

'You have obviously seen the newspaper article. Can you confirm the picture to be genuine? It that where it took place?'

'Yes, that has been verified. Special police units from Jakarta are investigating the problem.'

'So our man was involved without any shadow of doubt?'

'It would appear to be the case.'

'Thanks for your help.'

'There's something else. You should also know we are digging more bodies up.'

'Is this going to be another East Timor situation?' Turner asked, having already seen the preliminary reports.

'Not as bad but bad enough.'

'OK, keep me posted. Sounds like you have one hell of a job out there.'

'I dare say you're going to have your hands full in New York.'

'Thanks.'

'Anytime, Mike.'

Turner knew his day had just got worse. The story checked out. It would be easier if the financial director simply disappeared. The CIA would have their own way of dealing with awkward problems, but this was not the CIA. Somebody must have known about his secret habits and had tailed him all the way out to Sumatra. It could only be the paparazzi, but he was surprised at the poor quality of the shot. The image had to be enlarged, whereas the paparazzi would normally have used a telephoto lens. He couldn't fathom how they managed to get the photograph. It was only significant because it was the financial director who had been compromised. If any UN money had been used to pay for sex it would lead to the meltdown of the entire organisation.

There was also another matter to look into. The financial director had strongly supported just one of the bids for the rebuilding contract. If there were any financial irregularities, Turner knew he would lose his own job, and reputation. There was only one way of preventing this from ever happening. The bid had to go through but the man had to die and take his secrets with him. There were people in New York who could fix this sort of thing and maybe now was the time.

CHAPTER 45

HOUSE OF CARDS

B ILL FRAZER HAD ALSO READ THE NEWSPAPER article. The faggot had been exposed in Sumatra of all places, he thought to himself. He quickly considered what to do about the photographs of the man. They had been an insurance policy against losing the contract but it could now compromise his company if somebody found them. Even if nobody could trace the source, the fact that somebody had taken the photographs meant the Dutchman had been compromised. His decision to award the contract was therefore suspect and it had to be investigated. The photographs must be retrieved even if they were still within the UN headquarters. He thought of asking the investigator to do the job again but there was an extra part this time. He knew the investigator would not get involved with murder even for an extra payment. He looked up another secret number in his notebook. The investigator had done his job but it was now the turn of the cleaner. He liked using names. It was neat and to the point. In order to keep the building contract, he knew what had to be done. The photographs had to be retrieved and the Dutchman had to die. He called the number.

CHAPTER 46
NO WIN, NO FEE

TONY MARELLO'S PRIDE HAD BEEN BADLY DENTED from losing the contract. A lot of money had just gone down the pan for nothing and he wanted it back. Once upon a time, people played by the rules. They had honour. Now they played by different rules and this was all wrong. He tried to call the Dutchman but he never answered. Marello had no alternative but to set up a meeting. It was with an old acquaintance from another established Italian-American family. They met up in Tompkins Square Park, just by East Village. The two men walked towards each other with outstretched arms and greeted each other. The big hug and back slapping was part of the ritual but they both knew the score.

'Hey Tony! You don't see me for twenty years and now you call me in a hurry! What's up?' the smartly-dressed man said with a big laugh.

'Valentino, you're looking good. How is Momma?'

'She's not so good, Tony. Why you never come to see us any more?'

'I'm sorry, but I've been too busy.'

'You're now a big man in a big business. Cut the bullshit. What's so important you can't talk to me on the phone, huh?'

'It's about a deal I made. It went wrong.'

'How much of a deal?'

'One million.'

'Is that all?' the man laughed.

'I want it back.'

'What was it for?'

'The contract on the UN building.'

'Don't tell me! You didn't get it because you're an Italian company!' Valentino laughed again.

'I'm not laughing.'

'So what was the deal? Some schmuck said he would give you the contract for a million and then turned his back on you?'

'I'm getting half back for not getting the deal.'

'Tony, Tony! I didn't figure you for a dumb guy! Who's this jerk that pulled that fast one?'

'Some Dutchman from the UN. He's the finance man.'

'So you now want old Valentino to ask him for the other half a million?'

'Can you do it?'

'Sure, I can do it. It will cost you 10 per cent.'

'I need your word nobody will know about this. Get me my money back and you'll get your 10 per cent.'

'Tony, it goes without saying it will be done nice and neat. We come from honourable families. How do I find him?' Valentino asked.

'I don't know. He is not answering my calls.'

'What else do you know about him?'

'All his details are in here,' Tony replied, handing over a medium-sized brown envelope.

'There's something else I have to ask you, Tony. In my experience, this sort of thing is better done properly. After you get your money back, do you want me to get rid of him?'

'You mean kill him?'

'That's up to you. The price is the same. Dead men can tell no tales.'

'OK, do it.'

'That's a good decision. This thing can come back and bite you in the ass.'

'I trust you, Valentino. Do a good job,' Marello said quietly, without emotion.

'Hey, don't worry about it. We must eat together soon. You look too thin, Tony.'

'Maybe sometime, Valentino,' Marello replied, not wishing to offend the man.

Both men smiled and shook hands before walking away. Marello returned to his own car and drove off. The $50,000 deal was acceptable so long as he got the rest back. He knew the Dutchman would soon be part of the concrete section on a motorway bridge unless Valentino had changed his old ways.

Chapter 47

Media Pressure

T HE SCRUM OUTSIDE UN HEADQUARTERS HAD GATHERED expectantly. Well groomed reporters jostled for position as they searched for unanswered questions. They wanted to know how necessary it had been for the financial director to go to Sumatra and who else within the UN was involved in the paedophile ring. It was on every news channel. They also questioned the contract awarded to the New England Construction Company. If they were going to lynch the man by media pressure, they might as well go the whole way. With his integrity destroyed, everything he did would now be scrutinised in detail. They waited for their quarry to appear but it would be in vain. Mike Turner was kept informed of the situation outside. Very soon, he hoped somebody would know where the man was and then it would all be over. The Dutchman would be taken out with a bullet to his head unless the paid killer had other ideas. Turner could then bury this unwanted scandal and return some calm to the UN. It would hurt Turner's personal finances as he couldn't put this down on expenses but saving his job would be worth the price. What was ten thousand dollars after all?

Chapter 48

Final Solution

THE DUTCHMAN KNEW BOSTON WELL, HAVING WORKED there previously as a junior banker for one of the major Dutch banks. He had come a long way since then, changing jobs and rising up the ranks to reach the upper echelons of the UN. With Boston being only several hours away by road from New York it was a quick bolt hole to get to. The newspaper article had certainly caught him by surprise. His contacts had given him assurances about the little secret place in Sumatra but somebody had been there with a camera. The incident at Ludlow Street had already rattled him but he couldn't figure out who was stalking him and why. The secret network had already closed down and he couldn't communicate with any of his contacts. No doubt the internet police would be checking every source on the system.

He had stupidly posted pictures of himself with some of the children. Despite the encryption software to distort his facial image, the police had managed to use a programme to untwist the image. He could no longer hide his identity. His comfortable life had just come to an end and there must be a way of getting out of the United States. For now, he needed to hide somewhere. He bought a car from a dealer in the Bronx for cash, no questions asked, and headed to Boston.

The rented second floor apartment in the Boylston area looked out onto a park. The public area was a haunt for gay men at night, something he had discovered during his time as a young banker. The liberal American attitude towards sex was similar in his own country, which made life more interesting across the Atlantic. Despite being in a respectable part of town, the nocturnal activities in the park had largely gone unchallenged by the locals. Even the fake Cheers Pub was within walking distance, being just a facade for the popular show. He knew he would be safe there so long as he kept a low profile. He had left the car in the suburbs and took public transport into the city. To escape being traced, everything had to be done with cash. It wouldn't take long for his credit card details to show up. The knock on the door when it came was totally unexpected. He kept very quiet and hoped the person would go away. He heard the knock again, this time more insistent. The voice on the other side sounded desperate.

'Hey, my apartment downstairs is getting flooded out, man! If you're in there, open up,' the person shouted.

'I don't see any water in here,' the Dutchman replied through the door.

'Let me check it out. The water's coming in from all over the place so you must have a burst pipe.'

'Are you sure about that?'

'Yeah, I'm sure! Come on man! I don't want you destroying my property!'

'Well, can't you call the plumber or something?'

'I need to see where it's coming from.'

'OK, OK,' the Dutchman replied, opening the door.

The stranger walked straight in, keeping his head low beneath the baseball cap. He was wearing a Boston University sweatshirt, which went some way to reassuring the Dutchman. The man looked like some ageing student or ex-graduate.

'Thanks, buddy. You don't mind if I check out your bathroom?'

'Do you think that's where it's coming from?'

'I don't know. Let's go and see.'

The Dutchman peered outside on the landing before closing the door. He had to presume the man was from downstairs, not having met any of the neighbours since moving in yesterday. The stranger followed him to the bathroom. Without the Dutchman being aware, the man casually reached behind his jeans and pulled out an automatic pistol. The Dutchman only knew something was wrong when he heard the gun being cocked.

'Turn around,' the stranger ordered.

'What's going on?' the Dutchman answered, doing as he was told.

'Keep your hands up and don't do anything stupid. Move over to the living room.'

'What do you want?'

'Shut up.'

'Is it about money?'

'I said shut up.'

'Are you robbing me?' the Dutchman persisted, considering the possibility of that happening even in Boston.

The stranger suddenly hit him with the side of the gun, fed up with the questions. The Dutchman staggered before he was pushed roughly into the front room. His face had started to bleed from one corner of his mouth just as the ringing sensation still registered in his brain.

'Put your hands behind your back.'

'Why, what are you going to do?'

'Just do it,' the man said impatiently.

The Dutchman did as he was told. His hands were quickly tied behind him with a length of strong paracord, a tough but lightweight material used in parachutes. He felt his feet being tied next whilst he remained in a standing position. He still couldn't figure out if this was a robbery or not but the man didn't look like the police either. The Dutchman watched him tie another length of paracord to the overhead electric light in the centre of the room. He was pushed into position beneath it. Things turned kinky when the zipper on his trousers was pulled down. From the back pocket of his jeans, the stranger pulled out an object that made the Dutchman's eyes pop out. It was a hand grenade. The stranger carefully loosened the pin without pulling it all the way out, and gently inserted the grenade into the open trousers. He then tied the end of the paracord dangling from the light above onto the pin, checking the tension on the string. It felt about right as he carefully zipped up the man's flies, leaving the paracord trailing upwards.

'Shit! What are you doing?' the Dutchman cried out in fear.

'All you have to do is just stand still and you'll be OK,' the stranger replied reassuringly.

'Who sent you? Was it Marello or Frazer?' the frightened Dutchman asked, suddenly realising this was no robbery.

'I'm going to leave you now,' the man replied, without answering the question.

'Hey, wait, wait, wait! Just tell me what this is about? You can tell Frazer and Marello they'll get their money back.'

'It's too late for any of that.'

'Please, for God's sake, get that grenade out!'

'I don't think so.'

'Who paid you to do this? I'll pay you twice as much. Name your price!'

'No, you keep your money. I have to go now.'

'Hey, at least tell me how you found me.'

'I tailed you from New York. I knew where you lived and it was easy to follow after that. I didn't like the colour of the car you bought in the Bronx.'

'Is this to do with the contract?'

'No.'

'Then why are you doing this?'

'For personal reasons.'

'Oh God,' the Dutchman muttered before his mouth was filled with a piece of cloth.

The man turned without saying anything and walked out of the apartment, locking the door behind him. It left the Dutchman with time to think about who was behind this madness. Perhaps somebody had played a joke and this was meant to scare him. The grenade was probably a dud anyway. His mind raced to figure everything out. It had to be either Frazer or Marello because one of them wanted their money back. If he had to make a guess, it would be Marello. He didn't get the contract, but the Ludlow Street incident had happened before he met Marello. So, it must be Frazer. Now that the contract was his, he wanted the UN financial director to die in order to bury the evidence. He could think of other people who might want him dead. He had embarrassed the whole of the UN organisation. Perhaps the Secretary-General had ordered the hit himself. If not, then somebody within internal affairs wanted him out of the way to bury the scandal. Nothing made sense any more when the stranger said it was personal. All he knew was his survival involved staying absolutely still. Somebody would come back and get him out of this ridiculous situation. It had to be a joke.

Just over six hours later, the man in the sweatshirt reached New York after a slow and deliberate drive. He attracted no attention to himself, being just another long-distance commuter. Along the way, he had time to think about his life. It was his stepfather who had forced himself upon him one day in the woodshed. It went on for many years until he ran away at sixteen to join the marines. Military life suited him, making him forget about things, but he couldn't stay with the marines for ever. Since coming back to civilian life he had enjoyed the new job until the last assignment. He still knew many people in the Marines and the Navy. It was a like a big family. The email from Sumatra had made things personal for him. Everything about his life had clicked into place and he knew what his next mission was going to be. He had guessed the Dutchman would be leaving New York even before the press article came out.

The Dutchman had now stood in one position for over eight hours. He could feel his legs ache as his muscles shook from the strain. He was also mentally tired. Now convinced it was one big joke, he relaxed and sunk down to his knees. The grenade pin slipped out and he could feel the firing handle ping off inside his trousers. In the last four seconds of his life he suddenly remembered where he had seen the man before. It was in the apartment in Ludlow Street. There was a big white light before everything disappeared for ever. He had been blown to pieces.

The email that the investigator had received was from his buddy Charlie, who was out flying in a Seahawk over Sumatra. It didn't take much to figure out that it was the Dutchman who had been out there abusing the unfortunate children. There would soon be one child molester fewer in the world. He drank his coffee and lit up his fortieth cigarette of the day, smiling to himself.

CHAPTER 49

POTOMAC TWO-STEP

IKE TURNER WAS CALLED TO THE SECRETARY-GENERAL'S office on the 38th floor. He just knew something was up when the great man summoned him personally. He walked into the hallowed inner sanctum before sitting down.

'Thanks for coming, Mike. I want you to see this letter.'

The anonymous letter was printed on plain paper with no name or address on it. Turner read the contents, which were short and to the point. The letter had simply challenged his own integrity for running the department of internal affairs, citing his own possible involvement in the Oil-for-Food scandal. He knew what it meant. Because his integrity had been called into question his own department would have to be investigated. At a stroke, the whole review into the building contract had come to a grinding halt. Rather than being angry, he admired the person for showing their hand. He looked at the benevolent Secretary-General and smiled.

'It looks like somebody wants to stop me from doing my job.'

'Yes, it does, doesn't it? I'm sorry, Mike, it is out of my hands.'

'Pretty neat.'

'It won't take for ever. Once everything has been checked out, you'll be back in the driving seat.'

'How long will that take? One year, two years?'

'Whatever it takes.'

'And what about the building contract or the tsunami money?'

'Don't worry. It will all be sorted out,' the Secretary-General replied.

'Well, I'll go and pack up my things.'

'Yes, you do that. Let me know if you need my help at any time.'

'Thanks.'

Mike Turner left the Secretary-General's office. He knew who had thrown the ace card. Oil money was dirty, especially when family members were involved. He also knew the man had been the head of the Department of Peacekeeping Operations when the Srebrenica massacres took place in the lush pastures of eastern Bosnia. Incompetence and mismanagement had allowed up to eight thousand men and boys to be slaughtered. It was a small number compared to the million people killed in Rwanda when permission was refused to allow the UN commander to raid HUTU arms caches despite the warnings of mass slaughter. The man was due to receive a peace award for his achievement in the UN. Turner thought about the Potomac Two-Step. Perhaps it was time to play the game his way.

Epilogue

AFTER RETURNING TO EDINBURGH, NICK RENTED AN apartment in Morningside. He hooked up the laptop and found mail waiting for him. Much of the junk section was quickly binned but the one tagged 'Sumatra' caught his eye. He clicked it open and read the message.

'Hi Nick, this is Charlie, your Starsky and Hutch partner. Just wanted to say the kids we rescued are doing well. I looked out for the girl you called Annie. The good news is that the doctors couldn't find any evidence she was physically abused. She's getting on fine in the States and we are trying to adopt her. I emailed one of my ex-marine buddies in New York to find out more about this guy in the UN. I'll let you know what happened to him. Get back to me anytime. Charlie.'

Nick replied:

'Charlie, it's good to hear from you. I'm pleased to hear about Annie. Good luck with the adoption. We must meet up for a beer sometime. Cheers, Nick.'

He spotted another email marked 'Bali'. It read:

'Dear Nick. How are you? We saw the Komodo on the beach. Do you remember? Come to Cannes, OK? It will be nice to see you again. Serge says hi. Au revoir. Lilian'

Nick replied:

'Dear Lilian. It's a nice surprise to hear from you. I would love to go to Cannes but it will have to wait until next year or whenever. Still busy looking for a job. Yes, I remember the Komodo very well. It was a strange sort of day. Keep in touch. Nick.'

The news about Annie had been the tonic he needed. It was definitely time for a pint at The Canny Man's. No doubt Stuart would want to hear all about Sumatra but perhaps he should tell him about his deadly encounter with the Komodo dragon first.

The End.